UNEXPECTED

HER ILLUSIAN WARRIOR

ANNALISE ALEXIS

Unexpected (Her Illusian Warrior #1)

Unexpected (Her Illusian Warrior #1) is a work of fiction. Names, characters, businesses, organizations, places, events, and incidents either are the product of the author's imagination or are used fictitiously. Any resemblance to actual persons, living or dead, events, or locales is entirely coincidental.

Cover designed by Maria Spada

Editing by The Novel Fixer

Proofreading by Miss Bliss Author Services

This book contains content for adult audiences.

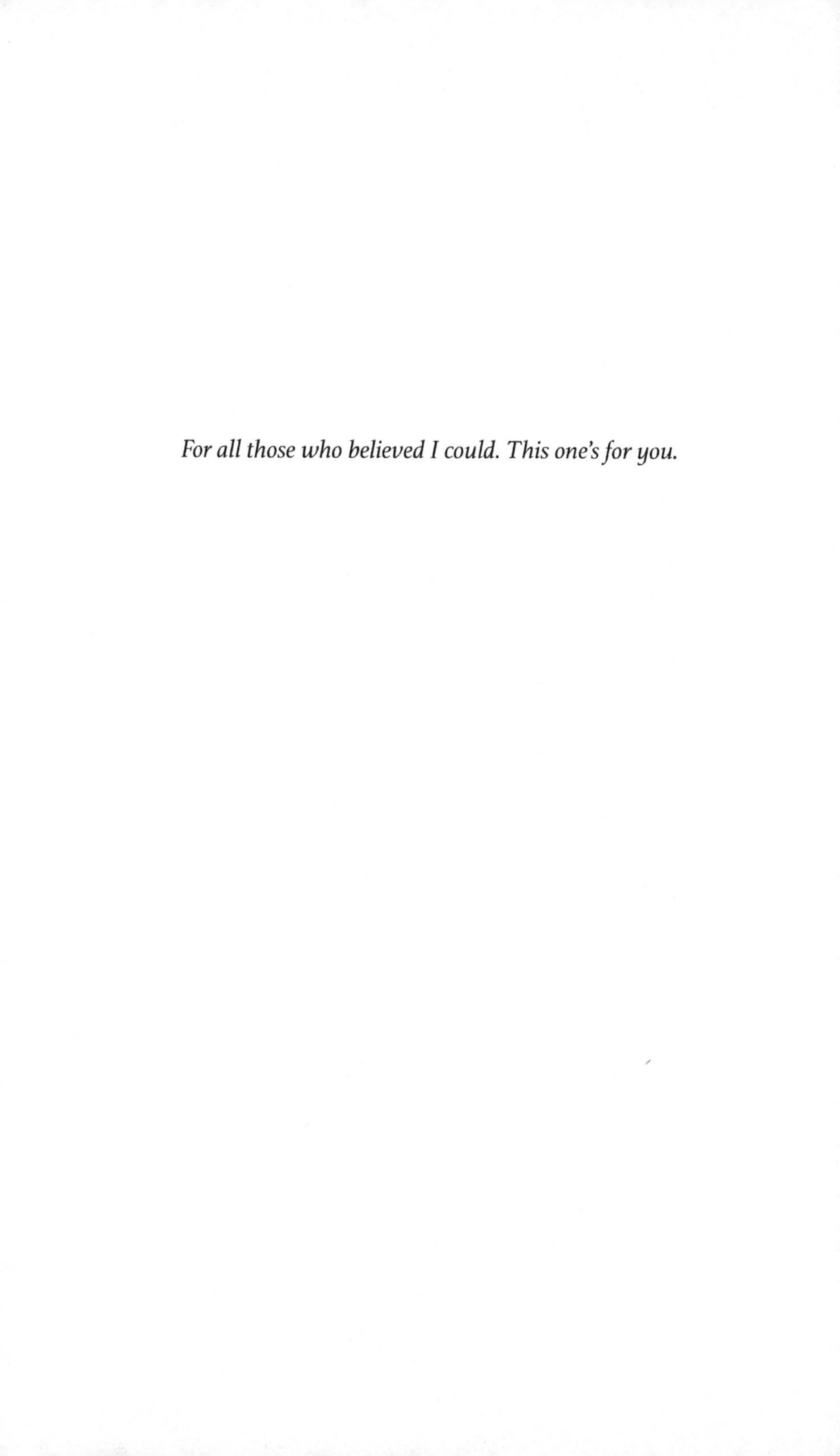

For all those who believed I could. This one's for you.

CHAPTER ONE

Jayla

THE ANTICIPATION IS *KILLING* ME. Arching my back off the bed, I wrap my hands around the hard planes of his abdomen and dig my nails in deep, giving him a not-so-subtle hint to move on. He's spent what feels like forever kissing on my neck, and I'm bored.

A hiss escapes his lips as he gives the delicate skin one last nibble, then flicks his tongue out, teasing the hard peaks of my nipples.

That's it, keep going.

Even in my dreams, I'm impatient as hell. Finally catching on, he moves his lips down the length of my abdomen. My muscles tremble with excitement as I spread my legs wide, eager to enjoy the warmth of his tongue.

Still unable to see his face, I'm not prepared for the feel of his rough fingers sliding into me. I buck my hips, urging him deeper, and gasp at what feels like multiple hands all over me. He's pinching. Teasing. Rubbing. All the combined sensations bring me close but aren't enough to shove me over the edge. I need *more*. Wrapping my hand around him, I tense as his moans shift from deep masculine grunts to much harsher wails that threaten to steal my concentration.

What the hell...? Whatever, just get to the good part.

So close, but still so far away, I know the only way I'm going to climax is if he shuts up and puts his mouth to better use. Attempting to ignore the increasingly loud and obnoxious change in his moans, I focus on the invigorating sensations still spreading over my well overdue body. Tired of waiting, I boldly grab the face still hovering over my navel, fully prepared to shove it where it *needs* to be but stop in shock as a familiar pair of eyes come into view. My passion dies abruptly, and my libido shrivels up with the revelation of my mystery lover's identity.

Oh sick. What's wrong with me?

Yanked out of my sleep-induced sexcapade by a combination of embarrassment, disappointment, and whatever the hell noise is screeching in my ears, I'm instantly pissed.

"Rett, I swear on everything high and holy, if you don't turn off your watch, I'm going to end you!" I yell, still stuck somewhere between awake and asleep, assuming my best friend forgot to silence his work alarm. After a few seconds of waiting with no answer, I force my right eye open, trying to figure out what the hell is going on. Oh, great. The general security tones are going off. *Again.*

Well, that explains the awkward moaning...

Extending my hand, I feel the bed beside me. The sheets are smooth and cool from disuse. I let out a sigh of relief. Thank goodness Rett wasn't here to witness my failed wet dream. He'd never let me live it down, especially once he found out which of our friends was in it. We've been inseparable since we first met, spending almost all our free time together. I've even become resigned to him coming and going as he pleases. Despite my numerous failed attempts at establishing boundaries, it isn't all that uncommon to find him passed out in my bed after he's slipped in during the night. At least he doesn't steal the covers.

I'm so tired, I don't want to move. Looking around, all I can see is a room swathed in darkness. The only source of light is the halogen bulbs casting a glow under my door from the hallway. Being one of the only two people willing to accept a medic position on this technologically challenged station and the only one able to speak over fifteen languages, I rarely get a day off. This is the first time in weeks I'm not expected to report to work at 6:00 a.m. and being woken prematurely by a malfunctioning alarm is irritating as hell.

Picking up my comm watch, I check the time, tapping on it several times before it finally uploads the latest available data. Rolling my eyes at the threadbare network that rarely works properly, I can see it is 2:00 a.m. and exactly three hours since I crawled into bed after completing this week's physicals.

Awesome.

This is not the first time the alarms have gone off by accident. The faulty wiring was supposed to have been replaced last week after the shipment of tools from UCom headquarters finally arrived. But apparently, that never happened. Being stuck in the ass crack of nowhere and not being a major hub of, well, anything, makes the work station I'm currently assigned to of little importance to the powers that be. Rarely getting anything but leftovers and bare necessities, the Universal Community—or UCom for short—personnel who live and work alongside me have learned not to expect much. You'd think after more than two hundred and fifty years of space exploration and the discovery of countless races and species of beings, a simple supply delivery system would've been created to ensure all employees are provided the basic necessities they need to do their day-to-day jobs. Not so much.

Designated as experimental, our station simulates what life was like a hundred years ago before AI superseded man's ability to think. In an effort to justify replacing all human tasks with a machine-driven workforce, the governing body of UCom forces everyone on board to carry out their jobs manually and submit weekly efficiency stats for comparison. I can't imagine those reports read well. Most of the time we just sit around doing nothing.

In an effort to drown out the ear-piercing warning bell, I cover my head with my standard-issue pillow. Frustrated, and growing pissier by the second, my irritation erupts into anger when my comm watch starts to ring. I answer without looking, the predawn hours inhibiting my already non-existent filter. It's Brandon, the only other medic assigned to Station U, and my night relief.

"Who's dead? Someone better be dead or about to meet Jesus, because, I swear, if you're waking me up for any reason other than to say you're about to fix that ridiculous alarm, I'm going to lose it."

"Get up. Get here now." The tone in his voice is serious and not dripping with its usual amount of sarcasm and inappropriate sexual humor.

"Get where now? What in the hell could be that serious at 2:00 a.m.? You know nothing ever happens here."

"The static on the call mixed with the volume of the alarm make whatever he's trying to say inaudible. I take a few steps to the right, hoping to improve the reception. "You there? Are Serena and the rest of the female mechanics threatening to strike over the tampon shortage again? Tell them they've been in the queue for a month and a half. They can just get over it and make do like the rest of us until they come in."

"What? Gross. No. I'm serious, Jayla. Fucking get up and come to the landing bay. We've got incoming, and they aren't answering our request for identification. No response on the comms at all. It could be a legit Unwelcome. Everyone who doesn't have an assigned role has been instructed to take cover. Haven't you noticed all the people running around like crazy?"

This is most likely a false alarm, but he thinks we're on the brink of a possible invasion, and is still uncomfortable at the mere *mention* of menstruation? Men.

"Shit, are you serious?" I flop out of bed and run to my door, peering out just to make sure this isn't another one of Brandon's less than humorous attempts to get a rise out of me. Rushing into the hall, I knock straight into Leandra—my favorite of the aforementioned mechanic bitch brigade. Her blond hair is dirty and thrown up into a messy bun, and her dark uniform is rumpled like she fell asleep without bothering to take it off. Abruptly closing the open comm line with Brandon, I make sure she's okay.

"Oh damn, girl I'm sorry. Are you all right?"

Getting up off the floor, she leans closer. "Yeah, yeah, all good. You hear what's happening? I'm on my way to the armory now. Me and the other mechanics have to load all the weapons in case things get bad." Her lips pull into a tight smile as she scans my face. "I'll see you out there."

She starts off slowly down the hall, then jogs up the stairs to my left. The bright red lights embedded high in the monotone gray walls are flashing rapidly, but their position makes it impossible to see them from inside the pods. What the hell is the point of that? If my sex dream hadn't sucked so bad, I might have stayed asleep.

Leandra pauses briefly at the top of the stairs, waving to get my attention. "Be careful, Jay," she says and turns the corner out of sight.

There's a strict protocol for ships seeking entrance into one of UCom's protected zones. If you don't answer the scripted questions, you're treated as a hostile or an "Unwelcome." It's pretty simple. Comply and receive protection. Refuse and get left for the wolves and space scavengers who go planet-to-planet raping and pillaging like the old-world Vikings did on Earth.

Completely militarized, UCom spans multiple planets and even galaxies. They've managed to maintain peace between numerous races of beings, all while protecting those who seek asylum—as long as they're willing to successfully integrate into the population. Unfortunately for us, since we're largely off the map, we don't have a military presence and have been given very little instruction on what to do in case of an emergency. The military officer in charge of our little heap of metal never checks in, and the only time anyone visited in any official government capacity, they arrested someone for letting their official work license expire.

Shuddering at our lack of preparation and disturbed by the possibility of a credible threat, I retreat back into my cabin and throw on my uniform. I allow myself another brief look down the hallway for Rett, making sure his nosey ass isn't skittering around. He *should* be in his pod safe and sound since his culinary skills aren't deemed necessary in an emergency. Sprinting up the four flights of stairs and six hallways between my quarters and the landing bay, I arrive just in time to see guns being distributed to the untrained group of blue-collar workers who make up our population.

The large open area surrounding the landing strip is still unoccupied. A small wave of relief washes over me at seeing the ship hasn't shown up yet. We still have a little time to figure this out. With no other way in or out of the station save for the waste removal hatch on the lowest level, the upper deck is only used to house three things: spacecrafts that arrive for transport and supply drop offs, my office and makeshift medical bay, and the main control hub for the doors, which everyone is currently huddled around. As usual, Brandon's sitting there being completely useless, letting his long, lanky arms hang at his sides while he watches everyone else work.

"What took you so long? What are we supposed to do?" Brandon snaps. My eyes narrow at his accusatory tone. Of course he expects me to take the lead and tell him what to do. As medics, we're both assigned to keep things orderly in times of an emergency, but since he spends his shifts sleeping or watching porn and has never bothered to participate in monthly crew meetings, it's obvious he has no intention of sharing our assigned task.

Staring at the sweat collecting in his busy eyebrows, I shrug my shoulders. "How the hell should I know? I'm just a medic." Brandon huffs. "What? I got the exact same training you did. You know, those two videos on the importance of maintaining *community relations*?" I find the whole idea completely ridiculous. Getting along with other species isn't difficult; you just can't be an asshole.

"You better figure it out. There's a ship one hundred and fifty kilometers outside our entryway that isn't responding to our demands to alter its trajectory. I double checked the logs, Jay. There are no scheduled drops and no cleared asylum claims needing temporary placement. They haven't slowed or made any attempt to steer out of our path. We either have to open up or risk them smashing into us. You know this rust bucket can't take that type of impact. It would kill us all!"

Annoyed by his overly panicked state and my rudely interrupted beauty sleep, I lose all remaining patience. There's something that's always bothered me about his face. Individually his features aren't bad, but his wide, slightly upturned nose and thin lips paired with the way he squints his eyes when you ask him to do *anything* really grates on my nerves.

"Seriously, get yourself together, dude, and grow some balls. Maybe they're friendlies and just don't speak Meta. Have you bothered trying any of the other languages?"

"Why would I need to do that? Everyone within the boundary speaks Meta. Don't be stupid."

"Don't be stupid? You asshat. You know just because fluency in Meta is required for permanent acceptance doesn't mean every single being who's attempted to learn it understands like we do."

"Well, then I guess it's a good thing you're our fearless translator, huh? Why don't you go stand up front and center and greet them when they arrive?"

"Oh, come off it, B. I don't know what has your panties in such a wad, but we'll figure this out."

Speaking of panties, I really should have changed mine...

I close my eyes, trying not to let the panic that's spreading like wildfire affect me. We've never prepared for anything close to this. An Unwelcome forcing their way onto a UCom-owned station is practically unheard of.

"Where's Ven?" I ask, his brotherly face fresh in my mind. A familiar tingle creeps into my cheeks, warming them. I don't need a mirror to know they're blood red. I have no idea how I'm going to face him after he starred in my dream. Brandon's eyes narrow, then scan the room around us trying to discover the motivation behind my blush. "Get him up here. He might be the softest Sinoa in existence, but he looks mean as hell and might be enough of a deterrent against anyone acting aggressively. How much time do we have before they get here?"

"About five minutes," he says staring at his feet. At least he has the decency to look embarrassed by his pathetic lack of manhood. Grabbing the black square comm attached to his wrist, he calls Ven to our location.

With Ven's pod only one floor down, he arrives quickly. Sinoans are an asexual race of gentle giants that hail from the outermost planet in the Andromeda Galaxy. Mostly farmers and artisans, they're the quintessential example why you shouldn't judge a book by its cover. With a form built for hard labor, Sinoans are made of layers upon layers of muscle. Add in their naturally weathered skin, large stature, and the extra set of hands, and they give off an intimidating vibe. Ven stands at least six-foot-eight and has to weigh close to two-hundred-and-eighty pounds. Too bad he wouldn't hurt a fly. I once caught him mourning the death of a rat he befriended after it stowed away in a compost fertilizer delivery from Earth.

I guess that explains the feeling of multiple hands in my dream...

Wondering how in all the worlds I was unofficially elected the person who makes the big decisions, I greet Ven in Meta and give him a quick rundown of what's happening. Still uncomfortable maintaining eye contact with him, I shift my focus to the rest of the now-armed rag-tag security squad and attempt to brief them on my *"stand there, look intimidating and try not to die"* plan, hoping everyone can hear me above the continued blare of the sirens.

Not successfully capturing their attention, I hop up on top of one of the empty plasma gun boxes and repeat myself. "Look, we all know there's a risk in opening the bay door, but there's an even greater one if we don't. Whoever has breached our perimeter may take our lack of response as an act of aggression and decide to openly attack. I think it's better to let them in and see what happens. There's always a possibility this is just someone who needs help."

Stepping forward with a pinched expression, Serena glares at me with a look of challenge in her eyes. Of course, she wants to argue. I square my shoulders and ready myself for whatever nonsense she's about to spew. Serena might get away with treating everyone else like a peon, but that shit doesn't fly with me.

"Are you insane? Just let them in? We have no idea who the hell they are or what they want. In case you didn't notice, we don't have an army." She holds up the gun in her hand. "We don't even know if these actually work. This is a fucking nothing station in the middle of nowhere." Looking around at everyone as if they're completely ignorant, she zeroes in on poor Zone, who's standing closest to her.

"If we were supposed to take in strays, we would've been cleared for it. There are protocols put in place to handle them. The UCom board would have sent all the necessary screening tools, supplies, and security to keep us safe. Do you see any of that?" She cranes her head dramatically. "If we open those doors, we could get slaughtered."

Staring at her ridiculously perfect creamy skin and long red hair, I'm annoyed. I can't help but agree with her logic. It's her blatant disregard for any life outside of her own that has me wanting to slap her upside the head. "Yeah. We could," I deadpan.

Throwing her hands up in exasperation, she turns to another one of her groupies beside her and continues to complain loudly.

Unable to think over the noise, I stalk over to the main control hub and start yanking out wires I'm pretty sure have something to do with our alarm system. The sirens cut off abruptly, and for the first time since waking, I can hear myself think.

"Ah, all better now." The disruptive chaos falls silent, and all heads turn my way. Judging by the large number of open-mouthed stares, most of the crew find my actions extreme. I'm not trying to make a statement; I'm just sick of all the damn screeching.

Zone, one of three electricians tasked with keeping our shitty floating paradise running, looks stunned. His lips are pursed in disapproval, but his perfectly smooth ash-colored skin shows no sign of wrinkling. Not even the blare of the red warning lights bouncing off the walls can compete with the irritation gleaming in his neon yellow eyes.

"You know that's going to take me a week to fix right?"

"Well, you're in luck. Dead people don't have to fix things, and we're probably all about to die." He nods his head in agreement at the absence of humor in my tone. We really could die, but what would freaking out about it do? "So, is everyone ready or what? Because by the looks of the radar, we have exactly forty-five seconds to open those doors or this place is going to get an unintentional facelift. Let's get this over with." I sigh as the group continues to squabble amongst themselves.

"It's against protocol Jayla," Brandon says, shuffling backward, away from where the master key rests inside the door lock.

"Of course it's against protocol! It's stupid! Why is this such a hard concept to understand?" Serena continues to gripe from the back. If her eyes roll any further back in her head, she'll be staring at her brain. Well, that's assuming she has one.

"They could need help. Jayla's right." Finally chiming in, Leandra moves from the outskirts of the group and inches closer to the center.

Serena snorts. "Oh, shut up Lea. We all know why you agree with her. I can feel you pining after her from here."

Leandra's brows shoot up. Balling her fists, she stomps forward. "No, I'm not. What the hell, Serena? Why are you such a heinous bitch?"

"Oh, for fuck's sake, *move over*!" I yell, pushing my way through the two bodies separating me from the control panel.

Determined, I turn the key. The group stares at me with a mixture of surprise, shock, and anger as they look back and forth between the entrance and me. Unable to hear anything outside of the eerie silence betraying the group's collective dread and the erratic rhythm of my pounding heart, I keep my gaze locked on the aged metal hatch, waiting for whatever potential disaster the next few minutes have to offer.

CHAPTER TWO

Jayla

THE ROUGH CLAMOR of grinding gears puts everyone on high alert as the worn-out joints of the bay door squeal under the strain of lifting its enormous weight. The previously smooth, gray metal, now rutty and rusted with age, moves slowly, almost ominously as it creaks and shakes to life. Standing in the middle of the room, alongside Brandon and Ven, I watch the others spread out evenly, flanking our left and right, anticipating the worst. Our unimpressive group of twenty is all that defends the remaining one hundred souls taking shelter in their pods.

I lean forward, trying to get a closer look, as the foreign ship comes into view. Its large, patchwork body hovers loudly as it putters its way into our terminal. Like a child's art project, it looks thrown together, piece-by-piece, and part of me wonders how it sustained the flight necessary to get here. Risking a look at Leandra, I see her green eyes narrow in confusion as she studies the bizarre exterior. She's no doubt cataloging all the safety regulations this thing is breaking. As its large, angular hatch rises, Ven's hands visibly tremble around his guns in my periphery.

So much for intimidation. What does a girl have to do to find a guy with some balls around here?

Shaking my head, I position myself in front of Ven, all five-foot-two inches of me, hoping to provide some comfort to the big guy. Reaching behind me, I offer him my hand. Taking it with no hesitation, he drops his gun and holds on for dear life. With the ship's main hatch now open, we're all stiff with anticipation, impatient for our potential enemies to reveal themselves. After five minutes of waiting with no explosions or knife throwing, I risk a side glance at Brandon.

"Well, this is anti-climactic as shit," I whisper with tight lips.

"Seriously, Jay. Do you always have to make jokes? This isn't funny. Why don't you think they've come out yet?" he asks.

"I don't know, asshole. Maybe they're waiting for us to approach first? We're all standing here with giant guns. Not exactly the friendliest way to receive guests, if you know what I mean?"

"Well, no one here wanted to *receive* anything. You made that choice for us, remember? This is your mess to deal with. Go say something." He taps his shoe in an erratic rhythm as we continue to argue.

"What do you mean 'say something'? Like what? 'Welcome, please don't murder us'?" My tone rises in pitch the more annoyed I get.

"Shit, I don't know. You're the one who speaks a billion languages. Try to get them talking. Figure out what they are before someone gets trigger happy and blows a hole in our wall and we all get sucked into space!"

"Fine. Give me a minute to think of something." Uneasy as I move into the line of fire, I start to hum under my breath until I'm twenty feet from the open spacecraft. One of my more annoying habits, I hum when I get nervous and always revert back to the song my grandfather sang to me as a child. Lyrical but completely foreign to everyone but me, it was something only the two of us shared. A long-forgotten nursery rhyme sung in a long dead language.

Close enough to hear the ship's occupants shuffling around, I stand tall and open my hands in the universal gesture of peace. Letting the melody calm me, I close my eyes and take in a deep breath, trying to dispel my anxiety. A cold burning sensation shoots across my neck and steadily spreads down to my toes.

What the hell is happening?

The smell invading my nose is incredible—a cross between earthy and sweet. My instincts are screaming for me to flee, but my limbs are heavy and immobile. Unable to control myself, I give into the scent swirling around me and let go of reality. I can hear someone in the distance yelling at me, but with my eyes still closed and completely relaxed, the rational part of me couldn't care less. I just want to wrap myself in whatever this is and stay here forever. Not until the cool nothingness relents do I notice the hand wrapped around my throat and the blade pressed against the side of my neck. The voice in my ear, cold and beautiful, whispers in a dialect no other living being should know.

"Move and I will end you. Speak, and I will relieve them of their lives."

Impossible.

Unmoving, I wait as whatever neutralized my instincts fades away.

"You understand me? Nod only once," the female asks.

I move carefully, wincing as the severe edge of her weapon cuts into my neck. The smell of iron and sweat overpower the blissful scent that enveloped me before. My captor leans in and runs her nose up the length of my neck, sucking in a deep breath. I tense at the feel of her rough tongue as she licks the blood slowly dripping from the wound. My skin prickles as her warm breath teases my skin and, despite being terrified, I fight against pressing further into her.

What the hell? Why are my nipples hard?

"You do not smell of our enemies and you do not contain the taint of their blood. How is it you possess knowledge of our language?"

Completely off kilter and confused by my feelings, I speak without restraint, my memory of the ancient language allowing for broken answers at best.

"I speak many languages, including yours, thanks to my father and grandfather. How the hell do *you* speak it? All your people are supposed to be dead."

Her grip suddenly tightens. "I should gut you for your disrespect," she hisses. "You think a group of simpletons like the Inokine could destroy a race as fierce and superior as the Illusians? We exist, as we have *always* existed, outsmarting our enemies, until they lie screaming beneath our feet.

Holy. Balls. If she's telling the truth, then this situation just got a whole lot more interesting.

Releasing her grip on my throat, she places her hand in my hair and curls her fingers through the long black strands, twisting until my scalp burns. Forcing all one hundred and thirty pounds of me toward my crew, she yanks my head back, keeping her blade firmly pressed against my throat.

"Have them drop their weapons. They are no match for me and I do not wish to shed any more blood on this day," she says, sighing.

I search the group for Ven and Brandon. Shock registers in their eyes—and something else. Desire, maybe? It's obvious neither of them plan on helping me.

How annoying. Guess I've got to save myself.

"If you can kill us all in a millisecond, why are you even bothering to talk?" I ask, pissed and completely over the confrontation.

"We are here for asylum. We only wish to seek temporary shelter until our males arrive. Our enemies discovered our location and launched an all-out assault. I have only females and their young onboard. Some are injured and need assistance. Lower your weapons, and I will release you. Keep them up, and I will dismantle every living creature on this ship piece by piece, starting with you."

Ugh, couldn't she have just started off with that?

Knowing what she is, at least who she claims to be, not only validates the painful clench of dread in the pit of my stomach but threatens to send me into an all-out panic. I'm not about to fuck around and get murdered.

"You'll agree not to harm anyone if they lower their weapons?" I ask, hesitant to believe her.

"You have my word. But none of your males are to touch my females or their offspring. It is strictly forbidden. I will not hesitate to end the lives of those who choose to violate our most sacred of laws. We will deal with you, and you only. Now have them stand down. I am losing my patience."

Speaking in Meta, I address the armed group in front of me. With guns aimed and steady, they almost look intimidating. *Almost.*

"Listen. I'm fine. Don't lose your asses okay? Don't panic, please."

Brandon is the first to respond, whisper-yelling like a complete moron.

"What do you mean, 'don't panic'? Did you see how fast she is? Have you seen what she looks like?"

"Does it look like I can see her, dumbass? They're just here for aid. They were attacked, the men stayed to fight, and the women escaped. Enough with story time. Just drop the damn guns so she'll let me go!"

"Drop our weapons? Are you completely botched? I'm not dropping shit!" My captor's head dips to the right as Serena's raised voice echoes through the mostly silent room. More than half the group nods in agreement, and my heart beats wildly in my chest. That bitch is going to get me killed. I swear I'm going to shave her head in her sleep if I get out of this still breathing.

"Look, I don't know what she's capable of, but from this sweet little intro, I can tell you all of us are dead if we refuse. Stop trying to be a hardass, Serena. You're going to get everyone killed."

I search their faces, mentally willing them one-by-one to stand down. After a moment of hesitation, weapons start to lower, and I exhale in relief. Clutching her gun to her chest, Serena steps forward and juts out her hip.

"I'm not getting anyone killed, Jayla. That's on you. I hope you know what you're doing. Don't come crying to me when she slits your throat in your sleep." Heaving the gun over her shoulder, Serena huffs. "I'm taking this with me. No way I'm letting some sketchy-looking space skank tell *me* what to do." With her gaze locked on the being behind me, Serena backs away slowly until she reaches the stairwell.

If she slits my throat, I won't be able to go anywhere, idiot.

Finally releasing her hold, apparently satisfied that everyone is complying with her demands, the Illusian female shoves me forward, hard. My knees grind against the rough, sandpaper-like surface of the floor as I lose my balance. Turning to finally catch a glimpse of the hard body that held me captive so easily, my mouth drops open in shock.

Expecting to see a terrifying space creature spawned from the depths of hell, I'm awestruck by the stark, almost comedic contrast in her appearance. At no taller than five-foot six, with a lithe, toned frame, her sun-kissed skin is covered in open wounds and bruises—clear evidence of the attack that led her to our door. With tightly rolled, shoulder-length dreads and a face that would put even the most beautiful human at a disadvantage, her crimson eyes scan her surroundings for any hint of a threat.

I have no doubt she's ready to unleash deadly force at a moment's notice. Her thin, stately nose, high cheekbones and full, silky lips are sensual, save for the razor-sharp teeth barely visible under her impressive pout. She's pure predator and can probably monopolize the attention of any being—male or female. Every part of her is designed to draw in her prey and appeal to the primal sexual need that calls to us all. Understanding now what my grandfather meant when he described this lost race of beings, I come to a harsh conclusion.

We are so fucked.

CHAPTER THREE

Jayla

SITTING by while the wounded female unloads her people has me feeling like a miserable hag. She winces as she escorts them—even carrying them at times—one by one to the medical bay. No one else is willing to help. Despite feeling drawn to her physically, something inside of them, inside of me as well, knows to get the hell away from her while they still can. There's something unnatural about her. The skin-tight, head-to-toe animal hide she wears is enough to make anyone slap their momma for a chance to get her naked. But the way she carries herself, her movements smooth and effortless, exudes unadulterated lethality. I shift, trying to ignore the cold, wet reminder of my pathetic sex life riding up my ass.

If the females are that hot, what do the males look like?

Resting my head on the worn plexiglass of the adjoining office door, I attempt to ignore my urge to help her. As one of the only medical personnel on base—and the only female—it's obvious I'm going to have to suck it up and go assess them. They need help. But I'd be a fool not to acknowledge my screaming desire to hide. If the red-eyed female is truly an Illusian, if they all are, we're literally about to rewrite history.

The mystery of their disappearance is a bit of a family-inherited obsession. My great-grandfather James disappeared when my grandfather was just a boy. James was a pioneer in the scientific community, and when space exploration really started to advance, worked directly with many of the newly discovered species. No one fascinated him more than the Illusians. My grandfather latched onto the stories his father used to tell and when old enough, researched them relentlessly. Convinced they had something to do with James disappearance, my father and grandfather compiled hundreds of manuscripts chronicling the series of events that surrounded the Illusians suspected demise. It seems the rest of the universe forgot they ever existed—or maybe they never knew. Too bad all those books are stored away in boxes on Earth with the rest of my dad's effects.

Knowing there's only a slim chance in hell she'll receive it anytime soon, I access my comm and send a quick message to my cousin Brittany—my only living family member. If anyone is willing to drop their plans and go digging through the mounds of crap my childhood home contains, it'll be her.

I can't recall much of what was spoken between my grandfather and I, but his tales of the lost warriors of Illusia stand out best. Thinking back to the many nights his outlandish stories lulled me to sleep, I can only assume the psycho I met earlier is what he referred to as a Keeper.

Romanticized as they were in his mind, Keepers are brutal; their violence and combat skills are only exceeded by those of their males. A group of huntresses whose sole purpose is to protect those of their clan who can't defend themselves. The ultimate warriors, they can slice a man in half before he can register their presence. Fundamentally designed to be irresistible in order to draw unwanted attention away from those in their charge, their appeal can be measured on a molecular level. Their scent, appearance…everything is used to lure in their mark.

Annoyed at the sudden emergence of my do-gooder side, I reluctantly leave the faux safety of the office and enter the poorly lit medical bay. Careful to make full eye contact with the Keeper, I move slowly. The last thing I want is to look aggressive and get my ass handed to me again.

"Is this everyone?" The scattered conversations stall as my knowledge of Illusian stuns them into silence.

"The Human knows of our kind and speaks our language. Do not fear her, she knows her place," the Keeper says, reassuring them.

My place? Oh, hell no.

I bite my tongue and continue. "We have plenty of medical supplies, food, and water here to last you however long you need. Unfortunately, there aren't a whole lot of places capable of housing all twelve of you, so this room is going to have to suffice." I stifle my attitude before I say something stupid. Knowing my smart mouth won't go over well with the Keeper, I try to keep my frustration to myself. Sizing up the room, the Keeper zeroes in on the lone entry point.

"This will be fine. Where are your warriors? You will need to anticipate an attack at some point. Our enemies will come for us, and when they do, death will be the least of your concerns. Your females closely resemble ours, which leaves you vulnerable to the vile and repulsive obsession they hold for us. The things they desire are, *unsavory,* to say the least. We appreciate your hospitality but, without the additional protection from our men, we are left… at a disadvantage. Send me your strongest, and I will brief them on what to expect if an incursion takes place," she says as she stands at attention in front of me.

"Congratulations, you're looking at her." I smile for emphasis. The Keeper's eyes narrow, unimpressed.

"You cannot be serious. You are but a whisper of a thing, less capable of defending yourself than a babe clutching his mother's breast."

"Look, this is a labor outpost. Everyone here works their trade and that's it. We don't have trained soldiers. What you saw earlier is as good as it gets." I shrug and busy my fingers with the hem of my shirt.

"Perhaps coming here was a mistake. You offer us no more safety than the void outside. Our males should arrive shortly. The transport vehicle we commissioned for our last-minute escape will not sustain flight. We barely survived our trip here. Be warned. You may know little of our kind, but you will need to brief your human males to take caution. Our warriors are lethal and hold the lives of their female counterparts above all else. Mated females are best left alone, even by you if they do not require immediate intervention. Any foreign scent can and will be seen as offensive, and their primal need to protect will not go unanswered."

My mouth waters at the thought of their males and I swallow hard. Walking over to the windows, I push the button that darkens them, allowing for more privacy from prying eyes outside. I lean back against the exam table and wait for her to make the next move. The Keeper winces as she turns to face the group. A raven-haired boy, no more than six, jumps up and runs to her in response. She quickly waves him off, returning him to his mother's open arms. His little brow furrows in confusion. He doesn't look wounded or ill.

I wonder what that's all about?

I gesture toward the clenched muscles of her abdomen. She's guarding herself, holding her stomach to stifle her pain. "Why don't you let me take a look? I get you can murder me in like two seconds or whatever, but it's obvious you're hurt. Let me see if I can help."

"No. Tend to them first. If I have not stopped bleeding by the time they are all whole, I will agree to let you examine me." She surveys her group before her gaze lands on a female at the far edge of the room. She's leaning against the wall, holding her knees to her chest.

"Xandria, you first."

Petite and golden-haired, Xandria approaches with caution, her nervous lavender eyes fluttering between her Keeper and me. Her hesitancy resolves with a single nod from her protector, and she scoots up on the table with a tight smile.

"Hello, my name is Jayla. I'm going to take a look at—"

"That will not be necessary." The Keeper blocks my hand and shifts closer to her charge. "I can tell you where they are wounded."

As Xandria is covered head to toe in some sort of soft animal hide reminiscent of leather, I can't see anything without lifting her dress or removing it. A quick glance around the room confirms they're all dressed in a similarly modest fashion and, judging by their overbearing nanny's response to my attempt at a full body examination, that isn't going to change.

"Okay..."

Reaching out, she gently places her hand on the back of Xandria's neck and closes her eyes. "Her legs, they pain her a great deal." I nod, curling my fingers around the hem of her dress. The Keeper moves closer, like she's ready to pounce. The muscles of my shoulders clench at the feel of her cool breath on my neck.

"Take care not to harm her, human, or I will leave you with scars to remind you of your carelessness."

Oh, fuck this.

"Easy, I'm just trying to help. I'm all for respecting whatever weird ass cultural thing you have going on, but I won't tolerate being threatened. You get a day pass for what you pulled earlier, but try that shit again, and I'm out."

A chorus of gasps echo through the room. Many of the females staring at me in disbelief. Half expecting her to gouge my eyes out, but only partially caring after my lack of sleep, I brace myself for the worst. Instead of anger, I get something that suspiciously resembles approval.

What the hell?

She sighs, annoyance and exhaustion creasing the corners of her red eyes. "You will continue, and I will keep my word. But tread lightly. Those I am tasked with guarding are of utmost importance. They are not to be touched without caution."

"Message received. Now, will you back up and give me some breathing room? You can kill me just as quickly from a few feet away."

Her eyes narrow and she steps back an inch.

Well, that's better than nothing.

A dirty pair of bare feet greet me as I lift the hem of Xandria's long dress. I'm surprised by how light it is despite its dense appearance. Soft and buttery, the material carries the heavy tang of dirt and wild animal. I can only assume the group spent their seclusion in the elements, dressing with whatever was available. Oh, my goodness, if my grandfather could only see me now.

Moving upward, I visually catalog several wounds from her ankles to mid-thigh. A mixture of deep blues and purples, her battered legs are covered in handprints, scratches, and something that looks suspiciously like large bite marks. With an anatomy that mirrors a human, assessing her takes only seconds. Meeting her gaze, I silently question the need to go higher, trying to allow her to maintain as much dignity as possible. She shakes her head, tears gathering in her eyes. The Keeper responds to her distress, answering for her.

"She remains intact. They failed to violate her, not that they did not try vigorously. You will see many wounds like this today and you are to speak of them to no one. You may fear my presence now, but if the time comes you are facing a similar circumstance, I will not allow you to be defiled. No being should be subjected to that type of cruel savagery."

With a lump in my throat the size of Jupiter and goosebumps coating my skin, I continue to care for the small group of refugees. One by one, each female comes to the table, and the Keeper stands faithfully by to direct my focus. I clean and dress wounds, reset bones, and administer antibiotics until I'm so weary, I can hardly stand. Six hours have passed since being woken in the middle of the night, and after re-examining my newly inherited patients once more for good measure, I see I'm not the only one beyond exhausted.

After completing the immunizations for both of the children, I sink down in my cheap, second-hand office chair and pick at the exposed foam. Leaning back, I catch a whiff of my armpits and wrinkle my nose. Damn, I need a shower. And a nap. Scratch that, I need to fucking hibernate. But there's no way I'll be able to shut my mind up long enough to sleep.

I'm on edge, the scattered thoughts rattling around in my brain demanding my attention. I can't get past the image of Xandria's thighs. It's making me physically nauseous. All but three of the females I treated will require additional care and dressing changes. According to the Keeper, the remainder will be fine waiting for the rest of their group, whatever that means. What the hell kind of beasts could assault a group of women and children? Feeling unsettled and driven to help, I open my eyes and force myself to get back to work.

After distributing the last of our standard issue, scratchy, mixed-fiber blankets and pillows, I watch as the Keeper, and who I think are probably the mated females she mentioned before, help the other females and children into their makeshift beds. It's clear by the way they interact there's a noticeable difference between the three groups. The unmated females are by far the most vulnerable outside the children. They display a certain air of helplessness and always look to the Keeper for permission.

The mated females are more confident and carry themselves with purpose—not to mention they fared physically better, perhaps possessing a sharper sense of self-defense. All equally beautiful, their bronze skin and violet eyes are so startling, only the profound scarlet of their Keeper's gaze draws me away. If a straight girl like me can't stop staring at them, I have no idea how I'm going to keep the men on this rig from getting themselves killed. Keeping them completely separated and out of sight is the only option.

Seeing the last of the group tucked into their beds, I pad over to the Keeper. She's the only one I have left to assess. I keep my voice low, hoping not to disturb the others. "You care a great deal for them. It's clear you take your duties seriously."

"It is not a duty. It is my life's honor to protect those who continue our lineage. They hold the key to our survival and must be protected at all costs. Surely, even a member of a race as prolific as humans can understand the sentiment."

"Is this all that's left? Of your women and children, I mean?"

She stares at me as if she's trying to decode my intentions. Satisfied with whatever she sees in my tired, tawny eyes, she shakes her head.

"No. Our numbers are much more significant, but because of the continued onslaught from those who seek to master our race, we are unable to live together in large groups and must remain spread out to ensure our survival."

"That's intense. So, you guys have been hiding your entire lives?"

Suddenly irritated, her eyes narrow, and a sneer pulls at her ruby lips. "Those of Illusia do not hide! We choose to be strategic about our survival. We do not wish to live under the thumb of another. That is why we have avoided your kind for so long. You humans wish to capture and abuse us just as our sworn enemies do, except you hide your intentions under the guise of providing security to those in need. We are free and choose to be so despite the high cost of our independence."

I draw back, offended by her characterization of my race and her obvious prejudice against humans. Sure, there are shitty humans out there, but I just spent *hours* helping them.

"If you hate us so much, why come here?"

"We had no other choice."

"Sure, you did. You could have roved around in space, waiting on your males. No one here asked for you to show up uninvited and bring your drama to our doorstep."

"You know nothing of our choices."

Her body grows rigid as my tone sharpens. "No, you're right, I don't. And you know nothing of mine. I've spent my entire morning caring for your people without asking for anything in return, not even simple gratitude. I've asked very few questions, even though my lack of knowledge puts me seriously at risk. I don't know what diseases you may have but still I'm standing here, covered head-to-toe in your people's blood. Don't you dare treat me like I'm a total piece of shit when all I've done is try to help."

The Keeper's aggressive posture relaxes, and a deep sigh escapes her lips. "You are right. You have shown us a kindness I know has come at a personal cost. I may not have understood the words used earlier, but I saw the way your people responded to our arrival. They dislike you."

"Oh, I don't give a shit what they think," I say, unable to control the smirk that crosses my face.

Still hesitant, she prowls forward and sits down in front of me at the table. "You may be physically weak human, but you seem to possess a certain resilience. Perhaps your population is not at as much of a disadvantage as I previously thought."

"Jayla. My name is Jayla, but my friends call me Jay. Now please sit down and let me look at you. You've nearly bled through your entire top. Can I at least clean out the wound and cover it for you?" She nods, then jerks away from my outstretched hand.

"Do not touch my skin without gloves," she says in a low voice. "It contains the remnants of a neurotoxin my kind can excrete. I have not done so while in your presence, but the residue always lingers. As someone with no tolerance, even the smallest amount can cause you harm. I trust you will not share this information with anyone else."

"Shit." Dropping my hands quickly, I retrieve a set of gloves off the table. "Am I going to burst into flames or something? I can't remember if I used them on everyone earlier."

"Fear not, only Keepers and rare alpha females capable of inheriting mating gifts can produce this specific toxin. None of the others can. Despite seeming cruel, even I would not have allowed you to compromise yourself in such a way."

"Well, that's a relief."

Her eyes narrow at the sarcasm in my tone. "I am Naya."

"I'd say it's nice to meet you, but my neck still hurts from earlier, and I'm almost positive you ripped out half my damn hair." My lips flatten into a muted smile as I focus my attention on her abdomen. I don't have to search long, finding a very deep, angry stab wound just below her navel.

"How are you walking around with this?" The jagged edges of tissue are raw and shiny, and the pearl-colored inner lining of her stomach shows through. There are also several layers of dirt and grime that needs to be cleaned.

"The wound needs irrigation before I can stitch it closed, and it's going to hurt like hell. Let me go grab some morphine before we start." She stops me as I turn toward the medication dispenser.

"I do not desire to stop the pain. It serves as a reminder of why I must protect them so fiercely."

"All right, but don't eat me, okay?"

With gauze and sterile water, I clean the wound, a little

harder than necessary. I'm still bitter about what she did when they arrived. I flinch as sharp silver barbs protrude from her fingers and pierce the fabric of her sand-colored hand wraps when the pain is at its worst. Relieved they were in place during her demeaning show of force earlier, I shudder knowing she could have snuffed me out with a single touch.

Fan-fucking-tastic.

Reinforcing the ragged gash with gauze and a thick stretch bandage to keep pressure on the still-oozing wound, I make sure to leave her with an antimicrobial ointment. After dimming the lights and showing Naya how to lock the door, I drag myself back to my pod and grimace as the tight muscles in my legs cramp with every step.

Twenty-four going on eighty. My back is screaming at me after leaning over our worn-out exam table all morning. It's been broken since before I reported to my post. My watch vibrates with a text from Rett. Word of mouth has spread about our new visitors and apparently, people are pissed. *Oh, hell.* I forgot to report in with my medical director and apprise him of the situation. I call him, dreading the conversation. By letting the Illusians on board, I've created all kinds of potential contamination risks, and now my job, and potentially my freedom, are on the line.

Screw them all, it was the right thing to do.

Since the powers that be aren't willing to pay a licensed physician to sit inactive on a rig like ours, and they aren't able to justify sparing one of the AI docbots, medics like me are the first and only line of emergency responders. Technically, I'm required to "consult" with my medical director on all patient cases to ensure that I'm not overstepping my boundaries. Whatever. There was no time for all that bullshit. After trying to dial out twice and failing, I give up. I did my due diligence, and I'm going to lie my ass down and try to sleep. Crawling into bed after ripping off my bloodstained uniform, I let my exhaustion pull me under.

My sleep is fractured by the constant thoughts tumbling

around in my mind. Picturing the arrival of the highly desired Illusian warriors has my body in a tizzy. After a year-long sex drought, the mental image of an absolute alpha male has my dormant libido stirring, and like an Earth bear waking in the spring, it's angry and hungry as hell.

CHAPTER FOUR

Ren

SQUEEZING the half-protruding spine in the palm of my hand, I search for memories, pulling and tugging at every image and feeling within its twisted mind. This piece of shit knows something, has been given information that will explain how we were discovered. My lip curls up in disgust, and my blood boils as I dig in further. The vile images of the females he abused stand out like mountains in his thoughts. He cherishes them, keeps them in the forefront of his sick mind as a reminder of the spoils of war. After several moments of ripping him apart, I have found nothing of use, and my ire rises with every breath the abomination struggles to take.

"Put it with the others," I command, dropping the now limp body and crushing it beneath my feet. I press the sole of my foot deeper into the gash my blade created in the side of his throat, enjoying the gurgle that escapes with the final mist of air leaving him. That is my favorite sound, the ultimate reward for ridding the universe of another repulsive Inokine. The memory of its filthy hands reaching out to pull at Xandria's exposed legs as

Naya ripped her from him mid-thrust, makes me want to tear the life from him all over again. She fought well, holding on until Naya and I could free her.

Already having annihilated the rest of the group, I reach down and pulverize what remains of his skull and revel in the tiny popping noise it makes as his green brain tissue oozes between my fingers. Orion nods his head and grunts in approval as he passes, dragging two lifeless bodies behind him. The rest of those in my immediate vicinity growl as a fresh wave of blood lust hits us all. Fuck, I need to find something else to kill.

Sol, Rivan and I take our time arranging what remains of the Inokine across the front of their freighter, leaving a small parting gift for the scouts who are never far behind. I anticipate their arrival within two moons of these assholes failing to report, so taking extra care to ensure our trail cannot easily be followed is our most important task. This is the first time they have managed to catch us unaware, and the emergent evacuation of our females leaves them vulnerable without our protection. I will not allow such an oversight to happen again.

"*Acia* Ren, we have loaded the rest of the supplies and have set fire to what was deemed unnecessary." Rivan gestures to the large plumes of smoke in the distance. "Nexx has successfully scrubbed the area of all remaining trace of the females and their young but made sure to leave enough blood for those dickheads to pull emotion memory from the remains." He mentions the last part excitedly, knowing I will be pleased. And I am. The thought of them reliving the violent deaths of their brethren, one at a time, is enough to make my dick hard. Then again, being unmated without a female to bury it in, my dick is always hard.

"Very good." I direct my attention toward Sol, who is advancing down our vessel's open hatch toward me. The most adept of our collective at technology, he was able to pilfer a few much-needed parts from the enemy ship to finish constructing a new communication hub. Living a transient lifestyle to remain undiscovered, we have grown exceptionally good at building whatever we need.

"Any word from Xen or the others?" I ask, taking one last look around the forsaken desert planet we have lived on for the past eight months. Deemed uninhabitable by most, this planet offers the solitude necessary for our survival. After spending the majority of our time here bunkering down in mud huts through sandstorms brutal enough to peel the skin from your face, I fucking know why.

"No. But chances are good you gave them enough warning to escape unharmed. His group was more than five hundred miles from our location, and I didn't pick up any other ships off in the distance. Are you able to access them through the bond?" he asks.

"No, they have gone beyond my reach, and I am unable to risk meditation. Xen is a strong leader. He will not fail. We will get our females and meet at the designated point. Are the fuel cells capable of hyperdrive? I saw Ragar slicing his way through the group of five trying to destroy them." I smile at the visual. If I awarded my warriors points for creativity, his unique ways of dismantling a body and his natural drive for violence would leave him far ahead of the rest.

We both look to my second in command as he scoops up the last of the body parts littering the sand and launches them on top of the Inokine ship. The various limbs and entrails splatter an inky sheen across the reflective shield and complete our bloody masterpiece.

"Good kills," Sol says, congratulating him. Ignoring Sol completely, Ragar grunts and acknowledges my attention, ramming his gore covered fist against his chest as a sign of respect. Shaking my head, I mirror the gesture and return my attention to Sol.

Sol frowns and turns back toward me. "What?"

I arch a brow. He knows exactly what this look means, and his frivolous question annoys me." Why do you insist on speaking to him when you know he hates you? I will not be held responsible when he tires of your games and rips your head from your shoulders."

Very atypical of our kind, Sol is not driven by his instincts. We are a rigid, militaristic, violent race of beings. He would rather spend his time nose deep in one of his creations than out in the dirt, learning how to better protect his future mate. Illusian males are born to do two things, fight and fuck, and he has yet to be interested in either. I moved Sol directly under my command when it became clear his lack of dominance and respect for authority left him open to violence from any unmated male who felt he is inferior. After working with him for over seven birth cycles in an attempt to mold him into a more acceptable warrior, all I have managed to teach him is how to piss me off.

"I think I am growing on him. He did not even growl at me this time." Not seeing the humor in the situation, I wait silently for Sol to answer my original question.

"Yes," he says, sighing at my lack of amusement, "they should be able to handle one more jump, but will be burnt to shit after that."

Anticipating him rambling on about the need for additional parts, I respond before he can continue. "We will obtain what we need as we always do."

Assured of our ability to get in the air, I shift my attention to Nexx as he continues to sample the ground, searching for traces of Illusian emotion. A race able to pick up on the feelings of others through any fragment of DNA, the Inokine are expert trackers. Leaving any type of signature would be a grave mistake. I instruct the others to reinspect the area. Any hint of fear from our females is enough to encourage the Inokine, and I would rather die than give them the satisfaction.

Confident we adequately sanitized the surrounding terrain, I order everyone back inside the ship so we can begin tracking Naya and the other females. I am pleased with her quickness in gathering the females into the makeshift escape pod Sol built. The responsibility of tracking them to their current location now lies solely on my shoulders.

"I still don't fucking like it, *Acia* Ren. Why couldn't we glean a single useful piece of information from them?" Rivan asks while securing himself in the pilot seat.

"Maybe they really knew nothing." Sol's naivety is vexing but not misplaced. He abandons the conversation to calibrate the boxy communication controls he just pieced together.

Ari takes his place behind Rivan. "They were some of the most pathetic we have faced."

"Bullshit. They knew something. How else were they dispatched to our location? Ren couldn't even see them being given orders, and he ripped them apart from the inside out."

A growl tears from my throat. Rivan's eyes widen at my warning, and the sour stench of his fear permeates the small space around us. Ragar rises from his seat behind me, ready to respond to my demand for discipline, but I call him off through the bond and he backs down. As long as Rivan remembers his place, there is no need for a physical reminder.

Rivan rushes to recover from his lack of formality and insult to my abilities. "I meant no disrespect, *Acia* Ren. But there are only two races capable of interfering with Illusian abilities, and the Inokine aren't one of them. What if there are others conspiring against us?"

Using my formal title—*Acia*—is the correct choice. Those inferior to me can call me by my first name only when I choose to allow it. I rarely enforce such an old-world formality, but Rivan should have chosen his words more wisely. To disrespect me is to ask for death.

"Then they will meet a similar fate. No one takes from our females what is not freely given." My teeth grind at the image of Xandria's terror. United in a single cause, all nine of us grunt in agreement as Rivan powers up the thrusters and we begin our ascent into the clouds. I close my eyes and recline in my chair. My channel must be wide open if I am to reach Naya at such a far distance. As I let the tether within me that links us all search for familiar energy, I am jolted by the recoil of the hyperdrive kicking in. The walls around us shake and rattle as we increase speed. Remaining on task, I let my mind drift and am bombarded by an unfamiliar pull near Naya's location. Choosing to ignore it, no matter how desirable it feels, I focus on the faint projection Naya's own abilities broadcast and send Riven in her direction.

CHAPTER FIVE

Jayla

I'VE SPENT the last fifteen minutes trying to fix my face, and no matter what I do, I still look like hammered shit. With a sigh, I throw my shoulder length ebony locks up into a half bun and splash some cold water on my face. Pressing my forehead into the mirror, I let the cool glass soothe my puffy lids. I got maybe three hours of sleep before the anxiety of my new responsibilities forced me out of the sanctuary of my bed, and I'm in desperate need of a pick me up. Grabbing my comm, I dial Rett, hoping his bubbly personality will pull me out of this hell of my own making. Answering on the first ring, he brings his usual level of jovial sass.

"It's about damn time you called me! I've been messaging you all night! Why the hell did you turn off the auto slide feature on your door? I couldn't even come to check on you because your passcode wouldn't work. What am I supposed to do? Pick the lock like a savage? Please."

I roll my eyes at his theatrics. Of course, I shut off my door. If not, Rett would have bombarded me with questions as soon as the gossip tree activated. Yeah, the crew knows a group of Unwelcomes showed up, but no one knows who they are. They Illusians obviously kept themselves hidden for a reason, and I don't feel right being the person to blow the top off their secret.

"Look, can we just meet up for coffee in the lounge? I don't have long, but my brain is non-functional, and I feel like I'm about to implode. Plus, I need your help convincing the cooks to prepare additional meals for our new bunkmates."

"Girl, you sure you want to show your face after yesterday? There isn't a single person in this place without your name in their mouth. You should hear the venom Serena is spewing; it's creative as hell." His voice is annoyingly amused. Rett loves this kind of drama. I, on the other hand, avoid it like the plague.

"Ugh, yes. Fuck them," I say, mumbling various insults under my breath.

"This is why I love you. Give me ten minutes. You're paying by the way."

"Of course, I am." I roll my eyes and purse my lips. Rett is ridiculously cheap, which is odd, considering he always has the nicest things.

"Don't give me that sarcastic tone. Consider it payback for the emotional stress you've inflicted on me these past twenty-four hours!"

"Twenty-f—please, it's been like twelve. Get over yourself. I'll see you in a few." I end the call, unable to contain my laughter at his extreme narcissism.

Replacing my sleep sweats with my required uniform, I stand out like a star in the clear Earth sky. Everyone else wears black with various colored stripes signifying their chosen trade. Medics, though, are forced to wear full-body caution yellow. Whatever idiot decided to put light colors on someone who has to deal with blood and other bodily fluids all day deserves a good punch in the face. The only benefit of wearing such a ridiculous get up is that no one else tries to steal my size mediums and claim them as their own. I may not be getting any action, but I still want to look nice, and with a chest as big as mine, if my shirts aren't tight, my clothes tent out and hide the rest of my curves.

Having to wear an unflattering uniform isn't the worst thing that could happen, considering there hasn't been a single noteworthy man on this rig in the past year. But just because I've settled for my vibrator doesn't mean I've abandoned all hope of eventually having a decent sex life. For now, I guess I'll have to live vicariously through Rett.

Rett, coffee in hand, waits at the table as I arrive. His neatly pressed uniform hugs him a little too tightly around his pudgy middle. Nearly snorting at the way his head follows the round ass of an electrician as she walks by, I finally see how he convinces so many people to sleep with him. He's unassumingly adorable. The pallor of his skin and his tendency to blush make him look more angel than ass, which he most certainly is. And the prim lines of his schoolboy haircut suggest an innocence he lost before he even turned fourteen. Shoving a cup in front of me as I sit down, he narrows his eyes in disapproval at my disheveled appearance.

"I thought I was buying?" I ask with a smirk.

"Yeah, well, some of us have important things to do, Jay. We can't all wait around for you to take your sweet ass time. You can get me later."

"Three sugars and three creams, right?" I inspect my coffee closely.

"Ew. Yes. Just how like you like it. You know you're not normal, right?"

"Haven't we already established that? Neither are you, bitch, that's why we work so well together."

"Please, I am perfect and you know it. Anyway, stop avoiding me. What exactly happened yesterday? I want to hear *every single word*." He fluffs his perfectly coiffed, short blond hair and takes a sip of his coffee.

"I don't have time for all the details. The short story? I went up there to translate because there was an incoming that wouldn't respond—"

"Yes, yes, I know all that. Hurry up and get to the good part. I overheard Brandon and Roe talking about them being scary hot. I want to know about that. He leans in and props his chin up on his hands, fully engrossed in the story.

Annoyed, I add another sugar disk to my coffee.

"You finished?" I ask, raising a brow. "Anyway, the first one out basically threatened to slit my throat in front of everyone. I had barely talked her out of it when Serena's dumb ass almost got me killed by refusing to drop her gun."

"So, *who* and *what* are they? No one has any idea. Ven said they look human except for their freaky eyes and unnatural hotness."

"What the hell, Rett? How many people did you talk to?" My mouth widens in faux shock.

"Enough, now get on with it." He waves of his hand, rushing me to continue.

Despite my less than warm encounter with the Illusians, I feel strangely protective of them and uncomfortable giving him the details. I know honesty is the best policy, but in this case, I'm going with Plan B: lying my ass off.

"Not sure. I mean they speak Keylani but that doesn't help much, it's pretty widely spoken." I hold my breath hoping he buys it. *I've got to come up with some better material. That language doesn't even exist.*

"So, when do I get to meet them? It's been like, weeks since I've gotten some, and I'm so not into sampling the masses after the Shane incident."

"Don't you mean Shane *and* Cora?" I ask, raising both my eyebrows.

"Ugh, you're like a damn Earth elephant. You never forget. Whatever, yes. I'm finished trying to balance a twofer. Being polyamorous is not for me."

I roll my eyes, knowing all too well about his short attention span. "Listen, I need your advice. I don't know what to do." My forehead feels cool against the table as I lay my head down. Too lazy to pick It up, I angle my face toward him.

"What's up?"

"I didn't exactly follow protocol after they arrived. I got so wrapped up in making sure everyone was okay, I kind of forgot to notify Dr. Issacs...or anyone else."

Rett reclines back in his chair a moment and I fidget around with the compostable fibers of my coffee cup, waiting for a response. "You're being serious? You aren't messing with me?"

"I'm dead serious. I'm such an idiot. Am I totally screwed?"

"Well, that is explains it." The fine lines of his forehead bunch with worry. "General Sterling was listed on the manifest this morning. I may or may not have seen it after having a midnight snack up in the comm room with Dita."

"Wait, didn't you just say you hadn't gotten any in weeks?"

"Well, I forgot about that one," he says, dismissing me with a wave. "You better stop worrying about me and start worrying about yourself!"

"Why? Who is General Sterling? Why do I know that name?"

"Probably because he was one of the leading contributors to that nasty anti-fraternization policy that almost passed and made bumping uglies with your fellow station workers a criminal offense. Thank God the governing board didn't approve it, or we'd all be locked up by now."

"That asshole? Why is he coming here?"

"He was recently assigned to our sector. A little bird told me he got caught red handed doing some very inappropriate things with a Blurg when he was stationed near Pluto."

"A Blurg? Aren't those the nasty, gray worm-looking things that regurgitate their own feces when they're excited?" He gives me a nod while sipping his coffee. "Sick," I shudder. "How long do we have before he gets here?"

"He's scheduled to arrive today."

Looking at my watch, I gasp. It's almost noon. "Shit! Is he already here? How the hell could he manage that if he weren't already on his way?"

"No clue. Sometimes they do surprise inspections or whatever, but it is pretty suspect."

"Oh, crap. I've got to go. The last thing I need is our new visitors murdering a high-ranking general because the idiot tries to touch them."

"Let me walk you there. Here." He hands me his coffee so I can down the rest of it, knowing I might need the extra shot of caffeine to face whatever shit mess I managed to get myself into. Rett heads into the main chefs' quarters located in the middle of the kitchen to order additional meal tickets for the Illusians and grabs several bags of already made food to take with us.

"Look, you can't actually get near them, okay? I'm serious. They're wild as hell."

"Yes, mother. You always know how to steal my fun." He groans and ducks out of the way as I try to smack him in the shoulder.

"I am *not* old enough to be your mother!"

The various dirty looks and whispers aimed my way as we head upstairs don't escape me. I'm suddenly over the moon to have a friend like Rett and my gaze lingers on his profile long enough for him to notice.

"You keep looking at me like that and I might blush." A coy smile crosses his lips as he blows me a kiss.

"You know I love you, right? Like honest to God, don't know what I would do without you love you?"

He smiles and nudges me. Knocking into his shoulder playfully as we round the corner, I run straight into a hard body and bounce off, hitting the floor.

What the hell?

Looking up, I come face to face with not one, but two

menacing soldiers decked out in UCom special teams' high-density armor. I cringe at the set of six-inch knives hanging from their belts and look to Rett for help. He's always been great at talking his way out of trouble.

"Lovely day today, isn't it, gentlemen? I'm Rett. Nice to meet you." Rett holds out his hand to the first soldier peering down at me. Blond and well over six feet tall, his pale white skin is peppered with mean looking scars. Not getting a bite, Rett then turns to the shorter of the two, a thin guy with midnight hair and eyes the color of warm shit. Rett's gaze cuts to the high-end laser specter clutched between his fingers, and he drops his hand.

"Right, then. If you'll just excuse us, my friend and I will be on our merry little way." Rett pulls me to my feet, then attempts to pass but the soldiers remain unmoving. Neither of them has spoken a word. "Well, that's just rude." He looks at me, completely at a loss for what to do. Apparently, flirting isn't going to cut it.

Channeling my inner mean girl, I opt for a different route. "Hi, Officers Gibbons and Petty, is it?" I ask, leaning in close to read the names stamped on their uniforms. I flatten my expression, trying to look unimpressed.

"It's Sergeant, little girl."

Oh, someone's a douche bag.

"Whatever. I'm Medic Shirley, and I need access to my office and medical bay which just so happen to be located on the floor above us. Unless you're planning on carrying my friend and me up those stairs, I need you to get the hell out of the way." Both men perk up and take notice of my name.

"Medic Jayla Shirley?" Sergeant Gibbons asks. Rett and I exchange a nervous glance.

"Yes, I see you did your homework. Now, move along." I gesture at Rett to follow as I try to push my way between them. Sergeant Gibbons' tactical glove-covered hand wraps around my forearm roughly and halts my attempt.

"You need to come with me. *Now.*" His grip on my arm tightens further as he pulls me away from Rett.

"Get your fucking hands off me, you cretin," I say through gritted teeth. How dare he manhandle me like this. Pulled forward despite my attempt to lock my knees, I fall as Sergeant Gibbons continues to drag me down the hallway.

"Watch your mouth, bitch."

"Watch my mouth? Watch your hands, dickhead," I'm still fighting to get my feet under me so I can walk as I look back to Rett for support, only to find him standing there dumbfounded.

Why are all the men here so useless?

"Calm down, little girl." The condescension in Gibbons' voice only feeds my irritation.

"How about you let go of my fucking arm, dude? I learned how to walk like twenty years ago." Ripping my arm out of his grip, I hold it close to my chest and massage the now painful muscle. "What the hell is this all about, anyway?" I ask, fighting my desire to kick him in the balls.

"You'll find out soon enough. This will all go a lot faster if you comply."

Comply with what?

With little knowledge to ease my mind, I focus on the heavy clang of his combat boots on the metal walkway as we head toward a section of decommissioned bio domes.

"What are we doing here? These haven't been used in months." I drag my heels in an effort to slow down our pace. Everything about this situation feels wrong.

"Shut your mouth and try not to do anything else stupid." Gibbons glares at me with his dull green eyes as he whispers into the comm hidden beneath his collar.

The bio dome door opens, releasing dust and other remnants of its dormancy into the air. I scrunch my nose as the scent of decay hits me like a ton of bricks and I lean back, trying to cling to the fresh air in the hallway. Not having it, Gibbons shoves me forward. Impatient prick. The toe of my shoe snags on the door, and I tumble over the threshold. Jerking my head up to cuss him out, I stiffen at the sight of yet *another* person who could potentially kill me for the second time in less than twenty-four hours.

I'm really getting sick of this shit.

CHAPTER SIX

Jayla

PROPPED up on an overturned manure crate like it's a throne rather than a discarded box of animal excrement, General Sterling makes an exaggerated show of turning off his comm and removing his ear piece. His beady gray eyes rove over my body with a mixture of lust and loathing before signaling Gibbons to turn off his comm as well.

"Ah, Medic Shirley, I see you have finally decided to grace us with your presence." His thin lips twist up at the corners as he beckons me closer with a curl of his finger.

What a fucking weirdo.

Now that I can see him up close, I feel oddly sorry for the Blurg. A light-skinned human male, standing only five-foot-four, his balding scalp is artificially dyed to appear full of rich mahogany hair. With an oily, pock-marked complexion, a bulbous nose, and a sweaty brow, he looks more like a troll than a man. The idea of anyone willing to peel the clothes off his nasty, overly-plump body makes me nauseous. If that isn't enough, the arrogance radiating off of him, combined with his heavily applied aftershave and the stench of rotten vegetables floating around us, have me fighting hard not to vomit. I swear if the General gets any closer, I'm going to spew all over his perfectly shined shoes.

I cry out in pain and my body contorts as Gibbons' steel grip clamps down on my hand and twists my wrist, immobilizing me. Unsheathing the knife hanging from his belt, he cuts through the band of my comm watch, and shoves it into his pocket.

"Hey dick, give that back!" I yell, holding my wrist protectively. "What's your deal? Use your words!"

General Sterling laughs. "Well, we can't have you recording this conversation, now can we?"

"Oh, is this a super-secret meeting? You about to ask me to join your club?"

The general's eyes narrow at my sarcasm. "Joke all you want, Medic Shirley, but you are in a world of trouble. Not only did you assist an unauthorized group of Unwelcome to board a UCom funded station, you then used government-issued supplies on said group and failed to notify the proper authorities of their arrival." General Sterling counts my infractions on his fingers one by one. "Not to mention, you placed every single being within these walls in danger from any number of possible contaminants the Unwelcomes may or may not have brought with them."

The general clucks his tongue as he continues to scold me. "You should be thankful I was scanning the coms when the anonymous tip detailing your infractions came in. If I were a less forgiving man, you would already be on your way to Earth in UCom custody, charged with a number of policy violations."

His eyes narrow as he stands and closes the few steps between us, looming over me. I know I should be intimidated but I can't stop staring at his incredibly poor dye job. Does he seriously think he's fooling anyone? I shake my head, trying to focus.

"Now, since I'm an understanding man, and happen to be of great importance, perhaps I can make a deal with you."

I snort in response and meet his shifty eyes. "What do you

want from me, General? You're obviously willing to go to great lengths to make a point, so spit it out already. And for the love of all things holy, call off your pet." I nod to Gibbons, standing behind me. "If he manhandles me anymore, it won't matter what you want, I won't be able to use my hands for anything."

"Aww, Sergeant Gibbons is sorry. Aren't you, Gibby?" The general's crooked teeth jut out as he turns his lips into a pout and rises up on his toes to ruffle the soldier's hair. Gibbons clenches his jaw, and the vein in his forehead pops out in a show of barely contained fury. I can't control my snort as I watch him try to reign in his anger.

"Gibbons, don't you have something to say?" he asks, placing his hands on his hips.

"Sorry," Gibbons replies through clenched teeth.

Uh-oh, trouble in paradise.

"Good. Now we can move on." The general directs his attention back to me, clasping his hands behind his back. The deep green fibers of his undersized jacket strain as he circles me and the gold buttons signifying his elite position look ready to pop off.

"I won't ask much of you, Medic Shirley, but I require your discretion. After coming here to ensure the safety of our crew, I was informed our new visitors show a particularly unique and ferocious set of skills. I wish to know more about them. In fact, I wish to know everything about them. You can understand them and speak their language."

He smiles at me, eyes gleaming with malevolence, and leans in close enough for me to smell his rancid breath. "What I need from you," he taps me once on the nose with his finger, "is for you to get close to them and continue your duties as their medic. To ensure you have ample time, I am going to reassign all your other responsibilities to your counterpart. You are to learn as much as you can about the Unwelcomes and report back to me."

"And if I don't?" I ask, boldly raising my chin.

Gibbons shifts closer to me, eager for a confrontation. The general's grin widens, daring me to refuse. "Well, if you do not comply with my very generous offer, you can consider yourself relieved of your duties and you will be on the first freighter back to Earth. I fear however, that due to our increasingly thin resources, your trip may be rerouted several times. Perhaps, to pick up prisoners from the more, how do I put this, unpleasant planets?" He taps his chin, pretending to think, and widens his unsightly smile. "You could spend weeks, months even, lost in transit between here and there, outside the bounds of UCom jurisdiction and could be subjected to any number of displays of savagery. And without your watchful eye, the care of our new guests will fall into my hands. I am a very busy man Medic Shirley, but I'm more than willing to take the time needed to provide the *special attention* such a ravishing and vulnerable population very clearly needs."

Wow. This douchebag has no idea who he's dealing with.

"How many men did you bring with you, General?" I return his smug smile.

"Ten of my most trusted and highly trained soldiers. Might I ask why you think that is any of your concern?"

"No reason. Just wondering how you plan to deal with the arrival of their males. I mean, since you're planning on providing their females *special attention* and all. I'm not an expert or anything, but I'm guessing if the women are that ruthless, the men are a force to be reckoned with."

"Don't you worry your pretty little head. Surely, you heard they narrowly escaped with their lives. I doubt we'll have to worry about any of the others surviving."

How does he know any of that?

My bravado dissolves, and I grow weary of the conversation. Adopting an air of boredom, I ask, "Are we done here, or what? I have things I need to do"

"Absolutely. I look forward to working with you. Glad we

could come to an understanding. The general shifts his attention to the sentinel beside me. "Gibbons, please escort Medic Shirley up to the containment unit housing our guests."

Forcibly directing me out the door by my elbow, Gibbons shoves me toward the stairs. Despite his firm grip, I feel more settled the farther away we get from the general's sketchy face. My relief turns into irritation as Gibbon's continues to squeeze my arm despite my compliance.

What is this guy's deal?

Coming up to the stairs, he releases me and pushes me forward with the barrel of his gun. I reach out and grab the bags that Rett and I brought earlier and stumble up the first step.

"Walk," he says, increasing the pressure of the weapon pressed into my back.

"Ease up, Commando Creep, I'm doing what you want." If this were a normal situation, I'd be giving him much more lip, but even *I* know to shut up when someone has a gun pointed at me.

As I stagger over the last step, my jaw drops as the makeshift biohazard containment unit they created comes into view.

We can't manage to stock feminine supplies and refuse wipes, but they can set up a fully functional isolation unit in less than five hours?

Unable to see past the fractionated privacy windows of the heavily guarded entrance, my concern ramps into overdrive. There's only one way in and out of this place, save for the refuse shoots, and it's now under the physical control of the person who just threatened me with rape and violence. If the general is willing to treat me so callously, what is he willing to do to someone he sees as a liability?

The guards stationed in front of the containment unit nod to Gibbons as we approach. They shift to the side, allowing us to walk into the first of two small chambers. After the doors glide closed and the vacuum seal takes effect, we're immediately assaulted with the heavy pressure of air. The anti-microbial infused fog steals my breath, and my eyes burn as Gibbons shoves my face against one of the four spray nozzles. I gasp, fighting against his hold, then knee him in the groin as the mist clouds his vision. Stumbling back, I crawl low to the ground, feeling along the seams of the room for a way out. *Finally, the door!* A burst of energy surges through me as I push and pull at the impassive hatch to no avail.

"You're gonna regret that, bitch," he says, leaning over, cupping his groin. "I like it when whores fight back." I claw furiously at the door, desperate to get it open, but only manage to rip up my nails. Cornered in the small space, I press myself against the wall, trying to hide in the thick fog.

He lunges, swiping through the empty air. "Show yourself, skank, the longer you hide, the worse it's gonna hurt."

My lungs seize as I hold my breath. He's *right* beside me.

"Here kitty, kitty, kitty." He slams his fist into the wall beside me, narrowly missing my face. I almost cry in relief when I hear the beep signaling the first step's completion. The erratic beat of my heart pounds in my ears as I shoot forward, trying to escape through the now open door. Gibbons snags his hands in my ponytail and shoves me face first into the wall. I struggle to stay upright, but the force of the blow is so strong, my vision narrows, and I stumble. The tender skin of my face screams as a boot slams into my back and kicks me into the second chamber. Cradling my cheek, I feel my disfigured nose, and try to stifle the blood pouring out.

Gibbons continues kicking me, landing blow after blow, forcing my body into the fetal position. I hold my breath in an effort to withstand the brunt of his weight as he steps on my chest and pins me to the floor.

"Not so talkative now, are you, bitch?" He chuckles at my attempts to gather enough air to scream for help. I panic, and tears fill my eyes. He's going to kill me. And for what? Being sarcastic?

I clench my abs, praying for the pain to end. With a loud ding, the second and final door opens. A deep well of disappointment severs my hope as I stare out into the bay. There's no one there to help me. I'm going to die.

Gibbons, unconcerned with any potential witnesses, lifts me off the ground and tosses me out of the containment unit onto the landing. Hitting the stiff metal floor with a loud thud, I crawl away as fast as I can, afraid of what will happen if he gets ahold of me again. My head's fuzzy, and my vision blurred. An otherworldly roar fills my ears and I scrape my hand over my eyes in a desperate attempt to see. There, in front of me, is a rage-filled gaze so intense, not even the fear of Gibbons can distract me.

Warmed to my core by his feral intensity, I fight my need to breathe, afraid that even the slightest movement might label me as prey. I glance up at him with a heated stare and study the rest of his face. His oblong pupils blot out all evidence of the color underneath. More cat-like than the average human eyes, they're framed by thick, uncontrolled walnut brows that meet a strong, commanding nose. His nostrils flare as he scents the air, enraptured with whatever he finds. Wrapped in the most beguiling shade of bronze, his pronounced angular cheekbones and sharp, masculine jaw lined with short, wiry stubble make him, without a doubt, the most desirable being I have ever laid eyes on.

I stare at him, despite the feel of warm blood coating my hands and the floor beneath me. *I must be bleeding more than I thought.* Not ready to look away, I use the corner of my shirt to put pressure on the gash on my head but break my gaze when it feels mostly dry. *If it's not mine, then where is it coming from?* I scan the floor for signs of the source and see the limp, still twitching body of Sergeant Gibbons lying on his back in a rapidly expanding pool of blood—a gaping hole where his throat should be. His cruel, lifeless eyes are forever frozen in shock. His violent end should disturb me. I should be appalled by the blood and gore now seeping into the soles of my shoes. But after what he did to me, I can't seem to find any emotion for him at all.

CHAPTER SEVEN

Jayla

People say there are precious moments where one choice can change your life forever. Up until this second, I always thought they were full of shit.

"You are wounded female," he whispers in a deep rasp, trembling with rage. The rope-like muscles wrapping around his shoulders and arms strain and bunch as he prowls toward me. Effortlessly gathering me into his arms without hesitation, he holds me flush against his naked chest and heads deeper into the landing bay. Still in shock, I allow him to carry me. Part of me knows how dangerous he is, but as the infusion of adrenaline I felt earlier wanes, my battered body gives me little room to concentrate on anything else. As we continue to move through the small utility area leading onto the platform where the Illusian females arrived less than a day before, I let the warmth radiating off his bulky frame ease some of the gathering tension in my back. Less than ten feet away from my office, I notice several small red dots swirling around in my vision, muddying his chiseled perfection with their artificial glow.

Great, that douchebag Gibbons gave me a traumatic brain injury.

Still there, no matter how many times I blink, I squint and look at the tiny lights closer. My heart drops as soon as I recognize them for what they are. Sniper sights. Targeting him.

"No!" I yell, flailing my legs and arms, trying to get free. Every single part of me screams in discomfort, but he just saved my life. I can't let him die because he chose to protect me. My savior grunts in protest as I wriggle out of his hold and slide down his chest. With no other way to shield him, I press my back against his chest and spread my arms wide, covering as much of his massive body as my tiny frame will allow.

"What are you doing, woman?" he asks, eyes glinting in amusement.

"Don't you see them? The lights? You're a walking target!" He examines his reflection in the grayed out medical bay windows, smiling in response.

"Shooting me is not so easy, little *Skara.*" His tone is affectionate, and he seems completely unconcerned with the impending threat.

Distracted from the startling sight of his predatory smile by the sound of heavy boots quickly approaching, I press closer to him. Staring back in the direction of Gibbons' body, five UCom soldiers come into view alongside a very angry General Sterling. All of them are decked out in black battle armor, and their weapons are aimed directly us. I can feel the second my savior grows tense; the well-defined muscles of his abdomen vibrate from the low-pitched growl that tears from his lips.

"What and who the hell is this?" the general yells, holding the collar of the officer assigned to guard the outer doors of the area. He shoves him in our direction and stares at him with a pinched expression on his face.

"We tried to contact you, General, but your comm was turned off. We signaled Sergeant Gibbons as well." The officer hesitates for a moment and continues on. "He also failed to answer. The group only arrived half an hour ago. Trang and I couldn't figure out how to work the ancient switchboard that controls outgoing transmissions, so we just assumed you were expecting them. Were you not expecting them?" He sounds increasingly unsure about his choice to let them in. "They haven't caused any problems and have kept to themselves. We tried to communicate but weren't familiar with their language, so..."

"So, *what*? You thought it would be a good idea to just let them wander around, unguarded, while you sat on your ass at your assigned post?" the general asks, exasperated, shoving the officer again.

"Well, no... but we can monitor the cameras remotely, sir. That's why we radioed when we noticed Officer Gibbons'... condition."

"His condition? *His condition*? You idiot. He was slaughtered! His throat was ripped clear out of his body. This is a travesty! Detain them both immediately!"

With my heart threatening to beat out of my chest and my equilibrium on its last leg, I realize that sometime during the general's tirade, I've gone from vigilantly guarding the hard body behind me to using it as a prop to hold me up. My fatigued mind is teeters on the edge of shutting down, and my body isn't far behind. Knowing I won't be able to take any more abuse, I weigh my options, fully aware if I give an accurate translation of this conversation to the warrior at my back, more people are going to die. Well, more *humans,* anyway. And if I don't, I'll be the subject of a lot more mistreatment.

Screw the general. I'm not going anywhere.

Looking up at the bronze god behind me, angling my face so my bruised cheek rests against his hot, battle-worn skin, I keep my voice low. "They want to take us after what you did to that guy. The one in the green jacket threatened me earlier. He's the one in charge. It was his lackey you put down."

"That human put his hands on you. He deserved worse." Rage flares in his eyes at the unpleasant reminder of my abuse.

"That isn't how it works here. These men are going to try to take us by force." The harsh baritone of the warrior's laughter soothes my ears and does wonders to calm my raging mind.

Not a man accustomed to being laughed at, the general narrows his eyes. "Remove yourself from that beast, Medic Shirley, or we will do it for you. You are to come with us, immediately. As for your friend here, he will be held responsible for poor Officer Gibbons' death."

Well, shit. This is going exactly how I expected. In a last-ditch effort to diffuse the building tension, I try to reason with the general one last time. "Your poor sweet Gibby spent the entire trip back from that shady-as-hell meeting you forced me into trying to rearrange my face. I would have died if," I jerk my thumb to the male behind me, "*he* hadn't protected me." Shoving my hair away from the tender, discolored skin of my forehead and cheek, I shudder as the weight of my words settles in. I really did almost die tonight.

"Nonsense. My sergeant did no such thing." The gizzard-like flap on his neck jiggles with each shake of his head. He can deny it all he wants. I didn't kick my own ass in the containment unit.

"You call this nonsense?" Pulling up my shirt, I expose the angry damaged skin already bruising.

None too pleased with what he sees, the already pissed off warrior at my back lets out a fierce growl, causing all six men in front of us to stand even taller.

"I am growing tired of this, *Skara*." My body sways, and my skin tingles as the warrior wraps his calloused hands around my arms.

"Medic Shirley! Remove yourself now!" the general yells, increasing the tension ten-fold.

I panic as the soldiers advance toward us and leave General Sterling behind to watch the action. Knowing my life will forever be ruined if I submit to the general's demand, I gather my strength, preparing to fight like hell. I barely know the being holding me, but I won't let either of us go down easily.

"Enough!" my savior growls. The bright lights around us flicker in and out with the swell of his power. "What do you think, *Skara*? Should we teach them not to play with fire?" With a slight tilt of his head, the warrior sends all five bodies closing in on us to the floor, writhing around in pain like they're burning alive from the inside out.

Holy. Shit.

Shocked at the impressive display of power, General Sterling stares at his men as their faces twist in agony. My eardrums vibrate with the intensity of their screams. The general's face transforms from outrage to pure delight as he watches his soldiers flail about trying to put out the imaginary inferno. Like a child staring through the window of a toy store, he openly displays his lust and intrigue at seeing such power in action. Even I can't tear my eyes away from their torture. This is what the general wants, what he expects me to do. Discover all of the Illusians' secrets, so he can use them for his own benefit. There are plenty of races able to move things or even use pyrokinesis, but being able to manipulate the mind of another? Being able to make someone feel, see, hear, taste or smell whatever you want? That's completely unprecedented.

Excitement flashes in the general's eyes as he forces his gaze away from the spectacle and focuses his attention on me once more.

"Medic Shirley, do you think you could ask your friend there if, perhaps, he would be willing to relinquish his hold on my men?" He peers down at the soldier screaming the loudest and kicks his outstretched boot. "I promise to be a good boy from now on, as long as you, of course, are willing to continue with what we discussed earlier." The taut lines of his face relax, no doubt confident in whatever plan his devious mind is forming.

"He dares to speak to you? Do your people have no sense of self-preservation?" I hear from the warrior behind me, feeling the rumble of his words.

"He isn't my people. He's trying to negotiate by saying he'll stop being a psycho and leave your group alone if you'll agree to stop torturing his men." I lean into my rescuer harder now, fighting to remain upright. His hands shift to my lower arms.

"And you, little *Skara*? What does he say of you?" he asks, peering down at me.

"He'll leave me alone as long as I agree to be responsible for you." *If I agree to spy on you.* Just the thought of betraying him makes me want to crawl out of my skin.

"You believe him? These men are all party to your mistreatment. Taking their lives as penance would not be unreasonable. My actions would be just."

Unsure what to say, I remain silent for a moment. He speaks of killing them as if it's a chivalrous gesture, like he's offering to murder them to restore my honor or something.

"Ugh, no. That won't be necessary. Thanks, though." As much as I despise the general and his men, I don't want to be weighed down by the burden of being responsible for the loss of life. I took an oath to protect and care for those around me, not pick and choose who lives or dies.

"Come," my savior whispers as he redirects me into his arms and ceases his mental assault.

Completely ignoring his recovering men, the majority of them still trying to put out imaginary flames, the general makes his way back toward the door, choosing to enter the first decontamination chamber rather than assist those under his command to their feet. Running back toward us before the doors can close, he leans down over Gibbons and carelessly turns his body over with the point of his boot. Reaching down into the dead man's pocket, he retrieves my comm watch and looks up in our direction.

"Oh, and Medic Shirley," he smiles and waves the broken band, "I believe you will be needing this. You can expect my call shortly."

Tossing the unwearable watch in our direction, he laughs as it skids across the floor, landing nowhere near us. Sterling was definitely the last kid picked for sports.

Unable to keep my eyes open, I remain silent as the warrior carries me through the medical bay door. My mind is starting to succumb to the battering ram-like pain coursing through my body.

Gently laying me down on the cold, hard, exam table, my savior leans over me and carefully covers me with a blanket.

"You should not touch her like that, Aren. You know it will upset the others." I recognize the stern voice as Naya's.

"Do not concern yourself with my actions, Keeper. This human attempted to save my life."

Fully attuned to my surroundings, I eavesdrop as best I can, taking in the conversation going on around me.

"Ha! She thought you required saving?" Naya asks, laughing as if she is shocked by such a ridiculous notion.

"Indeed, she did." He chuckles, tucking the blanket tighter around me. "Such a fierce female. Beaten within an inch of her life, yet willing to sacrifice herself for someone not of her own kind. She is quite remarkable."

"Do not let her distract you, Aren. You have an obligation to your people. The Inokine are regrouping. You said it yourself, they will find us within a matter of weeks, days even. We need to fix the carrier and meet up with the others."

So they brought another broken ship? The one the females came in is useless now, only good for parts.

"Do not presume to tell me what to do, Nayathiana!" Even from my supine position, I can feel the anger and frustration radiating off of him. Something obviously has him very tightly strung. "Leave us."

"You cannot be alone with her! Do not forget who you are! The others will tear her apart if they think she has gained your favor. You are of age, Aren. The unmated females have already grown irritable in your company. How do you think a fragile human like her will fair if they see her as competition?"

"No one is to touch her! And you will watch your words, Keeper. The only thing saving you right now is your sex." His unwavering conviction is unmistakable even to my foreign ears, but I'm confused by what he said. What does he mean by sex? Like, because she's a female? Or, are these two getting it on? I feel the familiar sting of jealousy rise up at the thought of them being together.

Where the hell did that come from?

"*Acia*, your scent is..."

"Do not say it. I am sorry I became cross with you Naya, I... I need to clean her wounds."

"Let me relieve you of the task. That will allow you to go to the others. I am sure after what you showed them of the human confrontation earlier they are eager to hear the details. Ragar has the entire group of males further down near the ship running through drills; the females are close by, out of sight."

"The young? Where are they?" The heat of his skin radiates through my clothes as he runs his hand reverently over my lower abdomen.

"Liral is with the warriors, observing them as you require. Jara is with her Life Giver." After a moment, Naya clears her throat. "May I speak freely, *Acia* Ren?"

He sighs. "I do not know why you ask if the answer will not matter, Naya."

"I wish you would not close off yourself to the bond in times of such unrest. The other warriors could barely control their lust for violence after smelling the scent of human blood and not knowing of the threat you were facing. If the females had not been in such a state of need when you all arrived, I fear they would have ignored my request to hold."

"There was no threat, Naya. I showed them all that was necessary. I have never felt the *pull* of a female before, and I have waited years to answer its call. Those moments were for me alone."

"You are letting your instincts overpower your reason, *Acia*!"

"Do not forget your place. My instincts are what have kept us alive and out of the oppressive hands of our enemies. I have never ignored their insight before and I will not do so at your request. I will be the one to care for her, Naya. The honor belongs to me. I will not gift it to another."

The conversation over, and my savior clearly finished discussing the matter, Naya leaves the medical bay. I let myself relax under his nimble fingers as he takes his time gently cleaning my wounds. I don't know how he's managing to do it without hurting me, but I appreciate it all the same. I fight the urge to smile as his large hands begin fumbling around the unfamiliar drawers and cabinets looking for the supplies he needs. I don't know all the cuss words in Illusian, but I can tell from the ones I recognize that his vocabulary is about as colorful as mine.

Removing my grime covered shoes and exposing my feet, he presses on my heel firmly in several spots, and the action noticeably dims the throbbing ache in my head. He might not be formally trained, but my savior definitely knows his way around combat medicine. Feeling his breath on my skin as he runs his face along my neck sends a shiver down my spine. The barely there sensation creates a wave of warmth that reaches all the way to my toes. The last thing I feel before fading into oblivion is the roughness of his calloused hands exploring the soft curve of my jaw and the light burn at the base of my neck where his fingers send waves of calming sedation through me.

CHAPTER EIGHT

Ren

I AM restless with Xen's failure to report. His silence is damning, no matter the cause. All Illusian leaders are expected to provide the current status of those under their command. To find a ship capable of reaching out. It is crucial to track the movements of our enemies, to anticipate their next move. I have no tolerance for weak excuses. Xen will forfeit his title. And depending on the cause of his silence, his life.

As a last resort, I can use my gifts to seek each individual Illusian out but I cannot afford to be anything less than full strength in such an unfamiliar place. After assigning Ari and Tor to gather intelligence on the layout and military presence within this compound, I am left with no other task to distract me from my thoughts of the fierce dark-haired human who fought to protect me. It has been less than half a moon cycle, and her scent is already driving me insane. It clings to my damn skin, and no matter what I do, it follows me, leading me in circles right back in her direction. After sitting with her long enough for my muscles to stiffen, manipulating her pain, I forced myself to leave her.

What kind of pathetic excuse for a medical facility has no neuronal pain suppressors? The only thing I could find was an injectable opiate that lasted for minutes and did not come close to controlling her pain. A fucking inexcusable oversight.

I find my urge to eliminate her pain through touch odd, since I can manipulate her from afar, but my instincts last night would not allow me to leave her. Refusing to release her mind until she had rested and her heart rate normalized, I stayed by her side. Naya and the others were made to wait for my return and they were displeased by my absence.

The unmated females have already noticed the change in my behavior. The last thing I need is Naya on me again about picking a mate so they will stop attacking each other. She knows it is her responsibility to control them. Female or male, no one will lay a hand on my human without meeting my wrath like that piece of shit who marked her. I should have killed him slower, made him suffer as I ground his bones into the floor with my bare hands. But by the time I felt the invisible pull toward her and recognized it for what it was, I could scent the blood seeping from her wounds and I lost control. The sight of her terrified and injured stimulated my prey drive, and in that moment, there was no room for logical thought. Only the intense need to kill the one responsible for her pain and suffering.

That entire group of human males owes her their lives. If not for her refusal, I would have crushed their minds and left them pissing and slobbering on themselves until their nervous systems shut down. I still might. The more I think about it, the more I want to ignore her request to let them live. The walls they constructed to keep us contained are a joke. The only reason I have not taken control of this puny station is because my instincts tell me something is not right with their leadership. That they are somehow involved. Their presumed dominance is our best weapon, and I will continue to play into the farce as long as it is to our benefit.

Feeling the shift in the air and catching his familiar scent, I look upon Sol as he trudges toward me. The male moves slowly, noisily. He follows my stern gaze to his feet, then begins picking up his heels, quieting his steps. Having already located the cameras recording our every move, I instructed my people to look and act as unknowing as possible. Even my choice to sit lazily at the control center is intentional. Sol lifts a brow, as if questioning whether it is appropriate to discuss his findings out loud. He knows the drones the human general are using to watch us are not capable of audio. But with my human well-versed in Illusian, we are not without risk of being overheard. I nod for him to continue, confident in her discretion.

"*Acia*, I was able to hack into the human communication system for a few moments before their security measures severed the connection. I sent a notification to our contact within the underground to be on the lookout for new auctions being held over the next few moons. I know Xen probably escaped but with his group being mostly female and the aged, I thought it might be wise since we have not heard from them."

Grunting in response, I continue to sharpen the blade I keep strapped to my calf. "You think Xen would fail to report such an occurrence?" I eye him wearily. He knows this is a test. Insinuating a highly positioned male is not capable of maintaining the safety of those under his protection is grounds for a challenge. As the highest-ranking male, I would have to accept on Xen's behalf in his absence. Sol would not survive. I am curious if he has learned anything of my lessons on protocol and expected behavior.

Sol closes his eyes and looks upward for a moment before answering my question.

"No, *Acia* Ren." His words are bored and drawn out. My jaw ticks in irritation at his refusal to acknowledge the importance of showing respect to those stationed above him. "Xen would absolutely report it if he were alive. The fact we have not heard from him is what concerns me." Sol's eyes lower to the left timidly before returning to my own. It irritates me when he does this.

He sighs, realizing his error. "Your Life Giver is on that ship, *Acia*. I only mean to protect them."

I stare at him for a moment before nodding my head. His instincts are improving. The female that gave birth to me is the eldest living Illusian female and holds the highest position among us. Having been mated to the previous alpha male, my father, before he returned to the dirt, she is the deciding voice should anyone challenge me as alpha. I carry a sentiment for her I do not hold for others, and it would be a grave mistake for the Inokine to harm her. They may be fools but even they know I am not one to be trifled with.

Our aged are held in the same regard as our young. Those who have gone before us and those who will lead future generations of Illusians are to be protected no matter what sacrifice is required. Sol took a chance in making such a choice without prior authorization, and it was a risk worth taking. Dismissing him silently, I shove the worry for my Life Giver to the back of my mind. I cannot do anything about the situation as it stands, and I will not reveal my frustration. My people will see it as weakness, and the last thing they need to worry about is my fitness to lead.

Like an invisible tether, something pulls my gaze back to the door separating me from my human. The idea of mating with her and creating young elite enough to lead our race into the future awakens my lust and pride. Her body stands out in contrast to the familiarity of Illusian females, and I find myself drawn to the uniqueness of her build. Her hips are wide and curved in a favorable way. The ease at which they could accommodate a large babe has me wanting to climb on top of her and bury my dick deep inside the cleft between her legs. Her thighs are strong, and her breasts are plenty. Mine. The urge to possess surges through me and my eyes search every male present. I am bigger, stronger —fiercer. I dare one of them to fucking touch her. My anger hangs heavy in the air. Ragar, recognizing the scent, stops sparring with Nexx long enough stare at me questioningly. I dismiss him, and he continues to fight full force by shoving his knee in Nexx's face. The blood dripping down Nexx's lip is evidence of Ragar's unrelenting force, and it stirs the violence within me.

We lay such a deep burden at the feet of our females, and the thought of introducing such a vulnerable species to the life we live seems unconscionable. Annoyed and uncomfortable with this newfound sentiment and foreign sense of conflict, I return my focus to the group of males sparring in front of me. I need to hit something, hard. Stepping forward to offer himself as a target, Orion kneels in preparation as I stalk toward him. Not interested in holding back, I lock eyes with Ragar. He is the only male capable of fighting me one-on-one without sustaining serious injuries. Returning to the middle of the circle, he grunts and assumes his defensive stance as I draw back for my first strike.

CHAPTER NINE

Jayla

After struggling for the last five minutes to get comfortable on the thin, coarse blanket I'm using as my makeshift pillow, I give up. There's no way I can ignore the pissed off muscles in my neck. I turn to the side, trying to relieve the dull ache, and a sharp bolt of pain shoots down my arm. Okay, note to self: Never sleep on this shitty table again. Cursing myself for using the last of my department funds to order a working coffee dispenser instead of upgrading the wretched exam table, I suddenly feel much more sympathetic for my patients who've complained in the past.

This table needs to go to hell and take the cheap bra digging into my tit right along with it.

Still refusing to open my eyes and face the consequences of yesterday's record-setting level of suckage, I pretend I'm still asleep. After gleaning so much information from the conversation between the warrior I now know as Aren and the Keeper, Naya, I can only hope continued silence will help me gain more insight into my current situation. For the first time in my life, I have no clue where I stand. What am I going to face when I walk out of here? Are my friends going to shun me? If I leave the confines of the isolation area, will the Illusians allow me back in?

"She knows we can tell she is awake, right?" someone whispers close by. The voice is high pitched and grates on my sensitive ears like nails on a chalkboard. Even the whimsical nature of the Illusian language doesn't camouflage the unnaturally whiny soprano.

"Let her be, Illaria. She has been good to us," a softer voice answers.

"Since when did you become so untroubled by a rival female, Amina?"

"I am not immune to the threat she poses, I just choose not to hate her without cause."

"Without cause? Aren is our most prized male. The fiercest of our warriors and one of the few unmated males left in our faction. He has never shown an interest in a female until her. You would relinquish your chance at mating him to appease the feelings of a human?"

"You know I would love to be destined for a mate like him. I have yet to feel something special for any of them. I guess I always assumed I would know when I met the one who is meant for me."

"Do not indulge yourself in fairy tales, Amina. You are no longer a child. Gone are the days when we could afford to hold out for emotion. We mate with those who carry the best traits and the most prestige so that our offspring will be strong. And if we are smart, we take affection when it is freely given. You should not have turned down Nico so thoughtlessly: he would have made a fine mate."

"Shut your mouth! Do not speak to me that way. I will choose a mate when I am ready. At least I do not shame myself by propositioning multiple males behind Naya's back, knowing it is forbidden!

"Better to stray from the rules than be the unprotected whore of an Inokine and forced to breed like an animal," Illaria yells, walking out, and slamming the door behind her.

Well, that escalated quickly...

"Is she always that rude?" I ask, peeking out from underneath my blanket.

"Most of the time, yes," Amina says with a sigh. Her kind eyes are covered in a fine sheen of tears. Most likely the result of Illaria's harsh judgement of her personal choices. With sun-kissed, sandy brown hair that reaches her lower back, smooth bronze skin and brilliant violet eyes, Amina is radiant.

"I'm Jayla," I say, hoping an introduction will ease her discomfort.

"Amina." The edges of her lips curl into a slight smile. I'm relieved she isn't as reluctant to talk to me as the rest of them have been. And that Illaria bitch? I'm going to have to watch her.

"Now that you are awake, I will alert Naya and the others. I am sure Aren will want to know as well." Getting up to leave, Amina straightens her ankle length dress and heads for the door.

"You could stay for a little while, maybe tell me what in all the worlds I've gotten myself into."

She pauses at my invitation. "I would but, we are not permitted to be alone with you."

"Why not?" My brows draw together in confusion. Do they really think I'd hurt them? After everything I've done?

"It is for your protection. The other females, those like me who have yet to select a mate, are prone to aggression around available males. With Aren taking such an interest in you, well, Naya thinks it is best to keep you separate from us." She looks around the room, then lowers her gaze to mine. "I should not even be in here now. But Illaria snuck in, and I do not trust her so..."

"I'm glad you're here. Is it really that big of a deal? I know he saved my life, but were his actions really that out of the ordinary?"

I sit up on the table, tired of craning my head to keep her in view. I catch a hint of pink creeping into her cheeks.

"Protecting our clan from those who intend to cause us harm is not only something Illusian men grow up learning to do, it is ingrained in their DNA. Our species reveres women and children, because biologically, we are who carry the young and, of course, the children are our future. What makes you unique is that Aren not only felt the need to protect you from those human soldiers yesterday, but from his own kind as well."

"Oh. And that's not how all the Illusian males act?"

She giggles at the question. "Well, yes and no. Illusian warriors are overbearing and aggressive but our community is built on respect. A mated pair belongs to each other. Members of the opposite sex do not physically interact with one another without permission from the respective mate. It is forbidden for any of the single females to interact with unclaimed males unless the male has shown favor and the female has answered his call. She raises her brows in a knowing manner.

"Yeah, I still don't get it." I shrug and chew on my nail.

"Aren is special. He holds a higher position than the others. His responsibilities enable him to bypass many of the rules, yet he has never taken advantage. He has never once considered any of us despite being of mating age for many years. His instincts called him to protect you, and what he did makes the other females very nervous. It is rare—but not completely unheard of —for a warrior to choose an outsider and Aren's primal need to care for you is one of the first signs that he has begun to pursue his intended."

"So, wait... you're saying you think he's into me?" Amina giggles and nods.

"And the other females are pissed? But you aren't upset with me?"

"No," she says, shaking her head, "I quite enjoy watching Illaria squirm with jealousy."

As Amina exits, I'm left alone and completely dumbfounded. What in all the worlds does that even mean? I don't want to get ahead of myself but, I'm excited about the possibility of the tall, dark, and delicious warrior from last night wanting me. Thinking back to the way he saved my life, the rational part of my brain points out that anyone in their right mind would react the same way. Maybe not the whole ripping out the attacker's throat part, but defending someone two seconds away from being murdered? That's just basic decency.

Tired and irritated by my growing confusion and the pain assaulting me in waves, I force myself off the table. Pins and needles shoot through my feet as my heels hit the cold floor. After gathering supplies with the intention of re-examining the females I treated the day before, I hobble out of the medical bay in their direction.

I take a moment to observe the group, watching the way they interact with one another. With yesterday's addition of nine males, their numbers total over twenty. Judging by the way they can barely keep their hands off each other, six of them are paired. Just as Amina revealed, the mated couples keep a good distance from one another, and the single males and females don't physically interact at all. I can see how Aren's treatment of me yesterday could look inappropriate. Convinced it was most likely a gut reaction in the heat of the moment, I still refuse to get my hopes up. I search the crowd of abnormally attractive beings but can't find him anywhere. Not letting yesterday's shit show affect me anymore than it already has, I muster up as much confidence as my worn ego can manage and silently pray I don't accidentally stare at anyone's mate too long.

Oh, man. This is going to get messy.

Dragging my feet from exhaustion, I catch my boot on a raised piece of flooring. A loud clang rattles in my ears as the small tin filled with medical syringes and ointment I was holding skids across the metal walkway. Groaning loudly, I try to force my stiff joints to cooperate, but my pathetic attempt to bend down is interrupted when Aren suddenly appears in front of me. Standing silently with the traitorous tin box in the palm of his wide hand, he looks irritated. His furrowed brow makes the inhuman curve of his eyes appear wider and causes the subtle blue of their depths to be even more enticing. My throat goes dry as I stare at him. He's so fucking beautiful. I'm drawn to every single inch of him, and the urge to crawl back into his arms and stay there forever is starting to distract me from my duties. Where in all the worlds has he been hiding?

"Why are you up female?" he asks, pulling me into his arms.

"What are you doing? Put me down!"

The few Illusians who hadn't noticed me before are staring, their expressions a mixture of surprise and confusion.

"You should not be on your feet. Go lie back down." There's no mistaking the command in his tone. Unfortunately for him, I've always had a problem with authority.

Disappointed that his chest is no longer bare, I poke the traitorous leather-like hide firmly stretched across his broad, firm muscles. "I have work to do. Almost all of your females need additional medical attention. Let me do my job."

Aren's strong grip on my legs is undeterred by my repeated attempts to kick him as he carries me back to the medical bay. I manage to wiggle out of his arms when his height forces him to lean down to enter the room. After both my feet hit the floor, I stumble backward several steps until I'm flush against the counter. He prowls toward me slowly and places his arms on either side of me. With only a few inches between us, I'm hyperaware of his every movement. Aren drops his head low enough for the lights above us to reflect on his bare scalp, then straightens, inhaling deeply on his way back up.

He opens his mouth to speak but stops as if he's decided against whatever he was about to say.

"How are you feeling, *Skara*?" he asks, letting his gaze bore into mine.

He knows my name is Jayla, right?

"I'm all right." Unable to tolerate the intensity of his stare, I avert my eyes.

"You should be resting. Your body has yet to heal from your injuries."

I wince slightly as he brushes the hair out of the cut on my forehead. "None of the other females have gotten to rest. I should be no different."

"But you are different, *Skara,* and I will treat you as such." He guides my chin upward with his finger.

"My job here is to care for people. Several of your females need treatment and I can't sit here and do nothing when I know there are people who need my help."

"There are only three females with wounds that have yet to heal, and Naya has already treated them after she observed you the other night. She can assist them until you are well."

"No, that isn't possible. I saw all their wounds myself. Most are way too deep to heal in half a day."

"There are things about our kind you do not know. Perhaps in time they will be revealed to you."

The intensity of the energy buzzing between us is making me dizzy. The tease of his cool, crisp breath offers a stark contrast to the scorching heat pouring off his immaculate frame. He still wears the evidence of his battle from a few days ago, the scratches and bruises on his neck and arms fading slowly.

"Aren, why do the others heal so fast and you are left with these?" My hands caress the edges of his cuts with a featherlight touch. His jaw clenches, and he leans closer.

"Ren," he whispers. "You may call me Ren."

"Ren," I say as my heart tumbles around in my chest. I can feel every single inch of space between us. Caught between wanting to launch myself at him and running away, all I can manage is to stand there awkwardly until the jolt of the door nearly being ripped off its hinges startles us both. Naya, with Rhia in her arms, comes rushing in. Already gone before I can register his movement, Ren hovers over them. Rhia's mate, Rivan, follows close behind.

"She has not felt the babe move today, and there was blood on her bedding this morning." Naya lays Rhia gently on the table. "Rivan has tried to calm her, but she will not listen to reason. She is convinced the babe did not make it."

"This is the third one, Aren! The third babe we have lost. I cannot bear the sadness." Rhia turns to Rivan. "I cannot bear it, my love."

Turning to the tearful female in her arms, Naya soothes her as Rivan covers her with a blanket. Ren faces away from the group and stands by the door.

"Rhia, do not fear. Let me know if anything hurts," Naya says, rubbing her hands on Rhia's pregnant belly. She continues to feel around, trying to coax the baby to move.

How the hell did I manage to miss that during yesterday's exam?

"Why don't you let me take a look?" I ask. Naya's shoulders grow tense as Rivan and his panicked mate both look my way. I hold still, afraid to move as the sound of Rivan's growl resonates through the air. My hair stands on end when my brain registers the threat behind it. Ren shields me with his body and tries to diffuse the tension.

"Be very careful, little *Skara.* What do you mean, 'take a look'?"

"I have a machine that lets me see the baby inside the womb. Or, whatever you guys have. It's completely safe and painless. The software is out of date since we have little use for it here, but I can show you if it will ease your minds."

"You will not touch her," Rivan says darkly. I cling to Ren as the promise of violence laced in Rivan's demand sends an errant chill down my spine.

Taken aback by the deep, sinister growl emanating from Ren, I quickly grab the ultrasound probe to my right and turn it on. Able to project its findings into the air, the ultrasound picture appears directly above me. Using myself as an example, I run the cool wand over my abdomen, so they can see how it works.

"Look, all you do is move the probe around," I say, holding it up, then tracing it around over my stomach, "and the image pops right up. Here, you can do it yourself." Leaning closer to Naya, I hand over the ultrasound and show her which buttons to push. "You center the baby in this box here and push the button, it performs a quick scan, giving you all the information you'll need."

Naya examines the probe for a moment before looking to Rivan and Rhia for confirmation. "You will do it," Naya says, handing the machine back, "but tread lightly, Jayla. I will not be responsible if Rivan gives in to his baser instincts." Her words elicit another growl from Ren who continues to stand in front of me protectively. I don't mind the unobstructed view of his incredible ass but having to reach around him constantly to get the angle I need is getting old very quickly. Even Naya's crimson eyes hold irritation at his ridiculous display of machismo.

The tension in the room is so thick I can practically taste it. Ren is glaring at Rivan. And the mated male continues to give me the stank eye while hovering over his pregnant wife, or mate, or whatever she is. With all this aggression, I have no clue how this group has managed not to murder each other into extinction. A nervous giggle escapes as I place the cool wand on Rhia's abdomen and begin the scan. Finally getting the entire body in one smooth swipe, I freeze the image and let the machine analyze the data. All four of them stare, enraptured with the tiny baby projected above them.

I exhale a sigh of relief at the report that pops into view a few moments later. The baby is healthy by human standards, male, and very close to being born. Well, if Illusian gestation is complete at forty weeks, that is.

"What does it say? Is it healthy? Will the babe live?" Rhia's words float through the air, cutting through the remaining tension.

"Yes, he's perfect. Since there are no species-specific criteria, I used a human profile for comparison, but according to this your baby is around eight pounds and is clear of any obvious deformity."

"You said him? It is a male?" Rhia asks, unable to look away from Rivan. Their passion for each other is palpable. Ren opens his stance, relaxing a fraction and uses his fingertips to rub circles on my lower back. His hands feel hot through the material of my shirt and the sensation of him touching me has me feeling all kinds of filthy.

Something tells me Ven isn't going to be the star of my dreams tonight.

"It is." I point at the very obvious male parts. Rivan stands a little taller at the sight and both he and Ren let out a grunt of approval. Noticing the fine hairs floating around in the water of the baby's protective sac, I look at her belly.

"What?" Rhia asks, clenching her fingers in the blanket at her side.

"How far along do you think you are?" I ask as cautiously as possible.

"She last bled thirty-two weeks ago, but with this being the first that has survived this long, we are unsure," Rivan says, answering for her. He seems more settled after seeing the baby, but I have a feeling that could change very quickly.

"I hate to break it to you, but this baby is ready and could come at any time." Expecting the news to inspire happiness, I'm in complete shock when Rhia begins to visibly panic.

"No! Rivan, I cannot have this baby here!" Rivan responds to her distress, using his tender touch to try and soothe his frantic mate. Concerned, I leave the ultrasound in place to continue monitoring the baby for as long as she remains on the table. The rhythm of the rapidly beating heart helps to calm some of the chaos.

"Naya?" Rhia calls out, "you need to check the others." Shaking her head, Naya refuses.

"It is unnecessary. They are much earlier in their growth. You are by far the furthest along."

"We will check them," Ren says, leaving little room for Naya to argue. "You know we have to leave as quickly as possible. We should examine all those with child to ensure we do not have to move up the timeline."

Reluctantly nodding her head in agreement, Naya leaves to gather the others. Two ultrasounds and twenty minutes later, all is well in baby-making land. As I watch Iana ease her way off the table while still cramping and bloated in the early stages of pregnancy, I'm surprised by the warmth of her delicate hand as she places it on mine. Even more shocking, her mate Orion doesn't look like he wants to murder me when I squeeze her fingers back in response. That counts as progress, right?

"Thank you for this." Iana rubs her hand over her tiny baby bump. "We rarely find ourselves in an environment with machines like these. I will not forget the gift of seeing our child." I nod in response and watch as Orion rests his hand on her back and leads her out the door.

Reclining back in my worn exam chair, I can't contain the smile that pulls at my lips. It's rare to have my efforts noticed. The people who come to me for help usually do so as a last resort or when they're forced by a government mandate. It completely blows my mind that a scared, pregnant, refugee being hunted into extinction is the first to thank me since I've accepted this post.

I guess humans really are the assholes of the universe.

CHAPTER TEN

Jayla

AFTER HAVING BEEN CONFINED to the medical bay by a moody Ren and forced to rest for the last several hours, I can't stand being stationary any longer. Desperate for a shower and some familiar food, I gather up my things and sneak out, heading in the direction of the vacuum-sealed doors that separate the Illusians from my crew. I know I need to get over my fears and get back to business as usual, but my looming obligation to spy on Ren makes my skin crawl. I don't want to do it. I *won't* do it.

Screw General Sterling and his bullshit assignment.

He should be more worried about the possibility of the Inokine attacking us to get to the Illusians. He's responsible for protecting our entire population, and the duty to listen to and act on credible threats is part of his job. The gnawing hunger in my belly turns ravenous at the smell of the traditional Illusian cuisine they're cooking in the hull of their broken-down ship. I could turn around and try to interact with them, but after seeing how badly I upset the balance in their group, I know it's smarter to leave. The closer I get to those stupid sterile doors, the higher my anxiety grows, and by the time I'm within a few feet of them, I can barely breathe.

He's dead. It's just a room. Stop being ridiculous.

Leaning over, I brace my hands on my knees, trying to take a breath deep enough to keep my urge to vomit at bay. Images of my assault replay in vivid color, and the world around me begins to fade away. As my vision tunnels, the black spots floating in my periphery join forces and threaten to pull me into their abyss. Despite my best attempt to remain firmly planted in reality, my fatigued mind refuses to listen. Terror weaves into all my senses, demanding that I run. Fight. The pressure in my chest rises up into my throat. As I am about to plunge into hysterics, a pair of strong arms wrap around my trembling frame.

Ren.

"Do not be distressed, *Skara*. He cannot harm you where I sent him." The wiry stubble on his jaw are rough against the tender skin of my cheek, and his breath is warm on the cool sweat clinging to my neck. Not willing to waste a chance to be close to him, I savor the sensation and snuggle in deeper against his arms. Who knew a girl like me would enjoy being coddled so much? Tilting my chin up so I can stare into his soul-stealing eyes, I let the mystery and passion behind them blanket my terror.

"I know. I feel ridiculous. I didn't anticipate freaking out. I guess I underestimated how bad that experience really was. I've never had anyone..."

"Never again. I will not allow it." The steadfast promise in his words and the grit of his voice assures violence for anyone who dares to challenge him. I let myself enjoy the moment, knowing it will be over soon. He'll be gone, and my life will return to its less than stellar routine.

"You are leaving?" he asks casually. I can tell by the way his body curls into mine he doesn't want to let me go, but I've got shit to do.

"I need to check on the rest of the people here. Plus, I really need a shower." I can smell myself, so there's no way the essence de onion from my sweaty pits has escaped his notice. I squeeze my arms in closer. He tightens his hold, and buries his face into my neck, breathing deeply. I feel the rumble of his low growl all the way to my core.

Yep. That's going right in the spank bank.

"You smell intoxicating, *Skara*. You need only to remain here with me," he whispers, letting his lips brush against the space behind my ear.

"The rest of my crew is in danger, Ren. I have to let them know. General Sterling seems unconcerned with the threat in your wake, and I can't, in good conscience, sit here with you and ignore the possibility of an attack."

"My instincts call for me to keep you here, but I understand the drive to protect your people. You continue to affect me in ways I did not predict, my *Skara*." He reaches into his pocket to retrieve my comm watch, holding it out to me. "Take this with you. Sol was able to sync the frequency with the internal communication board on our carrier. You can reach me at any time. You need only press here." His broad finger skates over one button. Smiling at his thoughtfulness, I shift to face him and boldly press my hips to his. The impressive girth of what hangs freely between his legs hardens, rebelling against the thick material of his pants.

Holy shit, I'm going to eat him alive.

"If you do not leave now, I fear I will not let you go." His jaw strains as he clenches his teeth. His hips thrust forward, pressing harder to mine. I sigh, then let my forehead rest on his a second longer. Time to get back to reality. With one last look, I wriggle out of his arms and force myself through the doors of the dreaded decontamination chamber, shaking my head at the way he makes me feel. It's ridiculous how strong my response to his body is. One touch, and I'm primed and ready to go.

Seriously, who the hell am I right now? Dry humping a guy I've known for two days? Am I really that hard up?

I hold my breath during the initial blast of spray, remembering how bad it stung the first time around. After waiting a full minute to turn on my watch, I dial Rett on the off chance he isn't busy. If anyone knows how to navigate this situation, it's him. The man has more meaningless sex than a porn star. Unable to reach him, I lean back and log into my mailbox. I have to hold my watch exceptionally close to my face in order to see the screen clearly, making it difficult to discern if Brittany has sent a response. The screen lights up with a message from our general alert system. Sent in text form to every individual listed on the manifest, the messages are widely ignored because it's nearly impossible to miss the accompanying alarm tones when they go off.

"Warning. Code Black in effect, all personnel evacuate the receiving bay. System purge will begin in five minutes."

Code black? System purge? But why aren't the tones ringing? Where is the alarm?

Running through scenarios in my mind, I rush to figure out how the system could be failing. I recoil in horror as I realize what I've done. *I'm* the reason the tones aren't blaring. I ripped out the wiring when Naya and the others first arrived. No one else on the landing has access to the warning message. They're all going to die if they don't get out of there, and it'll be entirely my fault.

Armed with the terrifying knowledge of what's about to happen, I slam my hands against the door and begin screaming at the top of my lungs. I know the walls are soundproof but my blind panic at the thought of all the Illusians suffocating to death overpowers rational thought. I throw my weight behind my fists as I beat on the door like a woman possessed, pounding over and over until the bones in my hands scream at me to stop. Pausing my assault to cradle my rapidly swelling hands, I remember what Ren said, and find the watch button he programmed.

Static carries over the line. "Ren! Ren! Are you there?" I yell, waiting for an answer.

"You dare to be so casual with him?" A barely audible voice cuts through the static, and I immediately recognize its uniquely unpleasant tone.

"Illaria! Get Ren! You need to get out!" My words tumble over one another in panic.

"Your pathetic ploy to steal his attention from me will not work. I finally have him near, now that Naya is focused on the children, and you will not spoil my chance."

"Get over yourself! This has nothing to do with that! You're all going to die! Get Ren now!"

"Do not come back here, or I will kill you myself." The line goes dead.

Now hopelessly enraged, I claw at the door, trying to get it open. My waning strength doubles when images of my assault come plowing into the forefront of my mind. Using those memories to fuel my fight to get to the Illusians, I wedge my fingers in the crevices so frantically that all the tiny wounds on my hands cover the unyielding metal with my blood. Using my full body weight, I press against the door in a last-ditch effort to get free and fall forward as the hinges that cemented the door in place shatter.

Holy shit. Ren just ripped the door off its hinges.

Launching himself on top of me, he covers me with his body and searches for whatever has caused me harm. The tangy smell of my blood mixed with his masculine scent fills my nostrils as his feral gaze continues scanning the room. With a timid hand, I reach up and touch his face in an attempt to calm him and pull him back into reality. Time's running out, and we're all about to die.

"Ren. Ren... look at me." At the sound of my voice, he rises to survey my body and buries his nose in my clothes, sniffing every inch of me for hidden wounds. We're all going to suffocate if I don't figure out a way to diffuse his anger and get everyone out of this room in the next few minutes. Doing the only thing I can think of to redirect his attention, I shove my mouth on top of his for a brief moment, then grab his face with my bloody fingers. "Ren! You have to listen! Whatever you were cooking triggered the fire alarm, and all the oxygen is about to filtered out and purged. Everyone will suffocate if we don't move. Get everyone out of here, now!" He registers my words and only lingers for a brief second, before disappearing.

Gathering myself off the floor, I lumber after him, only making it three steps before the entire group races toward me with unnatural speed. Illaria glares at me as she follows closely behind Ren. From his position at the front of the group, Ren grabs my hand as he passes and pulls me along with him. Only letting go of me to wrench the second door open, Ren assists everyone out into the hallway just in time for the heavy steel doors hidden in the ceiling to slam down and cut the antechamber in half. The mass of bodies forced into the cramped hall take on an elegant formation now that they're exposed. Several of the males disappear, leaving Naya and the remaining males to encircle the females and children—an impenetrable wall of muscle and aggression. The few crew members unlucky enough to be passing by at that moment don't linger long. Ren and one other particularly terrifying male stand almost seven feet tall and carry an air of violence that anyone in their right mind would want to avoid.

As the only female not in formation, my vantage point allows me to see two soldiers being held up by their throats. Their panicked, confused faces redden as they fight for breath. Meeting their eyes, I will them to keep their mouths shut and pray it's enough to save them.

"Aren," I say, using his full name since we're among all of his people, "we need to get everyone out of the hallway. The landing will be unreachable for the next twenty-four hours. I have a place everyone can stay until it's ready." My proximity to him is the sole focus of all the unmated females, and I have to control my urge to eye roll at the number of distinctly feminine growls that permeate the air as he sinks down into a crouch and rubs his rough cheek against mine.

Oh, shit! Is he publicly acknowledging me?

I can't hide my appreciation for his closeness. My nipples are hard and sensitive against his muscled shoulders and I'm more than grateful to remain hidden from the rest of the group behind his back. Shifting his eyes from me to Naya, Ren nods, giving her the okay to move the group.

I escort them through the less populated corridors, trying to keep them away from the majority of the crew as we make our way down to my pod. I'm not only surprised they agreed to release the two men stationed outside the doors, but also that we manage to make it back to my room with no casualties. The task of shoving twenty bodies inside a room built for one is difficult, but with a little rearranging, we make it happen. Since max capacity has undoubtedly been reached, upholding the normal unspoken rules of interaction between those of a different mating status is impossible. Plus, now I'm stuck in a room with Illaria and the other two unmated females who would happily rip out my throat. Thank God for Amina, she's the only one who doesn't seem to want to kill me

To avoid sitting and staring awkwardly at everyone, I seek out Xandria while Naya, Ren, and the other males discuss what to do next. I approach her with caution.

"Xandria, how are you feeling?" I ask, having to yell over the cat like hisses from Illaria and another unmated female.

"I'm much better. Naya has been treating my wounds in your stead," she says before crumbling under the weight of Illaria's angry stare. I reposition myself in front of her, blocking Illaria's view.

"Has she changed them today?" Xandria shakes her head, and

I glance back at the occupied males. Exposing even the smallest amount of skin is seen as taboo for an unmated female. I scan the room, it's completely packed, and they've shoved my couch against the bathroom door to make room for a larger sleep space in the middle. With nowhere else to examine her wounds, I'll have to do it here, very carefully.

"Since they're busy, can I take a quick look? I can change the dressings on the lower ones without having to lift your dress too high." She nods.

After retrieving the black portable medical bag from under my bed, I return to her side to assess and rebind her wounds. I take extra care when removing the adhesive. The sensitive skin on her calves is angry and ripping off the tape will make her pain even worse. The round edges of the smaller cuts are healing nicely. The tissue is knitting together well, and there are no signs of infection. I'm most concerned about the deeper bite marks on her upper thighs. I press lightly on them through the material of her dress to ascertain the status of her dressings. As long as they remain in place and still cover the wounds, the antimicrobial infused gauze should keep any infection from growing. Xandria flinches slightly at the pressure, and her lavender eyes stare blankly at the ceiling above us while I reseal the edges that have come loose.

I know that look. I've seen it before back on Earth, where I treated the men and women who were touched by war. Not wanting to relive whatever trauma they experienced, their minds take them somewhere safe. My fear of the Inokine grows as I recall Xandria's mangled upper thighs, and if I could reach into her head and take those awful memories from her, I would without hesitation. Out of the corner of my eye, I see Ren look up and scent the air in response to my change in mood.

Holy crap, he doesn't miss a thing.

Standing after the last of her dressings is complete, my worn-out muscles refuse to cooperate and send me tumbling into an unsuspecting Illaria behind me. As soon as my feet leave the floor, she shoves me directly onto Xandria's damaged legs. In what feels like one very painful, fluid motion, Illaria yanks me back up, then slams me to the floor before Naya steps in and tosses me into a corner with Ren and the other males.

Naya grabs the kicking and screaming female by the shoulders and fights, ineffectively, to keep her still. Illaria screeches something vile and continues to fight against Naya's hold, trying to get to me. Two children scurry to the opposite corner, finding safety in their mothers' arms. I'm about to reach for Ren, but he's already moving towards Naya, and my heart seizes as he presses his fingers tenderly along the base of Illaria's spine and takes over for the Keeper.

Illaria melts into his touch and purrs as he continues to caress her face. When he offers what sounds like a very personal rumble in response, my pride crumbles into dust.

So much for feeling special. I'm such a freaking idiot.

I'm so sick of people putting their hands on me. Fuck this. Pushing to my feet, I make my way through the crowded room. After being nudged hard by someone on my right, I start to fall, and one of the unclaimed males gently wraps warm and unfamiliar hands around my hips to steady me. Not immune to his uniquely male scent and the inhuman beauty of his face, I let my eyes linger for a moment and give him a tight smile. The innocent interaction sends everyone into upheaval. Ren goes berserk at the sight of the male touching me and drops Illaria on her ass, sending her back into full-homicide mode.

The entire room turns into one giant brawl as several of the other males do their best to restrain Ren, who fights to get to me, and Naya tries to control Illaria. I bolt out the door, barely able to contain my tears. As I run down the hallway, there's only one place I want to be and it's nowhere near the group of assholes currently destroying my living quarters.

CHAPTER ELEVEN

Jayla

AFTER SPENDING ALMOST ten minutes trying to convince him to let me in, Rett agrees, and I collapse on his bed. General Sterling not only forced everyone to endure his hour-long bitch fest about allowing me to commandeer the door controls, but also confiscated everyone's watch comms as punishment. The entire crew is pissed because that's the only way to access personal mail and place supply orders without using the main comm. Not to mention, people have to communicate in person without the convenience of text or voice messaging.

"I can't believe I humiliated myself in front of them and let him fawn all over me like that when he obviously doesn't care." My whiny voice is muffled by the hand I dramatically splay across my face. I turn and burrow further under Rett's rumpled sheets, too sad to care about the smell of sex lingering there.

Seriously, does he ever wash these damn things?

"Girl, you didn't humiliate yourself. You just enjoyed some delicious eye candy while you could. Nothing wrong with that. I can't believe that shit with General Sterling and that GI Jackass though. Your face is a mess." He stops playing with my hair and reaches out to touch the bruise on my cheek.

"Ow, jerk! It hurts like hell. Don't poke me," I yell, smacking him in the side of the head.

Rett snatches his hand back and uses it to prop up his chin. "He really did that to your face for no reason at all? What did the general say?"

"That his poor sweet Gibby would never do that." I lift my shirt to reveal my bruised ribcage. "And that he would never do this."

"Damn, that looks rough! How are you still walking around? You look like you need a repair pod or something."

"Like they would give us one of those here. But for real, I'm fine, more butthurt than anything." I roll to my right and face him, tucking my hand underneath his pillow.

"Don't let Mr. Sexy get you down. I know delicious man meat like that doesn't come here often, but don't worry I'm sure we'll get some new recruits soon. At least one of them has to be bangable. You shouldn't be so picky. You know I would never turn down a girl in need." He wiggles his tongue between his fingers.

"Gross. No. You're like my brother. I'm not having sex with you. Plus, judging by these sheets, I'm pretty sure you're getting plenty of action."

My comment coaxes a boyish smile to curve his lips. "Well, I may or may not be getting me a little military action myself, but a girl never tells."

"What? Rett, you whore! Those guys are all assholes! Stay away from them, they aren't right."

"Hey, don't you dare judge me with your damsel in distress actin' ass. We all do what we have to do to get what we need to get." The two of us burst into a much-needed bout of laughter as he throws his pillow at my battered face. Blocking it at the last second, I grab it and shove it under the one already beneath my head.

"Ugh, whatever. Hey, do you mind if I hang out here for a while? I know you have to get back to prep for dinner but I'm *not* ready to go back and face the psychos in my room."

"No problem, love. Just lock up when you leave. If you're lucky, I'll snag you some left over lemon squares. We got a whole shipment of fresh lemons yesterday, out of the blue. I jacked a few and put my skills to work."

"That sounds amazing." I nearly drool at the thought.

Snuggling down deeper into his bed, I close my eyes and wait to hear the click of the door before I let the first tear slip through. My feelings pour out and bleed all over Rett's pillow. I'm struggling to keep myself grounded. Shit. Not only did I break several major laws and risk prosecution, but I also discovered a long extinct race is still alive, got my ass beat multiple times, and completely humiliated myself by getting wrapped up in a guy I know nothing about. The most upsetting part? How ashamed I am for letting myself feel valued. It was only in my head.

Frustrated with myself and the constant dull pain shooting through my sore limbs, I grab my comm and pull up the mail from Brittany I noticed earlier. She sent me a ton of files. After selecting to download them all, I force my worn body into the shower, hoping the hot water will ease my mind.

Not so much.

Despite thinking better of it, I wipe off the steam on the bathroom mirror and study my reflection. I hardly recognize the person staring back. Feeling like shit is one thing, but actually seeing the damage that a size eleven steel-toed boot creates is another. My long midnight hair is ratty and tangled. The crown of my head is red and tender. The skin underneath my tawny eyes is purple and swollen, more so on the left below the baseball-sized bruise surrounding the laceration on my forehead. Outside of a broken nose, the rest of my face is remarkably untouched. I count my teeth, opening my mouth wide to make sure they're all still intact. Not bothering to put on makeup, I grab Rett's rarely used work out sweats and head back into his room.

Settling down on his couch, I sink down into its spongy cushions and log into my mailbox. The sight of my grandfather's familiar handwriting hits me hard as I read the first of the downloaded documents. Several more tears escape as I think of how much I miss his voice. While sifting through the thousands of pages of information my dad and grandfather compiled, a small symbol catches my eye. No. Not a symbol. A randomly placed doodle of a man and his dog. I laugh as I picture my grandfather lost in his own mind as he scribbled furiously at the pages of his notebook. I continue on past the drawing to the paragraph below.

"With their DNA far more dominant than that of humans or any other race, even part-Illusian offspring almost always take on the traits of the Illusian. The fact that their DNA is able to universally adapt and merge with whatever species it is introduced to is a primary reason the Inokine continue to capture and traffic Illusian females capable of breeding. Although it is incredibly rare, some are able to pass down inherited abilities. The degree, of course, is completely dependent on the strength of the non-Illusian donor. Females who had proved capable of creating male offspring were sold for almost ten million EU..."

Skipping several paragraphs, I continue reading at the bottom of the page.

It appears that the unmated females are aggressive only when of breeding age. Able to vaginally secrete a neurotoxin capable of creating mind altering hallucinations, all Illusian females were highly sought after for sexual reasons, despite their age or breeding status. Rumored to be the preferred sex slaves of choice by the Inokine and other nefarious clans, the Illusians fought off their constant kidnapping attempts for half a century before their disappearance in 2090.

They can do what now? I nearly fall off the couch as I shoot up to lean in closer to the screen, running my eyes over the words again and again. Naya had mentioned the danger of touching her skin but she hadn't said anything even remotely close to what I just read. I'm starting to understand why they're all so psychotic. The wave of sympathy overtaking me pisses me off even more. They hurt me, and I deserve to be angry. I don't want a reason to feel sorry for the bitch who tried to pummel me, but I after learning about how awful things have been for them, I can't summon the rage I previously had. Unwilling to read any further, I close down my comm and decide to go back to my room. It is *my* pod after all and nobody, not even that bitch Illaria, will keep me from it.

CHAPTER TWELVE

Ren

PICKING at the grime beneath my nails does nothing to calm me. My urge to pummel something is strong, and Ari is within feet of me. I could close the distance easily. But I will not. Instead, I relive the satisfying crunch of my fist slamming into his nose and revel in the splatter of blood that sprayed my face. That will have to be enough for now.

I have upset my human. She did not approve of how I chose to settle Illaria's aggression. Even through the bitterness of Illaria's arousal, I could smell the anger pouring off my human's tiny frame. She was hurt. The scent hangs in the air, eating away at my restraint. I want to go to her. Remove all traces of ire from her eyes, but that is not an acceptable action. Not yet. Not now.

I calculated the risks. With limited space and Illaria's size and strength, the potential for violence against my human was too great. Naya was not fulfilling her duty and failed to control the irate unmated. Physically calming her was the quickest and most effective solution. I repeat the sequence of events in my head. I was correct in my actions. It was the most logical choice. Yet, I still feel conflicted. Why? Angered by the foreign sense of doubt, I jump to my feet. Orion and Tor take on a defensive stance in front of a still bleeding Ari. I scan his injuries. Minimal. A bloody misshapen nose, bruising at his throat. He will not be so lucky next time.

"*Acia*, you must remain calm. Ari has taken the knee," Nexx says, reminding me of Ari's submission. As an unmated male, I had every right to challenge Ari when I felt he had shown my human favor. If he had not bowed, relinquishing his interest in my female, he would have died. I would have ripped his head off. I grunt and narrow my eyes. I don't fucking care if he has taken a knee or not. If I feel like smashing his face, I will. "Get him out of my sight."

Nexx nods. "Yes, *Acia*."

"You need to make your choice, Aren," Naya says, smoothing her hair after her confrontation with Illaria. "It is the natural order of things."

"You should concern yourself less with my choices and more with fulfilling your required role, Nayathiana. One of your unmated damaged my female." Naya's cheeks grow red.

"You have not claimed her. She is not yours."

Clenching my hands around the edge of the counter, I squeeze, forcing the synthetic metal to bend and cave under the pressure. A rough growl tears from my lips. She is correct. How fucking annoying. "She is mine. No other male will touch her."

"Not until you make a decision, Aren!"

I cock a brow at her raised tone. Her eyes are alight with fire, and the veins of her neck and forehead swell. She is frustrated with me. Too fucking bad. "You know why I waited to choose. I have not heard from my Life Giver." I release the counter and shove up against its disfigured edge.

"I am aware, *Acia*. But you cannot continue on as you are. The tension is too high."

"Enough." I turn away, pointing to the broken furniture.

"Enlist the unmated. This room is to be returned to its original condition."

OUR DISPLACEMENT IS VEXING. Keeping up our farce of vulnerability is much more complex when out in the open. Without the shelter of our ship, we must remain vigilant in our ruse. There is clarity in chaos. The human general has become very active since our evacuation. Both Tao and Ari have witnessed him issuing orders for additional security to be placed within the air-locked space. His motivations remain unclear. Mine however, remain the same. That piece of shit will die. By my hand or another.

"*Acia*," Rivan calls out, approaching me in short strides. I sent him after my human to make sure she remains safe. I watch her. Or have her watched. I am unwilling to allow her to be left unguarded. "What have you to report?"

"She is with the red-haired human male." His nostrils flare. "In his quarters."

My thighs sting as my barbs pierce the skin where my hands have clenched around them. "Leave me."

There isn't enough air in this fucking room. Not enough space. Stomping out the door, I seek shelter in the hallway outside. She is with another male.

My human.

Mine.

What if she has...? No. Moving in the shadows, I make my way to the human male's room, lurking outside. I do not understand the language, but the inflection in her voice is clear. She is relaxed around this male. She laughs for him. The sound is remarkable.

She does not laugh for me.

Anger surges through my veins as I fight against images of her naked curves pressed against him. On top of him. I am going to kill him. Slit his throat and offer his still dying form to her as proof of my superiority. I am built to fight. I have spent my life training to protect my future mate. He cannot provide for her as I can.

I hear the shuffle of feet and smell the stale scent of human gluttony. He moves to the door. Her scent weaves through and around the remnants of sex wafting off him. He does not deserve her. A female is owed loyalty and devotion. Not a male with mixed intentions and wandering desire.

The door opens, and he slips out, padding down the hall. The opportunity is here. I straighten to my full height in the corner and, with nostrils flared, let her scent on him fuel my rage. Feed it. Encourage it. I pivot toward him, prepared to violently engage him, but stop as the rich scent of salt and water blanket my anger. Stepping closer to the door, I direct my energy to my hearing, blocking out all other senses.

My human weeps. Her grief slices through my drive to kill and leaves an empty hole behind. I do not like this feeling. I do not understand. The unmated are often tearful. But never has their lamentation bothered me before. The urge to soothe her is unbearable. A wave of outrage pulses through me. Whoever has caused her such sorrow deserves to be punished and should grovel at her feet, begging for forgiveness.

That human will be punished. My feet begin to move before I make a conscious decision to go to her. She will be avenged. Her pain will not go unanswered. Like a blow from one of Ragar's fists, the realization of my guilt tears through me, and I stumble, sliding to my knees in the middle of the hallway.

I am responsible for her pain. Her misery lies solely on my shoulders.

CHAPTER THIRTEEN

Jayla

I DRAG my feet down the hall toward my pod, dreading the moment I have to see Ren. What the hell do you even say after something like that? The closer I get, the worse I feel. Forcing myself to turn the corner, I stop, unable to breathe. The nervous ache in my chest explodes into full blow pain at the sight of him. Ren sags against my door, but immediately straightens when his pale blue gaze meets mine. His eyes are creased in worry. Part of me is relieved to see I'm not the only one upset about what happened earlier in my room. Even from a distance the clenched muscles of his strong, masculine jaw stand out. I stare at his full lips, unable to forget their dark taste, and I immediately regret being so obvious about it. He just humiliated me in front of a room full of people, and I can't manage to go two seconds without lusting after him. How fucking pathetic of me.

"Can you move out of my way, please?" I ask as I approach my door. His nostrils flare.

"You smell of another male." His eyes zero in on Rett's pants stretched across my hips.

"Your point?" How dare he judge me for wearing my best friend's sweats when he had his paws all over that rabid skank from earlier. He runs his hands over his bare scalp, and I can hear the rough texture of his callouses rubbing over his skin.

"I can smell your anger, *Skara*. It muddles your scent. I do not care for it."

"Angry? Me? I'm fine. Now if you will excuse me, I need to get into my room."

Refusing to be that girl and admit my jealousy, I relax my expression and jut out my chin. My heavy breaths and the light sheen of tears forming in my eyes betray my attempts at looking unaffected. Where's my resting bitch face when I need it?

"I meant you no disrespect. I was only trying to protect you." His brows scrunch together as he studies my face.

"By putting your hands all over another female?" I ask in a voice thick with vulnerability. I lean back and cross my arms in front of me to put some distance between us but can't summon the energy to move my feet. As if he can sense my fickle emotions, he stalks toward me, guiding me backward with his hips until I'm up against the wall. With one arm on either side of me, I can't escape. I can't deny the way my heart seems to beat only for him as he presses even closer and a growl of appreciation emanates from deep in his throat. He nudges my chin with his nose, seeking access to the sensitive skin of my neck. His breath teases, and my core clenches in anticipation. *He's so hot, and he smells so good*. I let my head fall to the side, giving him permission to do his worst.

"I do not desire to put my hands on anyone but you, *Skara*," he whispers against the hollow of my throat.

If he wants me so badly, why doesn't he just do something about it already?

He lingers there. Right above my lips, less than a breath away. Almost as if he is stuck in some self-imposed limbo.

"What are you waiting for?" I ask before my reason can interfere.

He traces a finger down my cheek. "It is not so simple. If it was, you would already be mine."

I swallow hard, fighting the urge to glance away. "It's as simple as you make it, Ren."

My words cut through our sexual tension like a knife. Ren straightens, dropping his arms. Once again feeling rejected, I duck around him and enter the door code for my room. The floors, the furniture—everything is *covered* with sleeping Illusians. There's barely enough room to walk between the bodies lying on the floor. Dreya, one of the females I treated, and her young son Liral, are quietly sorting through the children's books I use for new employees who need tutoring in Meta. Against my better judgement, I make my way toward them.

"May I join you?" I ask, keeping my voice low, trying not to wake the others.

Dreya smiles. "Of course. We were just trying to find one with pictures he likes." She holds Liral close, gently twisting his raven hair between her fingers.

"Here." I smile and reach into a nearby box, grabbing one of my favorites, and offer it to him.

After looking to his mother for permission, he accepts the book and opens it up to the first page. His eyes light up in recognition as he sees all the adorable Earth puppies.

"Mama, these look like the pictures Jara had back on—" he says, catching himself before he divulges their previous location, "—where we used to stay."

"Yes, baby."

Only six years old, Liral scans the pages excitedly as his mother helps him identify the pictures.

"Would you like to learn how to read it?" I direct the question to them both.

"You could do that? Teach us the Universal language?" Dreya asks, eyes wide in surprise.

"Yes. That's part of what I do. I teach Metaversial to all newly arrived crew. It's the main requirement for acceptance under UCom law, so I try my best to make sure everyone stays compliant."

"There are others that would like to learn. Would you be willing to teach them also?" she asks with a slight grimace. I know she witnessed what happened with Illaria earlier. She probably thinks I'm completely insane for volunteering to risk my life again.

"Absolutely. I don't know how long you guys have, but I'd love to help."

"May we start tomorrow then? Liral needs to sleep, and I can ask the others when we awaken, if you would like."

"I would like that very much." Liral frowns and pushes the book back in my direction. I give him a broad smile and nudge it back.

"Keep it; it's yours."

His eyes light up in excitement. "Thank you so much!" he yells, clapping his hands. Dreya winces at the loud noise and chuckles softly. The strained lines of her forehead smooth and her lips pull into a tired smile.

"Thank you. I will ensure he takes good care of it."

With the room filled to the brim with bodies, there's no way I'm going to sleep peacefully in here. Abandoning my attempt at making a point, I realize I'm much more comfortable passing out on Rett's couch than trying to fight for space in here. Plus, with my luck, the unmated females would murder me in my sleep. As I quietly make my way out of the room after bidding Dreya and Liral goodnight, I pass a warrior standing guard. Recognizing him as the male that helped me earlier, I give him a slight smile. His eyes remain fixed on the floor. This is, no doubt, Ren's doing. Right before entering Rett's pod, I check my comm again. I missed a call from General Sterling, and I know if I don't contact him, he'll come looking for me. If he discovers where I've stashed the Illusians, there's no telling what he'll do. I dial his number and try to keep whatever crap is about to roll downhill from spilling all over their shoes.

"General Sterling, you called?" My words are short and my tone annoyed.

"Yes, Medic Shirley. How are you feeling after today's exciting events?" The unnatural chipper tone to his voice grates on my nerves.

"Just peachy. What do you want?" I clench my teeth, fighting the urge to lash out at him.

Calm your tits, Jayla. Don't make things worse.

"You've failed to submit any briefings on your interactions with our new friends. An accidental mishap, I presume? Surely, you wouldn't be so quick to abandon our deal. You know what's at stake."

"No, I didn't forget. But I can't exactly sit there and write an essay detailing their habits while they hover over me, now can I?"

"Well, no, I suppose not. How about this, Medic Shirley? I will ask you some very simple questions, and I want you to answer them. Is that agreeable?"

"Sure. Go for it." My anger flares at the image of his smug face.

"What are they?"

"I don't know, and they aren't telling." *Lie.*

"All right, what of the females, are any of them with child?"

"How would I know that? The alpha female won't let me near them." *Another lie.*

"What about the children? Do they have any special talents? Anything like that murderous beast that killed Sergeant Gibbons?"

"No. The males are protective of their women and children. They won't let me near them."

"Okay, what about their anatomy? Does it appear... compatible with ours?"

"Not sure which parts you're referring to, but what I've seen closely resembles human."

"Good, very good. Now, how often do you think the mated pairs fornicate?"

The fuck?

I grip my watch tightly, resisting the urge to smash it into the wall. "What kind of question is that? I have no idea. You think they screw out in the open like wild animals?"

"Well, I don't know. That's why I'm asking you."

"I haven't seen anyone humping, and no, I don't know about any of their sex lives. They barely tolerate me in the same room, let alone invite me for pillow talk."

"Do you think you could get me some blood samples? Specifically, one from the male child?"

"Are you completely insane? Or do you just not listen to anything I say? They won't even let me speak to them and you expect me to draw blood?"

His tone grows more frustrated and condescending with each question.

"Maybe I overestimated your usefulness. Perhaps I should enlist the help of someone more willing and relieve you of your duties."

Knowing that he can and will follow through with his threat if provoked, I try to pacify him.

"Look, with the fire and everything, things are tense. Just give me more time. Besides, shouldn't you be worried about the psychos that forced them here in the first place?"

"Do not tell me how to do my job. I'm not the one who's forgotten my responsibilities. You have until the end of this week to give me something useful," he says. His voice keeps fading out, like he's distracted by something on his end of the line.

Wait. Was that giggling? Gross!

"Medic Shirley, I must go. Don't forget what you owe me."

Relieved I don't have to hear the putrid sound of his voice any longer, I put my comm watch in my back pocket and enter the code for Rett's pod. I'm relieved to find it empty. After such a shitty day, a night by myself is most welcome. Crawling onto the couch, unable to ignore the scent of sex lingering in his bed, I grab the blankets I used earlier and burrow down deep. I pull out the digital notepad I use to tutor Meta and adjust the language algorithm. After entering each Illusian character by hand and assigning them to the corresponding words in Meta, I instruct the program to construct a probable alphabet and learning structure. My aim is to just leave it with the group after our lessons so they can practice at will. After I complete the base language profile, I let my eyes close. Desperate to sleep but finding it increasingly hard to manage, I hear the heavy thud of a body against the door. Sneaking up to the tiny viewing screen on the door, I spot Ren sitting against the wall, vigilantly keeping watch.

I summon the image of his handsome face strained in frustration when I shut him down earlier. A realization hits me hard. I want Ren. Whether if I can have him for one night, one week, or a lifetime, I want him, and nothing is going to stand in my way.

CHAPTER FOURTEEN

Jayla

THE CUSHIONS on Rett's couch feel like deflated balloons by morning. My back muscles cramp and tighten as I stretch in an attempt to work out the stiffness from sleeping at such an odd angle all night. Grabbing my watch, I groan and fling the covers over my head. Only five hours have passed. No wonder I feel like I just fell asleep. My bed may not be much to look at but it's mine, and after giving it up for a group of people who tried to kill me, I refuse to spend another night slumming it in someone else's pod. Halfway through my morning shower, I hear the familiar beep of a text alert. Grabbing the towel folded near the sink, I wrap it around me and pad into Rett's room. I have to tap the screen several times before it lights up enough for me to read it. Oh great, they're extending the deoxygenation hold on the landing by another two days.

Well, isn't that just freaking fantastic?

My hopes of sleeping in my own bed tonight crash and burn into a fiery ball of bitter frustration. There's no way in hell I'll survive in the same space with Illaria and the other unmated females for that long, so unless I want to take part in another epic bitch fight, I need to find them somewhere else to sleep. After weighing my options, I decide to track down Ven and ask him for help. We need somewhere off the general's radar. Ven's been here for the last ten years, and if anyone knows a place safe for the Illusians, it's him.

Walking into the bio dome where he spends most of his time, I find Ven kneeling down in one of his twenty planter boxes full of soil, singing to his plants. Today, it's the tomatoes' turn to be serenaded. He stands up, dusts off his knees and wraps all four arms around me with a smile. After returning his embrace, I sit down on the edge of the closest box and explain in very little detail what I need. He listens while quietly trimming his plants. Making sure to set a timer for the misters, he holds the door open for me to follow. This is exactly why I chose him. He doesn't ask me a single question as he guides me toward whatever room he has in mind. A being of very few words, he's both kind and loyal.

He takes me down five or six rarely used corridors before coming to a stop in front of an unlabeled gray metal door. He yanks on the handle several times before using all four hands to pry it open. The hinges whine as it dislodges the rust that has formed from disuse. As he enters, the lights above flicker on. A stale, musty odor assaults my nose, and I take in the filthy, pea green walls. The paint is cracked and discolored from years of neglect, but the size of the space is perfect.

Having to squint through the poor light emanating from the ancient bulbs, I try to channel Ren as I analyze the room. The single-story, long-abandoned gymnasium holds the remains of an empty Olympic-sized pool in the middle of the floor. I can't help but shake my head at whoever thought putting a large free-standing body of water in space was a good idea. The layout is simple, and with only one way to get in or out, defending it would be easy. The last thing I want to do is spend all my free time exploring dusty unused spaces, but twenty Illusians crammed in my room is unbearable. Plus, there's no way in hell I'll be able to get Ren alone with all those damn she-wolves hovering over him.

I skip as I make my way back to my pod, stopping intermittently to do a little happy dance. I might look like a total idiot, but I can't contain my excitement. Plus, I get to work with Liral and Dreya today. They should be awake, and my tablet is up and ready to go. Imagining Liral's little face scrunched up in concentration trying to learn the sight words is doing wonders to lighten my mood. When I turn the corner that leads to the main level, I see several people crowding around the bench like tables cemented to the lounge floor.

Did I miss a meeting notice, or was I intentionally uninvited?

I snort, knowing it's most likely the latter. I enter through the back, hoping to escape any angry glances thrown my way. I spot Leandra and sidle up next to her, praying she doesn't hate me like everyone else.

"Hey, what's going on?" I ask, searching the crowd for more familiar faces.

"Don't know. One of General Sterling's men went door to door this morning and woke everyone up. We've all been standing here waiting for him for the last ten minutes. I hope he hurries the fuck up. I need to take a piss and my coffee is getting cold."

"Have you seen Rett?" I ask, still unable to find him in the mass of people.

"No. What are you doing here, anyway? Aren't you supposed to have left by now?"

"Wait, what? Why would I leave?" My nose wrinkles in confusion.

"Serena's been telling everyone she overheard Rett saying General Sterling threatened to send you back to Earth on a freighter."

"Yeah, he did. I'm just not that easy to get rid of." Leandra snorts in response and shifts her hips uncomfortably. By the looks of it, she really is about to pee her pants.

Just as boredom sets in, people scurry out of the way for General Sterling and his men as they enter the lounge through the door to my left. Assisting the general up on one of the tables, an officer I recognize from the hallway outside the containment unit hands him an amplifier, and the general presses the dime sized device to the base of his throat.

"Attention, ladies and gentlemen. I trust you slept well. We will be putting a curfew in place, aimed at protecting our community from the barbarians currently living within our walls. I have taken great care to ensure that they are kept away from the general population and was only recently informed that a fire had broken out, forcing them to relocate out of the landing bay for the next few days." A cacophony of concerned whispers drifts through the air, and my eyes nearly roll back into my skull when the girl in front of me grabs her boyfriend's hand tightly.

Oh, come on people. You can't seriously be buying into this bullshit...

"What that means for you all is, thanks to Medic Shirley's irresponsible and unauthorized decision to permit a group of unchecked Unwelcomes onto our ship, we must vigilantly maintain a strict routine and stay in our pods whenever we aren't working until their threat no longer exists."

The crowd complains loudly at the new restrictions, and Leandra's eyes flicker from the general to me.

"Thank you for your time. That will be all." The general ends his speech and removes his amplifier.

Why the hell he's spending so much time and energy fixating on the Illusians is beyond me, but I'm not letting his ass get away with ignoring the real danger. Jumping up on table, I cup my hands around my mouth and yell at him. "What about the Inokine and the threat of their attack? What have you done to prepare for that?" The loud complaining in the room goes silent as my presence in the crowd is revealed.

"Speak of the devil, Medic Shirley. Have you come to publicly apologize for the inconvenience you've caused?" The general's lips spread into a wide grin, revealing all his crooked teeth. The guy really enjoys humiliating people.

"No, I came to find out why you're so focused on a group of refugees minding their own business rather than figuring out a plan to protect us." Anger simmers under my skin, but I keep my face neutral. I can't let him know I've gotten myself emotionally involved.

"I know of no such threat."

Liar, he knows exactly what I'm talking about. "Well then, let me educate you, General. An attack by the Inokine drove the so-called *Unwelcome Barbarians* to leave their home and seek asylum here. They're convinced it's only a matter of time before those nasty little pricks come looking for them. Don't you think that's cause for concern?" The soldier closest to the general averts his gaze to the ceiling.

Yeah, you know he's full of shit too, huh?

"I'll investigate your claim, Medic Shirley. But until then, you will continue with your assigned duties. As for the rest of you, nothing changes. Still no comms, mind the curfew, and no external mail. Maybe that will teach you all to think twice before allowing a renegade like Medic Shirley to make decisions that affect the whole crew."

They crew start grumbling loudly about the new rule and the general's snotty voice is smothered by the background noise. Red faced and obviously irritated, he hops back up on the table.

"Calm yourselves! Listen! Do not panic!" he yells, turning up the amplifier. "The proper authorities will be notified of Medic Shirley's claim. When and *if* it can be validated, the appropriate supplies and manpower will be distributed. There is no cause for concern. Now, since there has been *mention* of a threat, protocol calls for each crew member to convene at least once daily to run through preparedness drills with an authorized trainer."

Curling his upper lip, the general adjusts his tie and glowers at me.

Leandra's smiles, almost as if she's amused by the general's angry stare. "Wow, that guy really has it out for you, huh?" I would probably snicker too, if I didn't know how dangerous he is.

"As *my* men are the only ones qualified for such a task, we will convene every morning at 6:00 a.m. to run through drills and will repeat those classes every hour until noon. Since we face such a *grave threat*, I expect you to attend at least two. Now, unless Medic Shirley has something else to add that will further restrict your freedom, we are finished here." Giving me a satisfied smirk, the general disappears, ignoring the questions the crowd shouts in his wake.

Ugh, that isn't exactly the response I was hoping for. If single-handedly getting everyone's personal freedoms revoked didn't excommunicate me before, being the reason they're forced to take part in mandatory drills seals the deal.

Slipping out the back before the crowd disperses, I continue toward my room and focus on the tasks at hand: relocating the Illusians and sleeping in my own damn bed. So absorbed in my thoughts when I enter the room, I miss the shoe left carelessly on the floor and tumble over it. The unmated male from the day before reaches out to catch me before I hit the ground. We tense as his hand connects with my arm, expecting Ren to make a scene, but I'm both surprised and disappointed to find him completely unbothered by the interaction. The thick muscles of his shoulders bunch as he glares at Naya, who stands across the counter from him. Oblivious to my existence, he's so engrossed in their heated conversation, he doesn't even bother to look my way.

Why doesn't he care now? What's changed?

"You should really watch where you are going, human. This is the second time you have almost plowed me over." An amused laugh escapes his pouty lips as my mouth drops open in surprise.

"Ha, yeah. Sorry about that. My name is Jayla, by the way, nice to formally meet you," I say, holding out my hand.

"I am called Ari." His grin grows wider as he places his hand in mine.

Shit, wait... am I not supposed to shake his hand? Is that slutty or something?

Flattered by his awkward, albeit obvious, attempt at flirting with me, I start toward my kitchen with a little extra zing in my step.

At least someone is flirting with me...

"Naya, Aren," I say, nodding at both, "I have something to show you if you have the time. I got a message this morning saying the landing won't be safe for another two days, and I know having everyone so close together is uncomfortable for you. I think I found a solution."

Naya agrees to follow me, but Ren remains with the group to focus on strategy with a few of the other males. It bothers me I can't speak to them casually. It feels weird to be around all the males for multiple days at a time and not interact with them. I know they avoid me out of respect for Ren but I don't like it. I've been able to figure most of their names from listening to Ren address them but I've been too intimidated to introduce myself. The high I feel at Ari's attention fizzles out and dies the more I think about Ren's change in behavior

"You should not test him like you do." The sound of Naya's stern voice pulls me from my thoughts.

"Excuse me?" My brows nearly climb into my hairline at her audacity.

"Aren. He struggles to focus in your presence. His inattention is something we cannot afford to allow to continue."

What does that even mean?

"He didn't seem to care too much this morning."

"You do not understand the heavy burden he carries, nor are you able to fathom what a place beside him would require. These are things you are not ready to deal with, Jayla. No matter what your hormones tell you. You cannot possibly know the constant level of control he must exert over his emotions. Your failure to stay away from the other males does not make it easy for him."

What the hell? I haven't even talked to them! Well, outside of Ari, anyway.

No longer in the mood to chit-chat, I remain silent, even waiting for her outside while she surveys the space to avoid engaging her.

"You did well, this room will serve our needs nicely."

A rare smile crosses her lips as she exits the gym and glides past me. Rather than follow her back, I stop by the lounge in search of supplies for the group. They've been away from their ship and their food for more than a day. They must be starving. The extra ration tickets I have are about to expire so I ask Lin, the chef on duty, to ring them up and make a wide selection of different options. After finding my pod blissfully empty, I jog to their new quarters, worried that something bad has happened in my absence. As I pass through the doors, I'm awestruck by the changes they've already made.

The room is free from debris and they've partitioned off the space to keep the various groups separated. The females are resting on a small pallet off to the right where they've laid out the few blankets I had stashed in my closet. Fully intending to head in their direction I turn but stop short as the scent of sweat-laced pheromones draws me forward to the pool. Peering over the side, my eyes widen at the mass of bare-chested warriors sparring inside the empty shell. All muscles and might, the sound of their fists and knees slamming into each other bounces off the walls and echoes throughout the room. Undeniably drawn to Ren, I find him in the middle of the group, fending off four aggressors at a time. The well-defined muscles of his chest and arms glisten in the dull glow of the lights, and I can't help but imagine how salty he'd taste if I ran my tongue down the length of him. Sweet mercy, he's fucking sexy. Watching him beat the shit out of four grown males ignites something deep and feral inside me.

He moves smoothly and meticulously as he transitions from defense to offense, disarming them with ease. An image of him thrusting deep inside me stuns me as he grunts with the force of each blow. Trying to calm myself down before I do something stupid, I retreat back to the females. As I set the food in front of Amina, she lets out a tiny giggle, and the sound gives me the distraction I need to pull myself out of my trance.

"What?" I ask, pulling out the various entrees I've brought.

"Now you know why all the unmated want to rip your head off." She looks at me with a glint of amusement in her eyes.

"I don't know what you mean."

"Sure, you do. I can smell it all over you. In a few moments, they will be able to as well." She nods her head toward the pool and continues to search through the food I've placed on the blanket in front of me.

"What do you mean you can smell me?" I give each of my armpits a quick sniff.

What the hell? I know I put deodorant on...

"You don't smell bad, Jayla. That is not what I mean." She leans in closer. "We can smell your arousal."

"You can *what?*" I shriek, causing all heads to turn my way. My heart pounds and my cheeks flush a deep scarlet. My panties *are* soaked, but damn, can't a girl get wet without the universe knowing? A brief look at the pool confirms my worst fear. Amina's right, the males can smell me, and all of them have stopped to stare.

"It isn't a big deal, Jayla. It happens to the best of us. Now, how you will deal with *him,*" her eyes flicker to a spot behind me, "is your real problem."

"Deal with who?"

I can feel his heat on my back as soon as the words leave my mouth. Unable to resist the urge to breathe him in, I inhale deeply, and my intention to feed the group dissolves as soon as my brain registers Ren's masculine scent. Slung over his back before I can yelp in surprise, he carries me out of the room and shoves me against the wall. His pelvis grinds into my already drenched heat, and he flicks out his tongue in one long, sensual stroke up the side of my neck. The feel of him against me is amazing. Tangling one of his hands in my hair, he pulls my head back roughly and presses his full lips to mine.

Damn, I've missed that taste. The rich flavor combined with the heat of his mouth unravels my control. My desire increases a hundred-fold as he continues to rub his hard length against my sensitive core.

Punishing his mouth like he is mine, I press into him harder and raise my hips to match his thrust. My fingers dig into the bare skin of his shoulders and I moan as he growls into my mouth. Using my weight as a counterbalance, he leans back and moves his hands down to my ass. I gasp as he spreads my cheeks as far as my uniform will allow and angles his pelvis, allowing me to feel the tip of him through the thin fiber of my pants. He's touching every inch of me, and the sensitive skin of my folds beg for more. Still not satisfied, I strain to get closer to him, widening my legs and pushing my hips forward. Answering my desperate demand, he yanks my legs apart, his hands under my knees, and rubs against me furiously. Unable to handle the barrage of sensual sensation, I come, moaning loudly into his mouth as he sucks on my tongue. Seconds before I abandon my inhibitions and rip open the front of his pants, Ren stops moving and releases his grip on my legs. He backs away from me with a painful grimace on his face and disappears back into their gym.

What the fuck just happened?

CHAPTER FIFTEEN

Ren

I CANNOT KEEP myself away from her for much longer. Forcing myself to separate from her, knowing how wet and ready she is for me incites a visceral pain I cannot describe. The need to bury my dick inside her is unbearable. Her sweet scent clings to my fingers, and the soft mewls she makes nearly drive me insane. I can barely stand in her presence without giving into my mating drive and claiming her without the ceremonial approval of the alpha female could leave her vulnerable. It is an old notion and rarely enforced, but without it, any unmated female could challenge our union if Jayla were to fail to provide offspring within a life cycle of the first coupling. My Life Giver is the only person who can seal our bond without question, and with no knowledge of her current whereabouts, receiving her blessing is not a feasible option.

I waited to give Xen time to make contact but trying to keep my need for her at bay is distracting. It is a fucking ridiculous notion that any female I choose could be subpar. The idea that a creature such as Jayla is anything but superior to us all is laughable. With the fire and inner strength of an Illusian queen and the kindness and empathy only a soft human upbringing can offer, she will make the finest leader we have had yet.

After further investigation, Tor and Sol confirm that her leader has taken no steps to protect his people from the Inokine. Without word from Xen and the others, I am anxious to leave and seek the missing out, but the ship remains unable to reach hyperdrive. Jayla will never be safe with such untrustworthy men in power. Taking her as my own will mean subjecting my people to even more strain. My duty to protect her will extend to the humans here, making them my responsibility to protect by proxy. Closing my eyes, I briefly lust at the thought of pinning that piece of shit general to the ground and peeling the skin from his bones. I could just reach into his mind and pluck out what I need, but that is far too simple and a coward's way out. There is so much more pleasure to be had by physically reducing your enemy into a screaming, hysterical mess, but for now, I cannot allow myself to indulge. I agreed to refrain from taking their lives and I will never disrespect Jayla by breaking my word.

My human is headed for the red-haired male's apartment again. Rivan continues to watch her in my stead, shadowing her the second she retreats down the hall. I do not like the human male. Nor do I trust him, but what say do I have if I have not laid claim to her? The distinctive sounds of Naya restraining several of the unmated females pierces my thoughts, and I cringe in annoyance. Enough with this shit. Sweet remnants of Jayla's arousal cling to my skin. Sex pheromones and the scent of my own lust cover me like a cloud of smoke, driving the unmated females to violence. They are crawling all over each other to get to me.

Sol chuckles at the spectacle. "*Acia*, I have never seen them so riled up before, they are nearly ripping each other's heads off," he says, coming to stand beside me. Scenting the air, he stops midstep and stares slack-jawed.

"You have decided, then?" he asks without further explanation. Not in the mood for games, I cock my brow and wait for him to continue. "To mate her. Your scent is one of a decided."

Taking a moment to observe my own scent separate from the sweet feminine one I am drowning in, I realize he has not spoken out of turn. How interesting...

CHAPTER SIXTEEN

Jayla

Not ready to face Ren and acknowledge our full-on hump session, I flee to Rett's room like a coward. Aw, hell. I forgot about the e-notebook in my bag with the Meta lessons for Dreya and Liral. Teetering between my pride and keeping my word, I drag my feet back to the gym. Popping my head through the door, I signal Naya, and she emerges with a scowl and a fresh set of angry scratches on her face.

Taking the e-notebook from my hands, she shoos me away with a muttered curse. "You are not to come back until the unmated have calmed themselves. Go now, Jayla."

Over all the drama, I beeline for Rett's room in hopes of cracking open the bottle of 2040 scotch I've been saving for a special occasion. After my less than classy dick whipping in the hallway and Ren's fluctuating affections, I think today is special enough. I need a damn drink. After I grab the bottle from my room, I bang on Rett's door, hoping to find him true to form, napping on the clock.

"Listen, bitch, I know you did *not* just wake me up from my nap." Rett gives me his best go to hell look after reluctantly opening his door. Unable to keep a straight face, he bursts into laughter five seconds later.

"Move over and let me in, we have some drinking to do."

Ducking under his arm, I head into his kitchen and set the bottle on his counter. I have to rearrange several boxes of contraband to make room, including an entire crate of fresh peaches. Where the hell does he get all this stuff?

"It is five o'clock somewhere," he says clapping his hands. "There's my girl. Where have you been? I thought you were done with tall, dark, and delicious?"

I pour us both a very generous finger of scotch. "Yeah, I did say that, huh?" Draining the glass, I pour myself a double.

"Yes. So, spill? Did you get a taste?" Rett lets out a low whistle as he steps back, giving me the once over. Rumpled clothing. Sex-mussed hair. Great. I didn't realize just how obvious I looked.

"Shit, Rett, not everyone thinks about getting laid all day." I slide my gaze to my empty glass, wondering if three drinks in a five-minute span is considered extreme.

Screw it...

"I see. He hasn't given it up yet, huh?"

"Ugh, no," I say, handing him his drink and then collapsing on the couch. "I don't even know if he likes me. Aw, hell. It doesn't matter. It's not like I can start something with General Sterling doing his best to kill me and a group of sadistic rapists possibly on the way." I down the rest of the amber liquid and lean back to study the bottom of the glass.

Rett's brows shoot up and he fans himself. "Damn girl, you got it bad."

"Aaaaah," I groan and cover my face with my hand. "I don't know what it is about him that has me all twisted up. The other females try to kill me every time I get near him. It's insane. Who willingly signs up for that kind of drama? Plus, they're about to leave and go off to God knows where. I have no idea what I'm doing."

"Seriously? Why are they so stabby? You need me to kick someone's ass?" Rett pretends to sprinkle his hand and slap the air.

I roll my eyes at his offer, then get up and lumber into the kitchen to grab the bottle. After pouring him another, I flop back against the cushions. If I don't slow down, I'm going to barf before I even make it back to my room. "Apparently, Ren is like scary awesome and on every single one of their hit lists. Leave it to me to have a damn bad boy complex."

"Oh, you poor thing. All hot and bothered and no one to play with. I'm gonna fix that. Impromptu pod party tonight!" He hops up and dances around the room, spilling his drink in the process.

I catch his arm and yank him toward me. "Are you ill? Or just already lit? People hate me! No one will want to come."

"Well, rumor has it the general will be otherwise engaged tonight, as will his men. I guess word got out that he came here with ten of UCom's most elite, and supposedly he didn't have the clearance to pull them off their stations when he did. I have it on good authority he's holed up in his room, licking his wounds after they levied sanctions against him."

"Great, now he has even more anger to direct my way. Fan-fucking-tastic."

"Stop whining! We're going to have a party. Now, should we do it here? Or maybe in the decommissioned greenhouse pods?"

"Oh, definitely not there." I wrinkle my nose remembering the sickeningly sweet scent of old animal turds and rotten vegetables. "That place smells like the inside of a dead cow's ass."

"Do I even want to know how you know this?" He fake gags then grabs the bottle and pours me another shot. "Look, let me spread the word. It'll take forty-five minutes or so for everyone to find out since *someone* got all our comms confiscated."

"Shut it! Don't make me feel any worse than I already do.

Speaking of feeling terrible, is my worthless counterpart shitting himself over all the added responsibilities?"

"Ugh, does Brandon ever stop whining? All he's done since Sterling reassigned him is bitch about how much work it is."

"Please. It's karma. He left me his night shift duties all the time."

"All right, enough chatting. Let's do this. Go get dressed and meet me here in an hour. Bring all the booze you have!"

"Hey," I call out, "make sure you invite the Bio guys. You know they grow more than UCom-issued plants in those hydro pods, right?" I waggle my eyebrows.

Rett's eyes widen, then narrow in understanding and a grin tugs at his lips. It doesn't matter how easy is it to get on Earth, mind-altering plants are hard to come by this deep into open space. Let's just say I've seen Ven singing to more than his tomatoes.

"I love you. Be back in a bit," he says, blowing me a kiss as he runs out of his room.

Back in my pod, I spend ten minutes getting cleaned up and another ten digging out all the contraband hidden in the back of my closet. Staring at the six bottles of wine and eight chocolate bars neatly laid out in front of me on my bed, I sigh and turn my attention to the suitcase shoved behind my extra set of linens.

Do I dare? Hell, yes, I do.

The scent of home engulfs me as I throw it open and let my eyes feast on the black faux leather jumpsuit I haven't worn in years. I spend ninety percent of my time in a shitty yellow uniform and the rest in whatever I have lying around. Most of my wardrobe consists of boring, loose-fitting shirts and pants, but this is my *sex on a stick* outfit. My *fuck this, I'm fabulous* go-to getup I keep on hand for self-esteem emergencies. And tonight, I'm going to wear the hell out of it, Ren be damned.

I peruse the stash on my bed, waiting for a bit more liquid courage to kick in before I yank the black body condom over my curves. Of all the items I could've snuck on board, I chose my grandfather's homemade wine and chocolate. Almost impossible to come by this far from Earth, chocolate is a hot commodity and can get you any number of favors. Staring at the bars, all I can think about is how adorable Liral would be trying the sweet treat for the first time. Not to mention, if Illusian women are anything like humans, this could seriously help take the edge off when I'm around them. Buzzing hard enough to think it's a fantastic idea, I load six of the eight into my bag and head over to the re-purposed gym.

When I peek through the door, the kids and most of the females are sitting on their knees, huddled around my e-notebook, while the males continue to beat each other into bloody messes. If I could just sneak inside...

My steps are heavy and uneven now that the liquor has taken hold of my less-than-stellar natural grace. I stick close to the wall as I make my way toward them, trying not to fall into the giant ass pool full of sweaty bare-chested males.

On second thought...

Making myself right at home on their pallet, I plop down and pull my bag into my lap. Amina rolls her eyes at Illaria's agitated hiss when Ren's scent wafts off of me and toward her. Shit, I should have taken a shower—or a hoe bath at the very least.

I reach inside to retrieve the chocolate bars. "Hey, I know things are still awkward from earlier, but I wanted to bring you guys a peace offering."

Naya's eyes zero in on my bag, like I'm about to pull out a sword or something. Opening the first package, I break the chocolate into squares and offer them a taste. No one responds for the first few seconds until Amina slowly reaches forward with a sheepish grin. Naya rips the chocolate from her hands and shoves it into her own mouth before Amina can try a bite. It makes me a little sad that after everything I've done to help them, she still doesn't fully trust me. Satisfied I'm not trying to poison anyone, she nods to the group and one-by-one, they empty the package. I wish I could remember the first time I ate chocolate, mostly because I wonder if I looked as ridiculous—and as beautiful—as they do.

"Jayla, what is this? It looks so awful but tastes amazing! Where did you get it?" Dreya stares at me with bright eyes as she takes a second piece.

"It's called chocolate. They make it on Earth. We aren't really supposed to have it here, but I snuck it in when I came. Do you like it?" I survey the group. Even Illaria isn't immune to the power its sugary goodness holds. She hasn't hugged me or anything, but she isn't trying to murder me either.

After seeing the pure delight on their faces, I hand over the other four bars, saving the last one for Liral and the little girl, I haven't met yet. Jara, I think? Dreya breaks off a small piece and hands it to her son. I tear up at the wonder and excitement written all over his face. I always turn into a huge sap when I drink. Without even trying to look at Ren, I leave and head back to my room to finish getting ready.

Trying to get through the door of one of Rett's parties is like trying to shove yourself into a can of sardines. By the time I get there, the party's already spilled over into the next pod. The awful techno music Rett loves assaulted my ears from two halls away. Not even dinnertime, and people are already close to plastered.

After finding Rett with a drink ready for me, I spend the next three hours dancing and laughing despite several nasty looks thrown my way. No one says a thing. They're too busy drinking all the free booze. Separating from myself, I float through the room freely, swaying my hips and moving my arms to the music. Despite the jovial atmosphere, my exuberance is wearing thin. Not even my drink-induced catharsis can keep my mind from straying back to the sight of Ren's handsome face. Suddenly sober and depressed, I hug Rett and pout all the way back to my room.

After taking a brief shower, I throw on a knee length t-shirt and slip under my freshly laundered sheets. I'm overjoyed to have my room to myself, and after rolling around in my bed and spreading my arms wide like a star, I vow never again to complain about anything pod related. Still wound up from the night's festivities, a little light reading is just what I need to help me fall asleep. Grabbing my comm watch off my bedside table, I pull up my mailbox and mentally prepare myself to delve in to my grandfather's notes a little more. No matter what I do, my thoughts always return to Ren and his people. Just as I'm about to get started, there's a knock at my door. Suspecting Rett, I don't bother putting on pants. The man has seen me semi-nude before, and even though he's a total hornball, he's never made me feel uncomfortable.

"Listen..." I start to say as I open the door. Unprepared, I'm sucked into a familiar set of hungry eyes. My muscles tense, and I blow out a breath at the intensity of his gaze. It's primal. Raw. Penetrating.

Ren stalks forward, forcing me deeper into my room. "My *Skara*." His deep rasp raises goosebumps on my skin. Heat pools in my belly as he cups the side of my face and uses his thumb to caress my bottom lip. "I have been watching you. Every night I watch you, and every night I grow more consumed by my desire to have you." He leans in, tasting my lips with the faintest of kisses. "To keep you." I whimper at the light sting of his teeth on my neck. "I tried to stay away, to convince myself it would be a grave mistake to bring you into such a dangerous way of life, but after seeing you tonight, so close to all those other males..." he inhales deeply, "I can resist the call no longer. You are meant to be mine."

A moan builds in my throat as his rough fingers trail in between my breasts. I lean into his touch, curling my body around him, begging him to go lower. "This," I yelp as he pulls me close and grinds his palm against my sex, "is meant to be mine, and I came here tonight to claim it."

Moving past my lips and down my neck, he softly nips at tender skin over the hard ridge of my collarbone. The sensuous combination of pleasure and pain sets my blood on fire and I moan into his mouth.

"Let me have you, *Skara,*" he growls between my parted lips. "I cannot promise you an easy life, but I swear on my honor to spend my entire existence serving you and treating you like the queen you are meant to be."

With the evidence of my arousal now coating his hand, Ren rubs me harder with his thumb and slides a finger inside me. *Holy shit, I'm going to come.* The feel of his fingers pumping in and out of me, possessing me, ignites a lust so primal, I groan and dig my fingers further into his corded bicep.

Yanking my t-shirt over my head, I give him my answer. Emboldened by his desire for me, I drag my hands down his chest, enjoying the feel of the hard ridges of his abs. He remains still, watching as I explore the body he's declared is now mine. Anxious to unwrap my present, I curl my fingers around his waistband, urging him closer. On my back before I register my feet leaving the floor, I melt under the searing heat of his gaze as he takes in every inch of me with those magnificent eyes.

"You are exquisite. No other can possess me as you do," he says in low timbre as he grinds his hips against mine. I gasp at the feel of his arousal, hard and hot against me. Knowing how bad he wants me shatters the insecurities that always hold me back. No longer willing to wait for what's undoubtedly mine, I slide my hands into his pants and wrap my hand around his girth.

My body clenches in anticipation, the thought of his cock sliding into my tiny sheath creating an unbearable ache. With a grunt, he uses a finger to separate me, rubbing up and down my folds. Abandoning his position above me, he slinks backward and begins to worship me with his mouth.

A moan escapes my lips as he licks and sucks like he's unable to get his fill. The sensation of his warm, rough skin on my chilled, exposed flesh makes me cry out as he continues to lavish me with the bold strokes of his tongue. Two fingers slide inside me, and my body catches fire for him as he roughly pumps them in and out. Every single part of me screams for more. Grabbing the back of his head, I grind into him like a wild animal. Finally, I shudder and scream as I'm hit with wave after wave of pure ecstasy.

After being deprived of sex for so long, I'm happy but nowhere near satisfied. I guide his swollen lips to mine, claiming his mouth, unbothered by the musky taste of me lingering on his tongue. I need him inside me. I can't stand this feeling of emptiness any longer. Desperately hungry for him, I buck my hips, rubbing his cock against my entrance. His tip is slick with desire and ready to split me in half, so what the hell is he waiting for?

"You are mine," he growls into my mouth as I continue to rock against him. "You must say the words, *Skara*. Tell me you are mine." Clenching his teeth, he backs away from me. Crazed with need, I continue to squirm underneath him, arching my hips and back, dying for his touch.

"Yes, now fucking get over here," I say, unopposed to begging.

"Say it." The veins of his neck pulse in time with the rapid beat of his heart.

If you won't do it, then damn it, at least let me do it myself.

The ache between my legs is too great, and my hands slide down my stomach, but he grabs them, intertwining our fingers and pinning my arms over my head.

"Tell me you are mine. I need to hear the words." His lips are on me once again, claiming my mouth with deep strokes of his tongue. I groan loudly and fight to free my hands so I can end my suffering, but he's too strong.

"Yes! I'm yours! Now give me that dick before I explode!"

With a primal roar, he uses his knees to spread my legs and slams into me, sliding deep. He's so big, I'm stretched to my limit, and the burn is sweet agony as he starts to thrust. All I can manage is a barrage of whimpers and cries as he quickens his pace. I bite at his lip and Ren pounds into me harder, using his massive weight to reach so deep inside me, I feel like I'm suffocating on sensation. His long, vibrating strokes send me over the edge twice before he comes and we collapse, sweaty and panting but nowhere near finished.

For the rest of the night, only the two of us exist until sleep claims us both.

CHAPTER SEVENTEEN

Jayla

For the first time in months, I wake with a smile. Snuggling into the warm arm wrapped around my waist, I open my eyes and study the massive, naked warrior beside me. He's magnificent. Something straight out of a dream. I trace the hard muscles of his chest, down through the defined ridges of his abs and even further to the most glorious v-lines I've ever seen. His dick is tenting the sheets and stands at least eight inches tall. The things he can do with it...

My X-rated thoughts are interrupted by a throaty chuckle and I cringe, embarrassed at getting caught ogling him. Awake and staring at me, Ren smiles wide and pulls me on top of him, moving in for a kiss. I lean back, self-conscious of my morning breath, but he snakes a hand through my hair and kisses me anyway.

"You are running away from me already?" He cocks a brow and reaches out with his wide hands to palm my butt.

"Are you kidding? After last night, you're going to have to pry me off your dick." Another deep laugh vibrates his chest and a sense of rightness settles over me.

"You should not doubt my desire for you, *Skara.* My hunger for you knows no bounds." He arches his hips, showing me he's ready.

"Oh, no you don't! I'll be surprised if I can walk after what you did to me. My girly parts need a little rest."

"Do you hurt?" Ren's fingers carefully asses my swollen sex and I hiss at the sharp sting of pain.

"Just a little. I'm sure I'll be good to go in no time."

Displeased by my answer, he scoops me up in his arms and carries me to the shower. Letting my muscles loosen under the spray, I shriek in surprise as Ren drops to his knees and starts licking between my thighs. My nerve endings jump to life, masking the soreness that accompanies the pleasant sensation. Using a single finger, he enters me, and the dual stimulation forces me to relax and let my hormones take over. The pain begins to fade away, and his light touch suddenly isn't cutting it. I want more.

I don't think I'll ever get enough of him.

I drop to my knees in front of him, taking in the way the rivulets of water drip down his naked skin. His starling blue eyes and sexy bronze skin inspire a surge of protectiveness and desire so fierce, I can't control my need to feel him. Ren's pupils blacken as I crawl into his lap and drag my hands down his chest. He captures my mouth, drinking me in with long strokes of his tongue. His heart beats rapidly against mine as he grabs my hips and forces my tender nub to grind against his hardness. My core clenches at the feel, and I raise up to guide him inside me. It isn't enough. I need more. I need it *all.*

I slam myself down and cry out from the combination of pleasure and pain. Ren steadies me, forcing me to slow my pace. His thrusts are muted, almost gentle as he guides me up and down on his length. A moan tears from my lips at the deep sensation. Our movements are unhurried, allowing me to feel every single inch. I continue to kiss him as he slowly drives me insane. I come hard, clenching around him, begging him not to stop. With a final thrust, Ren grunts and finds his own completion.

So much for getting anything done today.

My lady bits feel miraculously better after our romp in the shower, and as I get dressed, I notice the muscles of my back and arms are improving as well. Who'd have thought a night full of dirty sex was all the doctor ordered? Exiting my bedroom, I smile at the sight of Ren waiting and I'm hit with a wave of emotion. The butterflies fluttering around in my stomach are a stark contradiction to my usual disgust with cheesy displays of affection. He makes me giddy, and honestly, I am totally okay with being that girl. Initially, I try to maintain some distance between us as we walk down the hall, but all hope of remaining under the radar dissolves as he wraps his large hand around mine. People are staring. And the more they do, the more the defined muscles of his arm press into me. Ren's incredibly on edge. Staring down everyone we pass, he causes more than one person to trip over their feet in an effort to get away from us. *What in the world has gotten into him?* I assumed after we did the deed, he'd be able to relax but it seems to have only made him worse.

"You all right over there?" I ask, looking up at him with a brow raised.

"Yes. I just do not like these people looking at you." His shoulders tense, and he snarls at the electrician trying to pass in front of us. Even the two attractive Gemmian females don't escape his aggression, and I'm annoyed as they stare even harder after hearing him growl. Freaky skanks. They're widely known for having insatiable sexual appetites and a proclivity for biting.

I dare a bitch to try...

"Pretty sure no one even knows I exist, Ren. In case you haven't noticed, you're virtually impossible not to look at."

"I see only you, *Skara*." His hand tightens around mine.

"Please. You're telling me you didn't see those two incredibly hot Gemmys just now?"

He stops mid-stride and pulls me toward him, pressing his lips to mine in full view of everyone. "After last night, you really doubt my affections?" He smiles, hugging me tightly.

"Casual hot sex isn't all that uncommon in the human world, Ren. There's still so much I don't know about you, and I'm just saying I would understand if your eyes occasionally wandered, that's all."

I stare at my feet to avoid looking at him. This is a pretty heavy conversation, and with our relationship being so new...

He quickly picks up on my discomfort and raises my chin to meet his eyes. His pupils are small, allowing for the faint hint of blue to shine through the blanket of white. No frustration, only concern.

"I knew from the moment I smelled your scent, you were meant for me. I've killed for you. Protected you. There has and will never be another that possesses me as you do. You are everything and everyone I need." He kisses me, holding me close. "This all must be so strange for you. Us meeting under such violent circumstances, and you being thrust into a culture completely different than your own. Only a strong female could take such a leap of faith, and I will not tarnish your belief in me." Ren draws back to read my face. "If my words are not enough to convince you of the depths of my conviction, perhaps I should give you another demonstration." My mouth goes dry under the heat of his sweltering gaze. He leans in, letting his stubble tease the side of my cheek. "I desire you to no end. Now start walking before I change my mind and take you against the wall."

Mentally preparing to have my face ripped off by a horde of angry females, I stare at the door separating us from the other Illusians. Ren stifles a laugh as he takes in the look of dread on my face. Still gripping my hand firmly, he opens the door and leads me inside. Naya's crimson eyes zero in on our hands.

Raising her chin, she sucks in a deep breath and lets it out slowly. Her lips curve into a smile and then turn down into a frown at the sound of my stomach growling loudly.

"Have you not fed her?" she asks, narrowing her eyes in distaste.

"No, we came straight here."

"You mate a female and do not feed her?" She turns my way. "Come, Ajayla. Let me get you something to eat."

I peek over her shoulder as we walk. All the females, mated and unmated, stand up as we approach. Strangely enough, rather than appearing angry or frustrated, most of them seem more accepting. Even those who prefer to keep their distance are no longer shying away. Confused by the obvious difference in how I'm being received, I sit down when Naya gestures to the edge of the blanket lounge area. As she places several plates in front of me, I stare at the unfamiliar food and then turn to Amina.

"Um, what is this exactly?" I ask.

"It is called vari. It is a mixture of vegetables and dried meats."

"Wait, where did you get this? Did you go back to your ship?"

Amina looks to Naya until the Keeper nods. "The males scouted the area this morning; it is no longer inaccessible."

"But you're all still staying in here? Why?" Amina smiles at my barrage of questions and continues to scoop out a portion of food for me. "All of those things are better coming from Naya. For now, eat. You will need your strength, Ajayla. The effects an Illusian male has on their mate can be quite unpredictable."

I start to ask her why everyone's now calling me Ajayla, but the taste of vari distracts me. In love with the delicate flavor of the vegetables balancing with the heady taste of wild game, I devour the first plate and move on to the second. Satisfied with my appetite, Naya kneels beside me.

"I am sure there are many things you wish to know. But first, you must understand that Aren did not keep these things from you lightly. It is his duty to his people—and mine to him—that has not allowed for full disclosure. Tell me what you know of our kind."

"I know you disappeared over a hundred years ago. That you..." my eyes take in the various shades of violet surrounding me, "have been targeted for your bodies and—"

"Let me stop you there," Naya says. Her rigid posture is making me anxious.

"Illusian females are hunted, stolen, and sold to the highest bidder. That is if those who seek to commit such atrocities do not keep them for themselves. A hundred birth cycles ago, roughly one hundred of your Earth years, we thrived. Our home was beautiful and self-sustaining.

Never looking to outsiders for anything, the Illusians remained relatively peaceful within our own bounds. There are even stories of a human scientist being sheltered for a short time. As technology grew, our isolation shrank, until one sunrise, the skies were broken by the flares of a foreign ship. Taking great caution, the Alpha approached the bizarre looking craft, only to find its inhabitants unresponsive and wounded. After deciding to take them back to his encampment, the Alpha placed the small crew of three under the care of the unmated females tasked with attending to the elderly mated pairs. Their aggression had not yet been triggered by the natural instinct to mate, so their role in society was to nurture those who could not care for themselves.

During the night the group of three overpowered the guards, slaughtered the aged, and ravaged the females, taking the two that survived back to their ship. The encounter not only exposed a sacred aspect of our mating tradition, but when the stolen females grew heavy with child, it ignited the centuries long battle we face today."

"A tradition you have selfishly stolen from Aren," Illaria hisses from somewhere to my right.

"Illaria! How dare you say such a thing!" Dreya yells as both Amina and Xandria audibly gasp at the insult.

Excuse me? I mean sure, my lady parts aren't laced with LSD, but I didn't hear Ren complaining last night.

Naya rises from her position beside me, prepared to keep Illaria in line but stops as I wave her off. I am beyond over her entitled mean girl act.

"Yeah, yeah. I get it. You have a magical pussy. Maybe if you weren't such an evil wench, one of them," I nod over my shoulder toward the males, "would actually want to touch it." The room is silent until Amina snorts and bursts into laughter beside me. Illaria turns up her nose and leaves the circle after a few others start laughing too. I sit quietly and wait for Naya to continue.

"What started with just a few attacks quickly turned into an all-out war, and we were inundated with Inokine. They took several of our females in the final attack and gave us no other choice but to splinter our population. We spread to the far reaches of space in an effort to keep those savages off our trail. We have mostly eluded them since, losing very few of our own, until last week when they discovered our whereabouts. This was the closest outpost we found after our makeshift hyperdrive spit us out, so we came here until Aren and the other males could dispatch anyone who could breathe word of our location."

She looks at the males with eyes full of affection. Following her gaze, I see Ren watching my every move. Still just as affected by his obvious attraction fifty feet away, I try my best to focus on Naya's story.

"Aren believes the threat has been contained for now. All of those present for our attack are now rotting on display, where they belong. But the rest will seek their kin and when they discover the bodies Aren displayed beautifully," she closes her eyes and smiles, "they will eventually track us here. Our plan is to be long gone before then."

"What exactly are they? The Inokine, I mean?"

Amina shivers beside me and Naya pats her shoulder.

"They are a race whose threat of near-extinction twisted their souls. We do not know why, but at some point, their females became infertile. Those that could produce did not yield female children, so the entire race began to die out. Their genetic structure is not compatible with most other species, so interbreeding was their only way of life. Desperate to continue their lineage, they forced the females capable of breeding to do so with multiple males. Driven mad by their instinctual need to procreate as the last female died out, they went planet to planet, taking who and what they wanted until they stumbled on Illusia."

"And Illusian DNA would allow for a hybrid child to be born between the two races, in essence keeping them from dying out…" I say.

"Yes, that is what makes this battle such a burden. Many of those raised to hunt us also share our blood."

"So, what is my part in all of this? What am I supposed to do?"

Naya's eyes narrow. "Aren did not explain the duties you absorb before you solidified your bond?" she asks, glaring in his direction.

"We didn't do all that much talking…" I confess, loud enough for Illaria to hear.

So, sue me, I'm petty.

The rest of the females are all leaning in, hanging on every word.

"Aren is our alpha. Our collective group, and the entirety of our race, are sensitive to his specific inherited talents. He is our leader, Ajayla, as his mate, you are also called to lead."

"I'm sorry. What?"

CHAPTER EIGHTEEN

Jayla

"Did you, perhaps, fail to mention something?" I ask Ren after pulling him out of the gym. Leaning against the wall, I cross my arms and tap my foot as my patience wears thin. He should have told me. I fix my gaze on the ceiling above us, worried that if I keep staring at his stupidly beautiful face, my resolve will break and I'll give in. He needs to know this isn't okay.

"I have upset you, *Skara.*".

He reaches for me, and I make a point to turn away from his hand. I'm not letting him hump his way out of this. "Well, yeah. Don't you think you should have, I don't know, told me that magical dick of yours comes with some pretty serious stipulations *before* you put it in me?"

The lyrical sound of his deep laugh has me fighting back a smile. Ugh, that is so annoying and charming. But mostly annoying. And it *is* seriously magical. "I see Naya informed you of my position. In hindsight, that would be something worth mentioning..." He pulls at the bottom of my uniform top, playing with it. Twisting the material between his fingers, he tugs me closer.

I know what you're trying to do, and it ain't working buddy. Well, mostly...

"You think?"

This feels like more than an oversight. He should have told me, and I'm irritated I had to find out from Naya. I just wish my stupid hormones would shut up and let my brain work.

"Would you have chosen differently?" he asks, continuing to crowd me. He makes my brain short circuit when he's this close. I know I should shove him away and avoid his embrace but I don't. I like it when he's all over me, even if I am pissed.

Hearing a hint of doubt in his voice surprises me, leaving me feeling unsettled. It's funny really; I've never cared about what other people think. Yet, here I am, staring up at the male who just rearranged my world, and all I can think about are *his* feelings.

"Of course not. I just hate being the last to know, especially when it involves me. No more secrets, okay?" I mindlessly fiddle with a small hole in the right corner of his shirt.

"I did not intend to hurt you. I will do better," Ren says, wrapping his arms around me.

"Yes, you will. You don't get to push this all on Naya. I want you to tell me what's up with the Inokine. Especially if there is a possibility they might come for me now too."

Erupting into a full growl at the mention of their threat, Ren looks behind him, calming the warriors who have already poured out of the gym to protect him. After shaking off the rage-induced fog, he returns his attention to me.

"How about starting with how the hell they're able to do that?"

Grabbing my hand, he pulls me down the hallway, leading me back toward my room. Even though there's no one in sight, Ren isn't taking any chances on being overhead. Not two seconds after we make it inside, he grabs the hair falling down my back and wraps it around his hand. Yanking me against him, he presses his lips to mine and closes the door with his foot.

"Nope. Not yet. You're not getting any until you explain yourself." Wriggling out of his embrace, I sit on the opposite end of the couch, keeping my distance from him. He slouches against the cushions, causing the frame to strain under his weight.

"Come here," he says, rubbing his thigh.

"No. Not until you tell me everything." I'm serious about this, and no matter how much I want to feel him on my skin again, he's not getting shit until he tells me.

"And then? What are you going to do then, *Skara*?" My nipples harden at the deep rumble of his words. Empowered by his intense attraction for me, I tease him by letting one knee fall to the side.

"Whatever you want." Images of all the dirty things I've fantasized about doing to him flash through my mind, and I lick my lips at the memory of his taste. With my lady parts miraculously feeling better than before, they respond instantly to thoughts of his naked body on mine. There's just something so insanely primal about the way I lust after him. Refusing to give into my desire and determined to get the answers I need, I try my best to let my mind go blank.

"You play a dangerous game, *Skara*. Hiding over there like prey. I will give you the answers you seek." His pupils widened further, swallowing all evidence of color. "Then I am going to devour you, inch by inch, until I have possessed you so fully, even your soul has not escaped my reach."

Holy crap, that's hot.

Stunned into silence by the intensity of his ridiculously sexy threat, I retreat into my kitchen. Trying to refocus and ignore the ache in between my legs, I grab one of my last remaining chocolate bars from its new hiding place and sink back onto the couch.

"All right, I'm ready. Let me have it." He raises a brow at my unintended innuendo. "You know what I mean. Spill it already so we can get to the fun part."

Shaking his head, he leans further back, bringing even more

attention to the bulge in the front of his pants. "Illusians and humans both rely on a series of nerve endings to send signals back and forth throughout the body, telling it what to do and how to feel." I nod in understanding, keeping my eyes above his waist. "Some Illusians can tap into and manipulate those neuropathways, altering the way those signals are received. In essence, the one-way path, becomes a two-way path and those strong enough to utilize this skill can send and receive images, feelings, or sensations through our entire group. Not everyone possesses the mental dexterity necessary, and, as far as I know, I am the only one able to do it without touch."

"So that's what Naya did when she helped me the first night..." I say, thinking back to how she touched the females to figure out where they were hurt.

"Yes, Naya can access the pathway through touch. With the majority of signals being carried down the spine, the base of the neck is the easiest place to both read and influence another."

Suddenly remembering him touching that other female, I'm instantly pissed. "Oh, what the hell? So, you could have calmed down what's her name without putting your hands all over her?"

Amused by my blatant jealousy, he smiles as his pupils continue to shrink back to normal size. "Normally yes. If I had not been directing a large amount of my energy toward controlling my urge to mount you in front of everyone."

"Ugh. Whatever. Keep going." I don't bring up the mutual purring. Just thinking about it makes me want to strangle him. And her. More than once.

"*Skara*." He leans forward to comfort me.

Nope, not happening. My pride won't allow it. I avoid his eyes and continue to pick at the soft fuzz of my blanket. He exhales loudly as he retreats back to his end of the couch. "I want to know if I should be worried about the Inokine. Are they coming or not?" I say, changing the subject.

He rubs his hands down the sides of his head, then rests his chin on them. "The Inokine will come here. Your general should have called for reinforcements days ago. Whether we stay or not, your people will be slaughtered without protection."

"What?" I sit up. "What do you mean *should* have? And why am I just now hearing about this?" Irritation pulses through me. Again, the last to know.

"We were not mated. I could not tell you. The females of my kind are not involved with politics or war games. That is one of Naya's most important roles. She is their voice."

"That's the most ridiculous load of crap I've ever heard. Our females are the ones getting abused. They should have a say."

He turns his head toward me as his eyes light up with affection. "You have a say, *Skara.* You are mine. Your position affords you a voice of your own."

"That's complete bullshit. Having a say in the way you live your life shouldn't be tethered to someone else's dick."

He sits silently, his instincts no doubt warning him I'm five seconds from exploding. Annoyed with the conversation but still wanting answers, I get straight to the point. "How do you know the general didn't call for backup? And how have you been going back to your ship? And why have you chosen to stay packed into the gym when you could be more comfortable back in the landing bay?"

"Is that all?" His eyes narrow.

Oh, someone has got an attitude.

"For now." My anger and the sexual tension floating between us is making me one snotty bitch.

"We have been watching your general. We are limited by the vast amount of security measures he has in place, but we have been able to ascertain that he has not notified his superiors of the threat you made known." He stands up slowly and turns toward me.

"The answer to your other questions is simple. We have never stayed in one place, not really. You think we survived this long by trusting those outside our circle? That is why there was tension between Naya and me. Every night while I watched you, tormented myself with thoughts of you," he takes a step toward me, "the others had to carry my burden of scouting out this place and discovering its secrets. We returned to the ship because we tested the air ourselves. It has been inhabitable for over a day. Your general, however, has taken the time to install additional cameras there, to spy on us, which is why we have stayed where we are." He takes a final step. "My preoccupation with you has caused an uproar within our ranks, but no one will dare challenge me." Now in front of me, Ren sinks down to his knees and wraps his hands around my thighs.

"You are mine. Nothing and no one can keep me from you. Not duty, not war, and certainly not these." He runs his knuckle down the seam of my pants. The thin fibers do nothing to dull the heat of his touch. "Now if you are done asking questions, I am going to bury myself so deep inside you, you will not be able to breathe without feeling my length."

Throwing the chocolate bar behind me mid-bite, I launch myself forward, meeting Ren in a frenzied kiss. His scent and the taste of his tongue silence the worry swirling inside me, and the feel of his hot skin on mine erases my doubts. This giant of a warrior won't stop fighting until he's eradicated the threat against us. So, for now, I give into my endless need for him and let the rhythm of our bodies quiet my restless mind.

CHAPTER NINETEEN

Jayla

Lying in bed, I stare at the exposed lines of Ren's naked back, and not even the muscular curve of his ass can distract me from my thoughts. Moments after we collapsed, sated, the events of the last week started to replay over and over in my mind. Sterling made his interest in Ren's fighting abilities clear but that couldn't be his sole motivation for whatever he's up to. Not after he asked all those odd questions about their sex lives and their kids. He's a major sleaze ball, but he has to know a race like theirs would never accept him. So, what does he want?

"You should get dressed. Your red-faced friend approaches and he looks annoyingly anxious." Ren's voice is raspy and muffled by the pillow under his face. He reaches over and runs his hand across my lower abdomen.

"How do you know that?" I ask, leaning up to get a better look at him. He taps his temple twice. Oh, the bond thing. Of course. He has someone hidden, watching the door.

Looking around, afraid someone's going to suddenly jump out, I yank the covers up around my generous breasts, shielding them from sight. "There aren't like, any of your guys in here right? Only outside?"

Stiffening with my words, Ren is on me before I can blink, the black voids of his eyes less than an inch from my face. "Anyone who dares to violate the sanctity of our bond by allowing themselves to see what is only meant for me will suffer a fate worse than death. No one will ever disrespect you in such a way. My warriors will always remain outside." Nostrils flaring, Ren scents the air, breathing in deeply. A look of confusion washes over his face. Whatever he smells isn't something he expects, nor is it something he likes.

Off the bed just as quickly as he threw me on it earlier, Ren pulls on his pants. He positions himself between me and the door, as if to shield me from an unknown threat. Snickering at his antics, I throw my legs over the side of the bed and get dressed.

"He will not touch you if he wants to keep his life." His tone is subtle, his threat is not. Damn near crumbling under the weight of his possessive gaze, I slither my way toward him and run my hands over the rough stubble of his jaw. Damn, I love this face. He leans into my touch, then abruptly turns to open the door.

With his arm extended, ready to knock, Rett's features slackens in shock. His ruddy cheeks blaze cherry red as he blatantly stares at Ren, letting his eyes linger on my warrior's naked chest a little longer than I prefer. Ren would never go for it but, judging by the unmistakable look of lust in Rett's eyes, he'd slit my throat for a chance to screw my Illusian.

He and Illaria would be perfect for one another.

Rett lets out a low whistle. "Damn girl, now I know why you were so torn up over him." He dips down slightly, so he can see me past Ren's arm.

"He can't understand us, right?" Rett asks. I shake my head, sure whatever Rett's about to say will just embarrass me. "My goodness, I'm getting hard just standing near him. How did you survive this long? Two seconds and I want to eat him alive."

"Hello, to you too, Rett." I roll my eyes as he continues to ogle Ren and completely ignore me. "Hey, over here asshole. What do you want?" I launch my socks at his head, trying to get him to pay attention. They smack into Ren, and I mouth an apology as he reluctantly lets Rett into the room.

"I came by to check and make sure you were still alive. No one has heard from you in forever." Rett heads for the seat next to me but, after a rather angry warning growl from the man-child behind me, chooses the opposite end of the couch.

"Seriously, it's been less than a day."

"Is that all? It feels like longer. Plus, people are losing their shit about you not turning up at drills after you got everyone else sucked into doing them," he says, pursing his lips in disapproval.

"I am not wasting my time when it's obvious something bigger is happening. I tell everyone a sadistic group of slave traders may be on the way, and all the general does is force everyone into some bullshit drills? I don't buy it, Rett."

"Yeah, well, no one believes you, girl. Serena told everyone she thinks you made it up to get attention from Sterling. She thinks you want him."

Ren's growls, and I reach behind me to grab his thigh. He may not speak the language but his perception is uncanny. Relaxing a fraction, he remains silent.

"Please shut up or I'm going to vomit. That's probably the grossest thing anyone has ever said about me." I scrunch my nose and fake gag.

"Don't be so dramatic, Jay. He isn't that bad."

"Not that bad? Who are you and what have you done with Rett? The general is up to some majorly shady shit. He was all over me when Ren's people first showed but hasn't said a word to me in like three days. Suspicious, right? The threat from the Inokine is real, and we have virtually no way of protecting ourselves. Don't you find it odd that no one cares?"

"Well, you don't exactly have the best track record, Jay. No offense to Mr. Tall, Dark, and Delicious over there, but you did ignore everyone and let a group of violent strangers on board. Plus, you seem to be the only one not forced to deal with the consequences." His gaze falls on the comm watch resting on my counter.

"I'm so sick of hearing how dangerous they are. Has anyone died? Other than that twat waffle Gibbons? No. They haven't. Ren's people have done nothing but keep to themselves and no one..." my eyes narrow, "I mean *no one* here, has looked at them as anything but space trash."

My face grows hot as my frustration rises, and Ren stiffens behind me, placing two hands on my shoulders. "I will cut out his tongue if he continues to anger you."

Rett's eyes widen. "What did he say? Holy shit. Even his voice is hot..."

I squeeze Ren's hand, reassuring him. "It's fine. We're just talking."

He grunts and continues to glare at Rett.

"Seriously, what did he say? Does he like me?"

I shake my head. "Not so much."

"Don't shoot the messenger. I'm the only one left in your corner, babe. Anyway, I just wanted to stop by and give you the lowdown. I need to get back to work though. Oh, and Brandon said to tell you how much he hates you. Sterling has him redoing all the physicals for the entire crew. Apparently, he thinks everyone will develop some kind of flesh-eating STD now that your man and his hot squad are staying on the main floor."

"Aw, hell. Tell him I'm sorry. Everyone else okay?"

"Fine. Ven is still talking to his vegetables, Serena is sleeping her way through the electricians, and our girl Leandra is tinkering away at whatever project she has for the month. Lea and I miss you, Jay, and no matter how many people hate you, we'll still be your friends."

"Wow, you know how to make a girl feel good. Go do your thing. I'll come find you later."

Reading the room correctly, Rett refrains from his usual bear hug and blows me a kiss. The action is enough to send Ren into an all-out tizzy, but ten minutes of making out and a solid blow job later, he's back to his pre-apocalyptic level of aggression.

REN and I start back toward the gym. I made sure not to shower off the scent of sex, so I can further rub my status in Illaria's stupidly perfect face. I may not know all the cuss words in Illusian, but my *petty bitch* is flawless.

Deciding last minute to take a quick detour, I lead Ren down the hall to check the main communications room. Since all the wrist comms have been confiscated and mine won't make outgoing calls, I need to see if getting in there is even and option. I seriously doubt I'll be able to just walk in there and turn the comms array on, but it can't hurt to check. Trying to remain unnoticed, I pull Ren past the slight turn in the hallway to the green door nestled in between two bright red maintenance closets. Met with a glare from not one, but two sets of angry eyes, I intentionally keep walking past the guards, yanking Ren along with me. I have to stop and shove him from behind when he refuses to move. He *really* doesn't like the general and his men.

As we walk through the more populated decks, it's impossible to ignore all the dirty looks and whispers. It doesn't bother me all that much, but I worry about Ren's ability to control his rage. Luckily, most people are at work or in their pods, obeying the curfew. Distracted, I stub my toe on a lip in the floor as we enter the gym, and Ren grabs my arm to steady me.

"Aren, Ajayla, you have arrived just in time," Naya says, looking at me. "I have been trying to assist both the females and the unmated males with learning Metaversial, but we are all having difficulty with the tense. Can you assist us?"

"Of course." Giving Ren's hand a final squeeze, I follow Naya to the females huddled around my tablet. Searching for the males, I see them similarly collected on the opposite end of the room. It looks as if Naya has hand drawn the symbols and words for the males to practice writing while the females have the tablet.

Sliding in beside Iana, I marvel at the softness underneath my knees. The blankets I gave them before have been replaced with their own, and the space has a more personal feel now. Despite its boring sand color, the texture of whatever we're sitting on is smooth and cooler than the surrounding room.

"It is made of Woana hide," Iana says after noticing my fascination.

"It feels cool, how is that?" The tips of my fingers tingle as they flow smoothly over the patchwork.

A soft whisper of a laugh escapes her lips. "Woana hide is always cold. They only dwell on ice planets. Their skin self regulates to prevent overheating. Even after death, their cells live on within the walls of their hides. Eventually, the cells admit defeat and allow themselves to die, but this one has displayed an unnatural determination to survive. It has kept us cool for over six years."

"Man, I could use one of these at night. I get hotter than hell."

"Ugh, I know what you mean. Ori always wants to sleep close, and I cannot handle it. This baby makes me feel like I am going to catch fire at any moment." Her hand moves to cradle her tiny baby bump.

The exchange between us is so normal. Two people complaining about regular things. Feeling lighter, I turn my focus toward Liral and Dreya. Poor Liral looks beside himself. His little brows furrow as he stares at the screen. Dreya's cheeks are pink with frustration as she fails to calm her son.

I take the next hour to explain tense and answer their questions, relaxing as everyone but Ari finally understands. Only able to get near him with Ren hovering exceptionally close, I'm relieved when Ren's called a few feet away for a brief on something that Rivan has found. Ari's too nervous to concentrate with him there and visibly relaxes when he leaves.

"Ari, why are none of the mated males interested in learning Meta?" I ask as he stares at the screen.

"They do not need to if their mates are fluent."

"Oh, okay. I guess that makes sense. They're always together, right?"

"So, you and Aren mated?" he asks as he continues to read the practice questions. His low tone unsettles me. Why did he wait for Ren to leave before asking me that?

"Yep, are you having any trouble with the questions?"

"I am finished. I understand it better now," he says, lifting his gaze to mine. The longing I see in his eyes immediately causes my stomach to drop. Worried he's about to say or do something incredibly stupid, I try to end the tutoring session. As I reach out to grab the tablet, Ari's hand lingers, caressing my fingers with his thumb. My hand stings as Ren rips Ari away from me, jerking my fingers along with him. Cradling my arm, I look up to see Ari plastered against the wall, the barbs of Ren's fingers rammed through his chin and into his open mouth. He's driven his other set of barbs clean through Ari's shoulder and into the wall behind him.

"You dare touch what is mine?" he asks in a growl. The rage makes my hair stand on end. Naya and the other males immediately respond, trying their best to keep Ren from ripping Ari's head off. Still shocked by the display of violence, I stand up in a daze and head toward them.

"No, Ajayla," Naya says over the sounds of the scuffle. "You should not be near him when he has lost control. Even the weakest of Illusians are dangerous. The alpha is... deadly. Stay back."

I ignore her warning. Ren won't hurt me but he's going to kill Ari if someone doesn't do something. Not wanting to risk Ren's wrath, Naya lets me pass untouched.

Approaching from behind, I slide my hands up his back starting from the base of his spine. He tenses at my touch. Ari grows paler by the second, his life seeping away as blood drips down his chin. But no one can calm Ren. Even Naya fails to soothe him with her gifts. Ari gasps, struggling to breathe.

Unable to think of another way to distract Ren, I duck underneath his arms and force myself between them. Latching my mouth onto his, I suck his lip in between my teeth and bite down, hard. He growls in response as blood begins seeping into our kiss. Dropping Ari's unconscious body, Ren redirects his fervor to my mouth and begins ravaging my lips. With rough kisses, he consumes me, gripping and squeezing my curves. The room clears quickly as we tumble against the nearest wall and he tears at my clothing. Ripping my pants open, he yanks my underwear off in one clean swipe and plunges himself deep inside me. He claims me furiously, thrusting again and again until my satisfied screams echo off the walls. Still having the forethought to protect my spine from the abrasive wall behind us, he comes hard and fast. His chest heaves as he releases my hips and lets my feet hit the floor.

"Forgive me, forgive me, my *Skara*. I did not mean to take you so roughly." His sweat-drenched forehead rests against mine as he rocks back and forth. "Ari had no right to touch you. I saw the light he held for you in his eyes and I wanted to snuff it out and all traces of him along with it. I would have done so if it were not for your... less than conventional methods." A gruff chuckle passes his lips as he presses them against mine.

"You know I want you any and every way I can have you, right? But maybe next time, not in front of everyone, yeah?"

"Never again, my *Aciana*."

Removing his shirt, he slides it over my head, letting the long length cover my exposed legs. Still trembling from the strength of our encounter, I allow Ren to carry me through the crowded hallway full of staring Illusians back to my room. Catching sight of Ari, bloody but alive as we pass, I exhale in relief and sag into Ren's arms.

CHAPTER TWENTY

Jayla

My head is pounding, and my skin itches like hell. I'm sweaty and sore and exhausted. After all the drama between Ren and Ari and the stress of worrying about Sterling and the crew, I desperately need time to myself. My anxiety is so high, if anything else happens in the next few hours, I'm going to emotionally vomit all over the first person I see. Ren agrees to give me space while he checks in with Ragar and Sol, but only after insisting Orion and Rivan stand watch outside my door. His energy is so dominating, it leaves little room for me to concentrate on anything else.

When thoughts of my friends enter my mind, the worry and paranoia I've been trying to keep at bay bursts through and demands attention. How could I have spent the last week trusting their lives to someone like General Sterling and his men? Ren knows the Inokine will show up, following the Illusians' scent or trail or whatever it is they do. There's more than enough evidence to justify a need for reinforcements, so why hasn't the general done something? He doesn't strike me as a stupid man and he loves himself way too much to be suicidal, so what does he get from everyone being slaughtered? There's no way I can live with myself if I don't at least *try* to prevent it. If Ren says the Inokine are coming, they're coming.

Deciding to act now and apologize later, I change out of my uniform and into my regular clothes. Ren isn't going to like this. In fact, I'm pretty sure he's going to hate it. It isn't the *worst* idea I've ever had. I mean, all I'm planning to do is break into the comm room and illegally send a message for help.

Totally doable.

Right as I walk out, a throbbing behind my eyes throws me off balance. Grabbing a few pain pills from my dresser, I swallow them down, hoping they stave off my headache from hell. Something has got to give. Despite all the benefits of regular sweaty sex with Ren, my head has been pounding on and off for more than a day, and I'm about to bash my skull against the wall. No doubt a result of my consistent lack of sleep, dehydration, and my many ass kickings. I silently promise my body I'll take it easy tomorrow. Or next week. Well, sometime after I make sure we don't all die.

I'm relieved to see the monotone gray hallway empty as I peek out. The only audible sound is the low hum of the air condensers. After telling him how creeped out I get when his warriors hide in the shadows, Ren asked both Rivan and Orion to remain visible. So where have they gone? Not willing to waste what might be my only chance at freedom, I close the door behind me as quietly as possible and jog toward the east wing. Spotting Serena reading and sipping on tea, I alter my gait in an effort to pass by unseen. I make it about ten feet when the pain flaring in my head pitches me forward, doubling me over.

"You barely have a scratch on you. I knew Rett was exaggerating when he told everyone you nearly died." Her voice is flat and full of annoyance, like she's put out Gibbons didn't murder me when he had the chance.

Come to think of it, my bruises *are* almost healed and there's only a small scratch where my head wound used to be. It's not like I really have a frame of reference for getting my ass kicked, but I guess I'm a fast healer?

"Serena, what do you want?" I ask, still doubled over trying to keep my sudden bout of dizziness in check.

"You. Gone. But that obviously isn't going to happen anytime soon. Especially since you latched yourself onto those savages like a parasite. What? Since your own kind despise you, you think you'll have a better chance with them? From what Rett told me, they think you're just as pathetic as we do." Her eyes narrow in disgust as she sizes me up.

Her words sting a little. The revelation that Rett is spreading my business around hurts. I shouldn't be surprised, he's a major gossip whore, but we're friends. I thought he'd keep my secrets.

"Is there a point to all your bitchiness or are you just annoying me for sport?" The room comes back into focus, allowing me to stand up.

"I just thought you should know how inadequate you are. In case you missed it." Her perfectly painted lips pull up in a sneer. Flipping her candy apple hair to the side, she looks proud of herself.

"Thanks for that. Total piece of shit. Got it. Message received. You may hate me, Serena, but I was telling the truth when I tried to warn everyone about an invasion. The crew may not listen to me but they'll pay attention to you. Try to get through to them, or everyone's going to die."

Serena stares down her nose at me, puckering her lips. After catching a flicker of consideration, I brush past her, not wanting to ruin whatever progress I've made. I press my fingers to my eyes and push down, trying to relieve the raging pain behind them. My vision is blurry again, making it difficult for me to see. How the hell am I supposed to sneak around if I can't even walk in a straight line? Bracing myself against the wall, I stop for a second and take several deep breaths. After stumbling most of the way to the comm room, I turn the corner and find the door completely unguarded.

Finally, *something* goes right...

Fighting the urge to squeeze the sides of my head between my hands, I tiptoe inside. It's dark, but I can still see thanks to the dim glow from the hallway. It's smaller than I remember. Barely big enough space to house the massive switchboard, the room looks even tinier with piles of boxes and random junk lying about. There are several small makeshift cots set up, along with an extensive stash of guns and scattered food waste. This must be where Sterling and his men have set up shop. It makes sense logistically; this room controls all the data and voice traffic in and out of the station. But why in the hell would they leave it unguarded?

Careful not to disturb any of the bedding or trash, I head up the two slim stairs leading to the main controls. A series of large square panels full of flat, inlaid buttons and a single screen in the middle, it looks ancient. And it is. Shaking my head, I enter my login information.

Denied.

The system now requires an additional passcode to turn it back on. Why in the hell would they leave it unmanned? Aren't they concerned about missing reports from the outside? Don't they have someone to report to? None of this makes any sense, especially knowing how particular UCom is about their protocols.

The unmistakable sounds of heavy breathing interrupt my muddled thoughts. I sneak closer to the door of the storage closet. It's already cracked open, and I panic as I realize that if whoever's in there weren't so distracted, they could see me easily. Maybe I'll just take a peek inside...

I squeeze my size eight hips through the space in the door and crawl on my belly. The panting gives way to moans and the sounds of sweaty skin slapping together. I nearly giggle before I realize one of the two pleasure seekers is likely the general. Dry heaving, I choke back the vomit threatening to rise at the thought. The scents of sex and body odor permeate the air.

Well, I wondered why the room was left unguarded; now I know. Apparently, even the general's own men would risk a coup rather than witness his sexcapades. Unable to stand the sounds any longer, I back away, catching the heel of my shoe on his discarded pants. The movement exposes a faint light reflecting off something hidden in the material. I peer closer and find the general's comm watch tangled up in his dirty underwear.

Oh, for fuck's sake, really? Couldn't it have been anywhere else?

Grabbing it out of his briefs, I use my upgraded comm to sync with his and download the contents. Before he hated me, Brandon hacked my watch so we could share his stolen music. I should really thank him later. Covering my nose against the smell of sweaty balls wafting through the air, I wait for the entirety of his file cache to copy. My heart beats rapidly. Five minutes feel like fifty. Still going at it, the general and whoever was desperate enough to screw him are still blissfully unaware of my presence. After backing my way out of the closet, I scurry out of the room and narrowly avoid a group of UCom soldiers running down the hallway.

Relaxing at the click of my door as it closes, I turn the lock and rest my forehead against its cool metal. With the vise-like grip on my head finally gone, I let my shoulders relax and exhale in relief.

"Did you enjoy yourself?" Ren's imposing frame is stretched out on my couch, his posture deceivingly calm. Choosing to ignore his irritation, I go straight into the bathroom where I brush the awful bile taste out of my mouth. With the door left open, I strip and step into the shower without acknowledging him. His nostrils flare at the scent of sex on me. Rather than dropping accusations like a human boyfriend would, he says nothing and watches the rivulets of hot water run down my skin.

I scrub myself until it burns, trying to clean my mind and body of any essence I might have taken with me.

"It isn't what you think," I say, letting my gaze slide to his. Stepping out, I wrap myself in a towel and slink back into my room.

"*Skara*," Ren says, placing his hands on my shoulders. The contact soothes the tension between us. Wrapping his arms around me, he rests his chin in the crook of my neck. "I am not cross because I fear your affections for another. I would never think so little of you." I lean into him and let him guide me toward my bed. "It is your blatant disregard for your own safety that stirs my ire." The sheets feel like butter as I slide my tired, damp body underneath. Crawling over me to lie at my side, Ren strokes his hand down my arm.

"I care about my life. I just care about my friends more," I whisper, turning to stare at his face. His beauty distracts me... the strong lines of his cheek and jaw mixing with the soft curve of his lips. Masculine and so wildly handsome I can't believe he's real. All the males of his kind have eyes in varying shades of blue, but his are so light, the soft hue is almost indistinct from the white at its edges.

If I could just get him to stay calm long enough to let me look at them.

"Your desire to nurture is one of the things that drew me. I do not wish to stifle your drive to protect but I do not like you risking your life."

"I wasn't trying to piss you off. It's not like I just went in there willy nilly. I had a plan, snuck in and out, and managed to download the general's comm watch data." Leaning over the edge of my bed, I grab the leg of my pants and tug them. My sheet falls down around my hips, and Ren's eyes glaze over with lust. Damn, I love it when he looks at me like that. "I was a total badass, you should have seen me," I say, tossing the watch at him.

"I did see you. I was there the entire time."

My eyes widen, then narrow in confusion. "I'm sorry, you were what?"

Ren sighs, then rolls over onto his back. Unsettled, he returns to his side, facing me.

"I saw the moment you decided to go. I relieved Rivan and Orion and followed you." His fingers repeatedly straighten the rumpled sheets. It's kind of cute. He's nervous and even though I know he's about to piss me off, seeing him fiddling around lessens my urge to smack him.

"Since when can you do that? I'm going to need you to explain. Like now."

The look on his face tells me he wants to argue but doesn't. "I was not sure it was even possible. Few of my kind take an outside mate, so how our bond will affect you is unknown."

"That's a lame excuse, but go on..."

"I can see you." The words are quieter and smaller than when he spoke before, almost as if he is trying to minimize their impact.

"You can what?" I sit up fully and finger comb my wet hair as a distraction.

"Most mates share a mutual bond—a simpler more natural version of what I can do with the whole group. They can send images, words or thoughts to each other. It is not telepathy. The information is not fluid, just snapshots of whatever they choose."

Thinking back to what Ari said in the gym, it hits me. "So that's why the mated males haven't bothered to learn Meta." He nods in confirmation. "Which means you understood everything Rett said..."

He nods again and continues. "I don't know how—maybe it is a manifestation of my gift, but I can see your mind. I can hear you and see through your eyes."

He can what?

Startled by the revelation and feeling defensive about the massive invasion of privacy, I struggle to find my words. "So, what? It's like Jayla in real time? When exactly did you figure this out, Ren?"

"I suspected it after we bonded. I have been pushing fairly hard today to figure it out."

"So, you're the reason my head has felt like it was going to explode?" I glare at him, realizing his big intrusive ass is the reason I've been so miserable.

"I did not realize, or I would have ceased my efforts. I think you have to passively accept it. I suspect the pain is a byproduct of your mind fighting back." He reaches up to move a stray lock of hair behind my ear.

"Well, how in the hell am I supposed to do that? What if I don't want you poking around in my head? Wait, wait, wait..." I look at him in horror. "You could accidentally see me poop? Oh, God, I'm going to die!" His pupils dilate at the mention of my demise. "Calm down, I'm just being dramatic. So, can I see into your head then as well?" I ask, curious if it goes both ways.

"I do not know, *Skara.* But I worry if you could, you would not like what you see."

"Too bad, love. Get ready, because this is so happening." He smiles as I gesture in between us. Able to take his confession in stride, I lie next to him while he continues to play with my hair. All things considered, I think I'm dealing with the news surprisingly well. I didn't scream or cry and now all I can think about is all the ways this could come in handy. If I'm tired and want food, or I need something from across the room but am too lazy to get it. This whole mind sight thing might not turn out to be such a bad thing after all.

CHAPTER TWENTY-ONE

Jayla

I'VE CLEANED my entire kitchen. My legs are shaved, my pubes trimmed, and I've eaten everything in sight. Agreeing to wait for Ren before examining what I stole from the general was the worst decision ever. The suspense is going to kill me.

As I sit on my couch, staring at the damn watch, my mind is going in all the wrong directions. After cramming the last bit of my chocolate stash in my mouth, I have nothing left to do but contemplate how my recent decisions will affect the rest of my life.

I've avoided all thoughts of Ren leaving. We haven't discussed what happens after they fix his ship. Part of me, well, all of me really, doesn't want to admit I'll have to make a choice. There is no way Ren and the other Illusians can stay here. As soon as word gets out about him killing Gibbons and boarding without being vetted, the powers that be will be on their way with the sole intention of locking him up and making an example out of him. That would be bad. Really, really bad. He won't be their only target either. They will crucify me for putting everyone at risk.

Shit, *I* won't be safe here after they leave. There's no way the UCom leadership will allow me to remain at my post knowing I fraternized with an aggressive, undocumented species. They'd throw me in a lab and study me for the rest of my life.

If thoughts of captivity aren't enough to make me a nervous wreck, the small voice in my head warning that Ren could leave without me makes my chest ache. I know it's irrational. And that Ren wouldn't ever leave me. But what if the time comes and I'm not ready? Could I really walk away from my entire life for a male I just met? With nothing more to occupy my time, I trudge over to the bedroom and separate my laundry.

Halfway through the first load, Ren walks in, turning to knock after already inside. Unimpressed by his efforts, I raise a brow. After finding out he can just hop in and out of my brain at will, I set a few boundaries I can actually enforce. Now required to knock before he comes waltzing in, I don't think he really understands the concept.

"You know I meant for you to knock *before* you came in, right?" I look up from my seated position on the floor.

"I can go back and re-do it if you would like." The tension radiating off him makes me nervous.

"Everything go okay? Is the group all right?" I pat the floor. His hand finds mine as he sinks down beside me, and I cringe slightly as his knee knocks over my folded pile of clothes.

"We are fine. The ship is taking much longer to repair than expected. Naya and the others grow anxious, as do I. We never choose a place to settle without researching it extensively. There are so many unknown factors here, it leaves us vulnerable to attack, and we dislike it."

Ren's anxiety trickles through the bond and my heart sinks. "What else can I do? I hate just sitting here."

He raises a brow. "Did you not just risk your life for this?" Reaching over, he plucks the watch out of my lap. "You have proven yourself to be a resilient, resourceful female in your willingness to search for our truth. Do not dare mistake yourself for less than you are."

Eager to sift through the stolen files, I snuggle in closer and log in. The first twenty folders contain useless information. Just old flight manifests, notifications from UCom, and the general's personal resume. Ren lifts me and positions me between his legs. Curling around me, he watches as I read. I look for anything out of the ordinary. A set of symbols jumps out at me as I search the files marked for deletion. They're familiar, but I can't remember when or where I've seen them before.

"Do you know that language, *Skara*?" Ren leans further into me to better see the screen.

"I'm not sure. I need to grab my tablet from Naya. All my translation keys are inside the program my father wrote."

"Is there anything in there you can use?" He points to the watch. "I cannot leave you to retrieve it right now. Rivan is with his mate, and Orion is assisting Ragar with the ship. Neither are available to protect you. Rhia is not feeling well, and Naya is using your machine to check the baby."

"Should I go help her?" I ask, worried.

"No, everything will be fine. You are best used here, trying to figure out what information this contains." He takes the watch and taps it a few times, squinting at the tiny screen. "Rivan will be available in just a moment." I find his insistence on dragging Rivan away from his pregnant mate ridiculous, but after the Ari drama, he will only allow him or Orion to watch over me. There are two other mated males, Nexx and Tao, but I'm not familiar with either.

"All right. If you're sure." I lean back for a quick kiss on the cheek but end up on top of him when he flips me around. My anxiety morphs into lust the instant I feel his dick harden underneath me. *I need this distraction, if only for a few minutes.* Pushing me back into my already destroyed laundry, he shoves one hand behind my head and the other down my pants.

"You are always so wet for me, my *Aciana*."

I arch my hips to deepen his reach. "You like that?" I ask, feeling the right kind of filthy. Ren withdraws his fingers and brings them to his mouth. My eyes widen in shock as he sucks on them. *That is the hottest thing I've ever seen*. Shoving him onto his back, I launch myself on top of him, pulling and tugging at my pants.

"Rivan is here," he says with hesitation in his voice.

Aw, that's sweet, he thinks I care. *I don't.* "He can wait."

Ren lets out a throaty chuckle and lifts his hips as I scramble to free his dick. Insane with need, I impale myself on his length. "Oh, hell yes," I moan, riding him faster. Sucking my lip into his mouth, he grunts and bites down. The sting of it pushes me over the edge, and I come hard, clenching around him as he rams his way to a climax of his own.

"Sorry. Couldn't help myself."

Ren moves the sweat-drenched hair from my face and kisses my temple. "Your apology is unnecessary. I am yours to enjoy."

Damn right.

In the few minutes it takes me to shower, Ren has already returned. Connecting the tablet with my watch, I scroll down and highlight the sections for comparison. Whatever this language is, it only seems to exist in written form. I can't find any data on how it's spoken. I've always had difficulty mastering a language I can't hear.

Knowing I have at least a forty-five-minute wait for the search analysis to finish, I ask Ren to call Dreya and Nexx, her mate, over. Of all the females, she seems to like me the most, and I need her help to figure out my mate bond. After realizing he caused me pain, Ren has refused any other attempts at reading me, and we're both eager to further the connection. I feel guilty asking them to come to us, but after our very public gym romp, I'm not quite ready to face the others.

"Are you all right?" Dreya asks as I close the door behind Ren and Nexx. I asked them to wait in the hallway, not wanting to miss out on any girl talk.

"Yeah. I'm okay. Just a little embarrassed." I give her a tight smile while adjusting the gray pillow in my lap.

"You should not feel ashamed or embarrassed. We are all quite impressed with you."

"Impressed? Why?" I snort, nearly choking on my spit.

"Well..." She looks down at her sandy colored dress and smooths it with her hands. "You redirected a newly mated male, the absolute alpha no less, in the throes of a mate rage." The deep wells of her violet eyes meet mine. "Ari is one of our best warriors —obviously no match for the *Acia*—and you saved his life. He had no right to touch you. His actions were asking for a slow death but you prevented even more loss for our kind. Your instinct to intervene did not go unnoticed."

"Thanks, I guess." Feeling awkward I change the subject quickly. "So how does this bond thing work, anyway?"

"I am not sure how much help I will be, Ajayla. Nexx and I have a different kind of bond. Ours is much more passive than what Ren described earlier. Sending a thought or image to him is as easy as drawing one up for myself."

"Well, what were you doing when you first noticed it?"

Dreya leans back and relaxes her shoulders. "You have to understand; our kind grow up looking forward to this bond. Our survival depends on successful coupling, so they raise us knowing what to expect. Nexx sent me a picture of a Cendarian Ruka on our bond night."

"A what?"

"It's a rare flower that burns with the rising suns on Cendara and regrows overnight. It is the most beautiful shade of red at dawn right before it goes up in flames. "Ren is not the only Illusian male who likes flowers."

Wait, what? Since when does Ren like flowers?

"Oh, I know what might help!" She jumps to her feet. "I knew it was coming. The image I mean. Nexx and I were so excited to test it out, we stayed up all night waiting for it to kick in. It takes a while sometimes for the genes to commingle and the connection to manifest."

"So, I just have to know it's coming? Well, that's worth a try." Feeling hopeful, I get up to retrieve Ren and Nexx but stop when I hear a ding. The translation is complete.

"What is it, Ajayla?" Dreya asks as my eyes narrow at the screen. It identified the language as Indayu? But how? What in all the worlds would someone like Sterling be doing using a sacred religious language? It's dead. Only Elvarian monks used it to communicate, and even then, the number of beings that can actually read it is miniscule. I only know because my grandfather helped translate several of their texts for UCom's ancient history archives.

As I continue to read, my heart stops. I'm running for the door before my brain can even process the translations. Ren barrels into the room, nearly knocking me over.

"Oh, my God, Ren. He knew about it. He planned it. He's part of this whole thing..." My words tumble into each other in panic.

"Slow down. What do you mean?" He grabs my forearms a little too firmly as my hyper-excitable energy sets him on edge.

"Sterling. He's in communication with the Inokine. They know you're here. They've known this whole time!"

Nexx lurches forward, grasping Dreya. "How is that possible? The Inokine have never partnered with an outside race other than to arrange transportation or to obtain a buyer."

"I don't know, but it is all right here!" I point to the message. "There are so many left to go through but this one says he's arranging for our normal security measures to be bypassed. It doesn't specify when but it says that everything's ready to go."

Dreya sucks in a deep breath and Nexx lets out a growl. Ren closes his eyes briefly.

"Did you tell the others? You guys have to get out of here.

What if they are coming right now?" Ren's arm wraps around my shoulder. "Keep reading, what else does it say?" He looks to Dreya and Nexx. "Go to the others, help them get everything packed, but do not go back to the ship. I do not want the general or anyone else to know we are aware of their plan."

"Your ship. It isn't ready, is it? What are we going to do?"

"Concentrate, my *Skara*. What else does it say?" Ripping my focus away from his face, I skim faster, trying to skip the things we already know. "He's getting something out of it, something in return for letting them in. Some sort of package..."

"A package? We have nothing of monetary value on board." His brows furrow in confusion.

"I don't know, Ren. That's just what it says. Oh, shit. Leandra! Why didn't I think of her sooner?"

"Leandra?" He sounds out the name slowly.

"She's the best mechanic I've ever met. She can help fix the ship."

Ren shakes his head. "I know you want to help but I do not trust humans. Only you."

I stare at the ceiling in an effort to dampen my frustration. "You don't have a choice, Ren! I still have so much to read... what if it doesn't give an accurate timeline? You can't take that chance. Let me ask her for help." The vein in my forehead pulses as my blood pressure rises.

Ren sighs before gathering me in his arms. "Come. We need to discuss this with Naya."

CHAPTER TWENTY-TWO

Jayla

"STOP PACING, *Skara*. You are making the others nervous."

Oh, *I'm* making them nervous? Not the revelation that this entire thing was a setup and the Inokine are undoubtedly on their way? Me... walking around while I desperately filter through thousands of emails is offending their delicate sensibilities. Too bad. I resent being guarded like some delicate, helpless flower, and it's written all over my face.

"There is nothing else to do but wait," Ren says, analyzing my every move. The rest of his people continue to pack things around us.

"That's complete crap, and you know it. Let me get Leandra." My irritation with him turns savage when, in my periphery, I see a look of jealous outrage on Illaria's face. "What the hell are you looking at?" I glare in her direction. The satisfaction I see on her face makes me regret my reaction. Shit, I just showed her how to get under my skin.

"Just disappointed our poor excuse for an alpha mate is so

unbelievably disrespectful." Her smile is full of venom, and the way she eyes Ren pisses me off even more.

He grunts before coming to stand beside me, rubbing his eyes then narrowing them. "I will not tolerate your disrespect. You will remember your place, or I will allow Naya to remind you." Illaria shrinks under the weight of his voice.

"Can't I like… banish her or something?" I ask, not ready to let it go. Naya stiffens at my side. Illaria shifts her legs underneath her, but remains seated, refusing to stand as their decorum requires.

A sneer pulls at Illaria's lips. "The *Acia values* his females. I am sure he would not allow me to be cast out like trash over your insecurities."

"Yes, *Skara,*" Ren confirms, throwing his arm around me. "You could request Illaria be reassigned to a group led by a lesser male. To be under my direct leadership is a privilege."

Illaria sniffles and opens her mouth to speak but Naya holds up a hand to silence her. "Ajayla, stop fighting with the other females and finish reading that thing!"

Calm your tits, I'm working on it…

Moving away from all of them, Ren included, I sit up against the wall in the only unoccupied corner of the room and continue sifting through the general's messages. He's worked with the Inokine for months, first to buy an illegal sexual encounter and later to traffic large crates of stolen goods for them and another third-party investor. It doesn't specifically describe what was in the crates but based on the latest message dated four days ago, it sounds like living cargo. Continuing past several messages containing dick pics and other pornography, I catch myself wishing I hadn't translated the entire mass of data. The thing is a treasure trove for the desperate and depraved. Skimming right over it at first, trying to avoid any more images of his wrinkly balls, I stop at a message with the same Inokine signature that gave away their connection before.

"Ren..." My voice shakes as I stand.

"What is it?" Ren immediately rushes to my side.

I can tell he's fighting his instinct to crawl inside my head. At this point, I wouldn't even mind the pain. "What is today's date?" I ask, still glued to the screen.

"*Skara*, I do not know how you measure time." Duh. With no star large enough to dictate day and night where we are, our time is based on Earth's only in principal. Both date and time are denoted on our comm watches to help keep our circadian rhythms in check.

"Hurry, hand me my watch." After a few seconds of searching, Ren comes back empty handed. Looking up, I can see my bag propped up against the wall and the watch dangling out the side.

Seriously? He can't find it? Illusian and human males have more in common than I thought.

Summoning its image, I mentally hurl it at Ren. I have no clue what I'm doing, but the universe could implode in the time it takes him to find it without help. Ren's lips pull up into a smirk as he saunters over to retrieve it. Pulling me to him, he taps the watch and wraps his arm around me so I can see. I've got to be wrong. This can't be happening.

"It's tomorrow, Ren. They set the exchange to take place tomorrow."

The room erupts in chaos, but Ren remains steadfast. "Rivan, Orion, Tao. You three will remain here to guard the females. I know you will not feel comfortable separating from your pregnant mates and young. Ari and Fen, you will report to Nico and assist with whatever he requires to prep the ship."

"But your ship—" I start to argue.

He silences me with a kiss. "We leave tonight. You may call on your friend." His eyes narrow as I accidentally project the image of him saying goodbye. Damn, that was pretty easy to do the second time around.

"I will *not* be without you." With no explanation beyond that, he holds the door open, waiting for me to lead the way toward Leandra. Well, that settles it. The surety of his words removes all lingering doubt. He's leaving, and I'm going with him.

How do you even pack for that?

Ren and I waste no time getting to Leandra's pod. There's a good possibility she's still at work, but there's no way I'll be able to talk to her in the mechanic's lounge. If I can catch her away from Serena and the rest of the bitch squad, I'll have a much better chance of convincing her to help us. Everything about Ren screams dangerous, and even though I'm taking a risk bringing him with me, I hope seeing him in person will change her mind. People become a lot harder to hate when you have to look them in the eyes.

Coming up to her pod, I can hear the sounds of heavy metal music vibrating through her door. Half-naked in a towel, Leandra slings her door open, despite her exposed state. Ren immediately averts his eyes, and I can't help but smile at his reaction. He's just so damn old fashioned and, good gods, he's hot.

"Jay, what are you… Oh!" she says, pausing as she notices Ren. "So, this is one of them, huh?" She studies Ren while he stares hard at the opposite wall. "I totally get where you're coming from now. Good Lord, he's built like a tank." She looks back down at her chest, adjusting the towel to cover herself better. "Sorry, didn't mean to almost flash ya. Just got out of the shower, what's up?"

"We need your help."

"Come on in. Let me go throw some clothes on." Ren and I take a seat on the couch as Leandra gets dressed. He continues to stare at the ceiling.

"Seriously, I don't care if you look at her. But if you try to cop a feel, I will end you." The side of his mouth curls into a smirk and he squeezes my inner thigh.

"Don't you think you've caused enough trouble, Jay?" Leandra calls out as she crosses into her kitchen. She grabs three cups out of the cabinet and yanks a large unlabeled bottle from the back.

Leaning over us, she places all three on the table and pours us each a drink.

"You know me, always getting into something." I smile and slam the drink. Ren's hand covers my lower back as I cough and sputter, nearly spitting it out. The strength of whatever devil juice she just gave me has my throat on fire.

"Holy shit, Lea! What the hell kind of poison is this?" I grab the corner of my shirt to wipe the remnants of spittle off my chin.

"Homemade moonshine. My specialty." She laughs, downing the shot. "So, what is it you need? I know you didn't just come here for the drinks." My eyes flutter to Ren, silently asking permission. I guess we should have decided how much we would divulge before we made our way here. He answers me with a subtle nod.

"Well, the thing is, I'm going to sound insane but I swear it's the truth. The general is in league with a bunch of slave traders. They're planning to attack here tomorrow, General Sterling dismantled our security systems and shut down the main comm." I stop and take a deep breath. "The traders kidnap and sell women and children, Lea. It's not exclusive to Ren's people either, everyone here is up for grabs."

She sits silently for a moment before grabbing Ren's drink and swallowing it down. "No shit?"

"No shit," I repeat.

"What are you going to do? What can I do?" Unable to sit still any longer, she paces the room.

"We need to get Ren's people out of here. They're who the slavers really want. If we can get their ship up and running, it might keep the people here safe, but I need your help to fix it. You're the best mechanic here, and if anyone can figure out what's wrong with it, it's you." Leandra's pacing comes to a stop as she grabs the bottle off the table separating us. Taking a swig long enough to make me cringe, she slams it back down and grabs her tools from the counter. "All right, lead the way."

With Ren unwilling to expose the rest of the Illusians, we escort Leandra up to the landing ourselves. After she's introduced to Sol, she waves Ren and me off before disappearing underneath the ship. It's odd to see her working alongside them so unaffected. I know she doesn't have a pair of nuts, but if she did, they'd be bigger than any dude's I've met.

Well, except for Ren.

The need to do more nags at me, especially knowing all I'd need to do to get the comm passcode is beg Rett to hijack it from his lover boy. Well, if they're still banging. If I could get in that damn room and send out an SOS, we might all have a chance at survival. Startled by Ren's hands gently directing me through the doors of the gym, I look up and realize I've spent the last fifteen minutes completely in my own head. No matter which way I look at it, there's no scenario where Ren doesn't forbid me from going.

Wait a minute. Forbid? Since when have I ever let anyone forbid me to do anything?

Back in the present, I notice Rhia on the floor. Her color is way off. She looks gray. Something's wrong. Making my way to her, I kneel next to her. On her side, with her head propped up on a rolled-up blanket, she has her knees pulled up to her gravid belly. With a light sheen of sweat forming on her brow and her hair tangled behind her, she looks miserable.

"Rhia, what's wrong? Are you in pain?" My hands push the sweaty strands of hair away from her face. Noticing our interaction, Naya stalks over.

"I am fine, Ajayla. This baby is always making me want to throw up." Rhia lifts her left arm and rubs her lower back.

"How long has your back hurt?" I move the blankets surrounding her out of the way, and my hand comes back wet. They're soaked.

"All morning. Do human babies make you this miserable too?" Her beautiful face is frozen in a tight grimace as the pain grows stronger. I put my hand on her lower back and massage it. Fearing the worst, I look to Naya.

"Get me the ultrasound. Quickly." She drops the collection of clothing and blankets she's holding and grabs the machine from where it sits near the exit. I reposition Rhia on her back and use the gray blanket underneath as a cover while I expose her belly for the scan.

"We have a small problem," I say as Naya drops to her knees beside Rhia. Overhearing the conversation, Rivan hovers near.

"I think she's in labor. There's not much fluid left in the baby's sac, and the blanket underneath her is soaked." Not taking my word for it, Naya scents the air near her belly.

"She demanded I leave her after I told her something wasn't right. I cannot believe I missed this. The fluid is warm still, it must have just happened." Naya continues to palpate Rhia's abdomen.

"It may have, but I would bet good money that the back pain she's having is contractions."

Naya cranes her head to Ren, who stands near Rivan. "We have maybe an hour or two before she will become immovable."

"What do you mean you can't move her?"

She sighs and moves closer to Rhia. "Illusian births are extremely dangerous. The threat comes from the babe, Ajayla. Regardless of age, Illusian males have the ability to respond to anything they perceive as a threat. Most babies pose no real harm, and we take precautions out of habit, but if the child is male and carries the alpha trait, stress can trigger the dominant gene, and the fetus can become aggressive in utero. It can be fatal. It is of utmost importance the baby come naturally and undisturbed. In early stages, movement is permitted but the female must hold still once the baby begins to leave the womb."

Oh, shit.

CHAPTER TWENTY-THREE

Ren

I DESPISE BEING MADE to wait. I know it is customary for Jayla to remain with the other females as they prepare Rhia for birth, but I do not like it. I cannot see her face or feel her skin. I cannot even use my mate bond to observe her. The ritual forbids male participation and calls for a complete disconnect between the mates involved. I fucking hate it.

For a distraction, I survey the lounge next to where Jayla and Naya moved the females. Its location in the abandoned end of the hall near her sleeping quarters offers substantially more privacy. There are no monitoring devices within range, and it is easier to defend if the need should arise. My gut tells me it will. The room is small but sufficient to hold us. Most of our numbers are here, with only Sol and Ragar still at the ship. I considered calling Ragar, positioning him here, but he prefers solitude, and most of the females are unsettled in his presence.

After Jayla discovered the connection between the human general and the Inokine, our hope of leaving before another battle quickly dissolved, leaving a raging eagerness to decimate our enemy in its place. With his failure to report, I have to assume Xen is dead or has been captured and given something to block our connection. With my Life Giver a part of the missing group, my bloodlust awakens. If they are mistreating her...

I know she still breathes, that her heart still continues to beat, but that is all my connection to her allows me to see. The blood bond between mother and child can never be severed completely. I share no such connection with Xen or the others in his group. The urge to slaughter anyone standing in between us nearly overpowers my reason but anchoring myself to my mate restores my calm. I will find my Life Giver, and when I do, suffering and agony will befall any who have harmed her.

The human, Leandra, identified a problem with the ignition system but is still building the parts needed to repair it. By my calculations, facing the Inokine here will lead to a favorable outcome for us but the number of human lives lost could be catastrophic. I can hardly stand the excitement surging through my veins at the thought of spilling filthy Inokine blood. The scent permeating the surrounding room is one of aggression and anger. Feeling our collective rage build as the seconds go by feeds my desire for vengeance until the pressure of my need to kill pulsates through my veins.

My lust for violence morphs into lust for my mate as she enters the room. Coming up behind her as she turns to close the door, I wrap my hands around her hips and slide them down around her thighs. I cannot stop myself from touching her. Even with the threat of a massacre being brought to her door, she remains calm and provides crucial insight into planning for the safety of our group. Her devotion to me and mine knows no bounds and I will forever worship her for it.

Her curious brown eyes take in the surrounding scene, and she gawks at the hulking males crammed into the room. Her gaze falls on the arsenal strapped to my body. Looking up at me with a brow raised, she offers me a sensual smirk.

"Why do you guys all carry knives? I mean, you can do the whole mind control thing and have the whole finger barb thing going on. Why the need for all the pointy stuff?"

Enjoying the feel of her gaze, I gave her a predatory grin. "Do you eat for taste or for survival?" I ask as I shift my hands around to her ass. The softness of her curves is addictive, and her scent reels me in. She smells of sweet fruits and rain water and it drives me insane.

"Both I guess. Why?"

"Illusians do not fight with our fists out of necessity. We fight because we love to feel our enemies break beneath our hands." I lean in closer to nibble on her ear. "The only thing sweeter than what your flower holds for me is the sight of my enemy's blood on my blade."

I can feel the shift in her weight as her knees weaken, and fuck, I love the way she responds to me. Holding my nose close to her skin, I can smell her arousal, and despite current company, have to restrain myself from spreading her legs right here. Pulling back, she drops her smile and flattens her lips. "We need to talk."

No good can come from those words.

"I'm going to the comm room again. I have to at least try to send for help." Her voice does not waver. She has made up her mind.

"No. It is not needed, we can sufficiently contain the threat. There is no need to place yourself in harm's way." I turn away from her the same way I do with my warriors, using my body to close the lines of communication. They retreat without question, interpreting my dismissal as a no, but my mate is unaffected and continues to stand her ground. Damn, she is fierce. Her refusal to take orders is frustrating as hell, mostly because my dick will not see reason. Apparently, I like it when she stands up to me. It is a good thing too because I have a feeling it will become quite common.

"I'm sorry, did you think I was asking permission?" Her shoulders drop, and she puffs out her chest. I know that look, she will not back down from this obscene idea without a fight.

"Your intention does not alter my decision. You will not go," I command, crossing my arms.

Without acknowledging my refusal, she turns away and heads for the door. Raising a hand in the air, she displays her middle finger, before slipping into the hallway. I am not familiar with that gesture, but after smelling the anger, hurt, and frustration pouring off of her, I grab her hand to stop her.

"Let go of me, Ren," she snaps, jerking her hand away from me. Naya and the other females pour out of the birthing room to circle around her. We should not be arguing this close to Rhia. She does not need the stress.

"You might think you guys can handle things without a problem, but there are a lot of women here. If I can help keep them safe, then damn it, I'm going to." She rises to full height. "You might be the best thing that's ever happened to me, but there's no way in hell you're going to stop me from doing what's right."

Damn, I want her. Realizing that I may have underestimated her stubbornness, I offer a compromise of sorts. "Then I will go with you." I will not allow her to risk herself unaccompanied. If she refuses to yield to my initial demand, then she should at least agree to my request.

"No. You can't go with me. You need to be here with your people, guarding the females. If things get out of hand, you're the only one who can do your mind thing." She crosses her arms. "Let me go alone, Ren. I'll be fine."

Despite my best efforts, I am drawn to the fullness of her breasts, and no matter how many times I try to look her in the eyes, I cannot.

"Seriously?" The corner of her mouth turns up slightly in amusement, and then as if she remembers our standoff, goes flat. We continue to stare at each other, neither one backing down, until Naya speaks up.

"This is not healthy for Rhia. Clearly, Ajayla, you will not back down." Naya turns to Ren. "The ceremony is complete, and now all there is to do is wait. As long as you and the other males stand watch, I will accompany the *Aciana* on her task."

Aciana. Fuck yes. She is my Queen. Every warrior in the room places a fist to their chest at Naya's use of Jayla's full title. *Acia* is the Illusian word for King. I allow my people to shorten it to just the letter A if they so choose, but for a keeper as highly respected as Naya to address Jayla so formally goes a long way to solidifying her place within our ranks. As our Queen.

"You will guard her with your life, Keeper." Nodding, Naya gathers some additional weapons. Reaching out for Jayla one last time, I let my hand connect with hers and pull her toward me. "I will not live without you. Come back whole. Do not make me come find you."

She leans forward and puts her lips to my ear. "I love you too."

CHAPTER TWENTY-FOUR

Jayla

WE TAKE the long way to Rett's, doing our best to avoid the general's drones. Naya is tense beside me. Anxious, even.

"If you're that uncomfortable being away from Rhia, why did you come?"

Her shoulders stiffen, then settle slightly as she turns my way. "You do not listen, Ajayla. You are stubborn and headstrong," her mouth pulls up slightly, "but you also represent change."

I what?

"You doing this, standing up for your beliefs, it is important for everyone to see. Our females have always been coddled, kept out of sight. Never allowed to participate in their own protection."

"So, you think they should learn to fight?"

Her jaw ticks. "I will not speak on that matter. It is forbidden, but mandates can be changed and traditions altered."

Oh. I see where she's going with this. She wants me to change Ren's mind.

As we approach Rett's door, Naya disappears out of sight. We both thought it would look suspicious if she showed up with me. My heart stutters at the sight of her scaling the wall and disappearing through the tiled ceiling. I don't know if I'll ever get used to their strength.

Rett better freaking be here. There's no telling where he is, and I have zero time to waste searching for him. It might be midday but it's unlikely he's in the kitchens. That boy never actually works. Raising my hand to knock a fourth time, I jump as Rett opens the door in his robe.

"Girl! You have the worst timing ever!" He rushes out into the hallway and closes the door behind him. Already feeling Ren's nosey ass trying to peel back the layers of my brain, I close my eyes and relax, letting him in. Rett seems irritated by my silence and begins tapping his foot. "What's up? I'm going to meet up with Serena for coffee in fifteen and was just about to hop in the shower. It's nutrishake day, and girl, you know I can't be strutting around smelling like plant proteins."

"How is it you managed to be a chef and hate most foods?"

"Does this story have a point? I've got to go. What do you need?" He flails his hands like he's outraged. I love Rett, but sometimes his attitude is too much.

"All right, rude ass. I need a favor. Get your booty call to give me the passcode for the comm system. I want to turn it back on."

He looks toward the inside of his pod. "Ugh, hold on a second."

I cover my mouth in surprise. "He's in there, isn't he? *Hi, boyfriend.*"

"Shut up, Jay. Don't be so loud. Maybe he is or maybe he isn't. Give me a second, let me get what you need." I try to sneak a peek as he re-enters his pod, but he closes the door too quickly. Five minutes later, he hands me a small piece of paper. "You didn't get this from me, okay?" His eyes linger on me a little longer than normal. Confused by the guilt I see beneath his baby blues, I give him a kiss on the cheek and start toward the comm room. Naya drops down from the ceiling, seeking cover in the shadows to my left.

Only one hallway from our destination, she steps out to sniff the air.

"We need to leave now, Ajayla." My brows narrow in confusion. There isn't anyone near us. What in the world has her so spooked? Oh, I am going to be so pissed if this is a ploy she and Ren dreamed up to give me the illusion of freedom. I swear if he pops out and tries to take me back, I'm kneeing him in the balls. I continue forward, ignoring her warning, but look to her for an explanation.

"The scent on your friend, I have smelled it before."

Rolling my eyes, I approach the unguarded door and cringe at the thought of walking in on the general again. I know the drill taking place in the lounge has drawn most of the soldiers and staff away, but the idea of having to witness those sad, wrinkly balls in action has me wanting to wash my eyes out with liquid nitrogen.

"I'm sure you have. Rett and I are best buds. We share clothes all the time." I dismiss her concern and scan the room. It's even filthier than last time. *Don't these pigs ever clean up?* Making my way up the stairs quickly, I lean over the dark screens and hit the sequence to boot up the array.

Naya hovers near me. "No, Ajayla, you do not understand. The scent on your friend is not yours. We need to leave now." Her words are hurried, and she begins pulling me toward the exit. I swat her off.

"Look, we're almost done. I can't believe those assholes made this so easy. Just a few more seconds and I'll have the message out and all will be good."

Typing in the passcode and logging in, I boot up the comm and curse at the disabled mic to my right. Great. Now I have to type the words manually. Unable to see well, I hunt and peck for each key, nearly completing the message before Naya turns on the lights.

"Naya turn that off! People will see!" I rush to finish the call for help, then look up to find out why the hell the lights are still on. My heart drops at the sight of General Sterling standing in the doorway.

Ren is going to be so pissed.

"Well, hello, Medic Shirley." His voice grates along my spine like cement on fresh skin. Naya's gone—or at the least, completely out of sight. I'm glad she escaped, but I'm also terrified because there's no way out of this. Sweat drips down my temple as the general's men flank me. I scramble to hit send before the goon to my left lunges forward and wrenches my arms behind by back.

"Too late asshole, UCom is going to know exactly what kind of nasty shit you're into. You're finished. Just give up and leave." I lift my chin proudly. These jerks might kill me, but at least they'll get what's coming to them.

Sterling slaps his knee and laughs so hard, he has to stop to catch his breath.

"Oh, how cute. You think we didn't plan for that?" He looks to the blond-haired soldier at his right. "She thinks we didn't plan this whole thing." He clucks his tongue, slowly approaching. "I have a man on the outside capable of deflecting any signals sent from here. Your sad, pathetic excuse for an SOS isn't going to reach anyone. But I give you points for effort. You are much more resilient than expected."

With a nod from the general, the soldier holding me tries to drag me toward the door. I fight wildly, kicking and screaming as I send the image to Ren, giving him a detailed look at their faces. The joints of my shoulders pop in protest as the soldier wrenches my arms even closer together, and I squeeze my eyes closed, gritting my teeth through the pain. He suddenly releases his grip, and I jerk my eyes open, confused. General Sterling lets out a gasp as the top half of the soldier holding me slides to the floor, leaving his legs upright and twitching.

Naya didn't leave after all.

Chaos breaks out as the general calls for backup. Naya fends off our attackers, using the blades strapped to her thighs like sheers, slicing through anyone who dares to get too close. A tall, black-haired solider rushes into the room, and I whirl, scanning the room for a place to hide. The general snickers as the new guy points his gun right at my chest and I freeze, afraid to move.

Naya slows her movements, no longer fighting at full speed. I've seen her spar with Ren. She's lethal. The way she's now dancing and parrying seems drawn out, like she's toying with them—or wasting time. Ducking out of their reach, she lunges toward me, pulling me flush against her. I wince at the contact. The neurotoxin on her skin creates a tingling sensation that radiates into my palms, burning my hands. Her bare hand wraps around my neck, and she silently sends me an image of her tied up. The message is clear. *"Let them take me."*

Confused, but smart enough to follow her command, I pretend not to see the soldier behind her. He grabs her by the waist, and she flails, making a show of being captured. She plays the part well. Smug pride shines brightly in the general's beady eyes, and he stands a little taller as Naya and I are ripped apart. We are held with our arms behind us on opposite ends of the room.

He actually believes he got the best of her.

"No!" she cries in perfect Meta, digging in her heels to drive herself forward to get to me.

The general raises a brow at her knowledge of the language. "You three have this under control? Or do I need to hold your hands?"

"Nah, boss. We got this," the soldier behind Naya says, waving the general off. As soon as the general leaves, the one holding me begins to complain. "Fucking prick. I don't know why I let Gibbons convince me to join this shit show..."

Standing in the corner of the room, a burly green-haired soldier watches. His eyes are trained on Naya and her curves. Stepping forward, he runs his fingers through Naya's dreads. She whimpers, licks her lips, then leans into his hand. *Oh, shit this can't be good.* He reaches out, hand trembling, and runs his thumb across her lips. She purrs at its taste, then sucks it deep into her mouth.

"Dee, stop fucking with her. Let's go," I hear from behind me. The soldier holding me looks... uncomfortable. Sorry even. I recognize him as one of the two who were stationed outside the containment unit. They would have died if I hadn't suggested the Illusians let them go.

"Fuck you, Riggs. This little minx is purring like a damn Earth cat." He pumps two fingers into her mouth. "Yeah, I bet you like that, huh?" He chuckles and looks behind her to his friend. "This slut is a savage, bro. Look at her, deep throating this shit." He continues to thrust his fingers into her mouth roughly, before slowing his pace. Naya pouts and opens her mouth wide, inviting him back in. As expected, he pushes his fingers down her throat, making her gag. I close my eyes. I don't care what she's doing or why she's doing it, watching him humiliate her like this makes my stomach turn.

"Stupid bitch!" I jerk my eyes open. Naya bit down on his hand, severing his entire thumb and the two digits he had shoved in her mouth. She chews on them twice before spitting them out in large chunks on his shiny black boots. Cradling his mangled hand, Dee slaps her, hard. Smiling through the blood seeping from her busted lip, she sucks her teeth and spits out the remaining flesh.

Ha! Serves you right, asshole!

We fight the rest of the way to the lower level to where Dee, Riggs, and whoever is holding me throws us into the cage. It's a large, barred area about sixty feet wide created as a security measure to hold people who had gone crazy from being unable to regulate their sleep cycle this far into space. The rest of the room is sterile, no more than a blank space. Decommissioned after being deemed cruel nearly fifteen years ago, it has sat unused and out of date like the majority of things on this station.

After the door clangs shut, Dee taunts us with a wave of his mangled hand, then disappears around the corner. Thankful to be far away from the refuse shoots that occupy the opposite end of this level, I slide down the bars and onto my butt.

"What do we do now?" I ask Naya, making myself dizzy trying to follow her as she paces the cage.

"We wait, Ajayla. The *Acia* knows what has happened. He will come." Her tone is flat and without emotion. Almost bored.

I startle, jumping to my feet. That's exactly what the general wants. And it can't happen. "No. Tell him to stay away. It could be a trap!"

"It likely is. But he will not listen to reason where you are concerned."

"He has to stay with Rhia and the others."

Naya considers my words. "I cannot tell him Ajayla. I do not have that gift. The *Acia* calls on me and I answer, not the other way around. You must do it yourself. He will not be pleased, you know. Those humans have already sentenced themselves to death."

"Damn I forgot, you use touch. Okay, here goes nothing..." With my back against the cold bars of the cell, I close my eyes and search for Ren. I imagine our connection the same way he described before, like a two-way street. Crawling my way toward him, I reach out with my mind and picture myself crashing into him. My knees give out and my chest burns as I'm flooded with a rage so deep it threatens to steal my breath. The walls are whizzing past at an unnatural speed, and I panic as I realize what's happening. Ren's on his way, and death's coming with him.

CHAPTER TWENTY-FIVE

Ren

Pumping my arms, I charge through the hallways. They have taken her. *My* mate. And they are all going to fucking die. Sweat drips down my brow, and I pant—but not from exertion. From anger and outrage. I stop for a second, to register the faint scent lingering. Left. My *Skara* is left. Picking up speed, I swing around the corner, throwing the humans out of my way as I go. I have no sense of empathy for them. They should have known to get out of my way.

My body trembles with rage. They touched her. Put their filthy fucking hands on her and caused her pain. She showed me their faces. I have memorized them, down to the last freckle and scar. There is nowhere in existence they can hide from me. I will find them, peel them apart, strip by strip, until they are reduced to nothing but a puddle of scraps at my feet. I am going to eviscerate them and watch as their entrails spill on the floor before me—"

"Stop!" Her voice blares through my head, silencing my murderous thoughts with a sudden wave of pain. I fling my body

forward, trying to control my speed and remain upright, but she commands my legs to stop. How is she doing that?

"Enough with the killing, Ren. Is that really what you think about all day?"

Shocked by the sudden interruption in my own thoughts, my rage dampens. The sultry voice of my mate, alive in my head, has me feeling a mixture of relief and fury. I told her not to get caught.

"Like I meant to..."

There she is again. She can hear my thoughts? And can speak as if she is occupying my mind as well?

"Yes, Ren. We don't have time. Stay there. Naya and I are fine."

I resume jogging toward her, slowly gaining speed until I am again at a full-on sprint. I can smell her fear, and it is unacceptable. They dared to take my Queen, and I refuse to tolerate their foolishness any longer. I am done playing games.

"Ren, stop! I'm serious. Go back! You can't come here. You know it's a trap."

"I will not leave you there, Skara. Let them try to stop me, it will be fun."

"The Inokine could show up at any moment and our people need you there. If anything happens, you can come kill everyone and finger paint in their blood or whatever. Just wait. Let's see how this plays out."

Finger painting? How had I not thought of that before? *"You do not know what you are asking of me. I will not be complicit in your abuse. You are my mate and you will be treated as such."*

"I'm not asking you to be, I'm all right here, Ren. Naya won't let anything happen to me."

I growl in frustration and slam my bare fists into the wall. I don't like this. There is no way those pathetic humans and their weapons could overpower me if I went to her. She would be in my arms before my next breath. But she is correct in assuming that abandoning the rest of the group would leave them at a greater disadvantage if the Inokine arrive.

Even though it would take me mere seconds to end them, the Inokine have killed with less opportunity. I have never in my life felt more conflicted about protecting my people. I have served since birth, placing their needs above my own, but now that I have tasted what it means to be connected with another, I refuse to relinquish the feeling. I can never be sated; my desire and need for her is immeasurable. My mate runs through my veins just as wildly as the crimson that gives me life, and I will never fucking tolerate her mistreatment.

If I am to deserve the gifts she so willingly offers, I cannot ignore her voice. It would be a great disrespect to devalue her wishes and the ultimate insult to place my needs above hers. Damn. Now I see why our kind holds females in such high regard. The power they hold between their eyes and legs is beyond what I could have ever imagined. It defies all logic that a tiny human—less than half my size—can influence me in such a way.

I am the most powerful in strength and mental fortitude, the most skilled in battle, and bred to lead my people into the next century. Yet, here I stand, in the middle of a hallway, willing to ignore all my instincts because of the unexplainable trust and belief I have in her. It is completely illogical. And I will kill to keep it.

"I will yield, Skara. I will turn back and honor your request. But if I so much as feel a hint of displeasure through our bond, I am coming for you, and there is not a fucking soul in all the depths of time and space who can stop me, not even you."

"I would expect nothing less."

Closing my eyes, I inform Naya of my decision, then return to the lounge where I find Sol with news of the ship.

CHAPTER TWENTY-SIX

Jayla

BREAKING my connection to Ren hurts like hell. Like someone's playing tug-of-war with the right and left hemispheres of my brain. Forcing my way in was worse though.

"Damn, that stings," I complain, wiping at the blood dripping from the left side of my nose. The raging pain dims as Naya presses her hand to the base of my neck. Ren's gentle presence still lingers in my mind but fighting to remain in his was exhausting. Not to mention, the poison Naya excreted all over my skin has left me inflamed and irritated. No matter how many times I try to wipe it off my hands on my pants, the fiery itch remains—even worsens. I catch Naya following the repetitive motion of my hands.

"I feel like I'm going to explode. Why did you touch me?" I ask, remembering her warning the first night we met.

"You have bonded with Ren. I can smell a change within your genetic makeup. I assumed that included our races immunity to the toxin."

"What the hell Naya! I could have died!"

"My estimations were correct. You are indeed still alive. It was necessary for me to remain with you after the soldiers utilized their weapons. I could not risk your life."

"Why didn't you leave me? I would have understood."

Her crimson eyes study mine as she continues to pace the expanse of the cage. "You were not born of us, Ajayla, yet you sacrificed to give us shelter. You could have remained with Aren and sat idly, but you chose to risk your life to get us the answers we need. You may not be of my blood, but you are mine in spirit, and I will not abandon you in your time of need. I will stand beside you, *Aciana*, even if I must give my life."

My heart drops at the thought of losing her. At losing any of them. "No one here is dying today, lady. Well, neither of us anyway." I know good and well Ren is going to murder half the population if he has to wait for me much longer. He isn't a being known for his patience.

But wait...

"Naya, why didn't you just kill those soldiers in there? I've seen you fight. I know you could have taken them."

"We need them to remain alive, for now, until Aren can harvest their memories. The mind begins to degrade shortly after death and takes the information it holds with it. If I had killed those humans, the *Acia* would have been forced to come salvage before the bodies grew cold."

THREE HOURS LATER, all we've managed to do is wait. No one has come, and Naya has grown restless.

"What is it? You're wearing out the floor." She's stiff and anxious. Her confidence remains, but there's a crack in her composure. The only reason I've been able to hold my shit together is because I know she can handle anything thrown at her. I need to know what has her so rattled.

"It is time," she says in a quiet, detached voice.

"Time for what?" I climb to my feet.

"Rhia. The child is ready. He will be coming soon." She clutches the bars in front of her, looking out, eyes unfocused.

"How do you know that?" I ask, confused.

"Aren showed me. Amina just came out to announce it."

Naya's sole purpose is to care for the females and their young. Her role in the birthing process is considered the most important. It's her duty to take away the pain during the final stages of birth to lower the chances of maternal and fetal demise. Her not being there means Rhia will have to give birth naturally. And if she isn't strong enough to bear the discomfort, she could die. If anything happens to Rhia or that baby, I'll never forgive myself.

"I can connect with Ren again, and have him fill me in on what is going on," I offer, hoping to give her a sliver of comfort.

"You need to save your strength, Ajayla. Channeling the bond with a mind as strong as Aren's will weaken you, and at this early stage in your mating, maybe even kill you. I have much more mental dexterity. He can use me. I will hold the connection as long as I can." She sits in preparation and sighs almost immediately after her butt hits the ground. "He is aware of my request and agrees with my concern for your life force. He will utilize me until I am no longer able to sustain him." Naya closes her eyes and leans against the bars.

After forty-five minutes of nothing, I begin to nod off. My vision tunnels while I fight to keep my eyes open. Jumping to her feet, Naya begins pulling at the joints of the door, the bars, anything, looking for a way out. Like caged animal, ready to fight, she's wild-eyed and hyper-vigilant. Glancing up at her, I take in the mixture of dread and aggression displayed in the heavy frown lines around her mouth. "The Inokine have come."

My stomach drops, and my heart begins to race. They're really here.

"We must hurry," she says, squatting beside me. "You need to know what to expect." Anxiety and panic threaten to overtake me, and bile rises in my throat. We have to get out of here. Knowing any mention of my desire for Ren to come get me will result in him doing just that, I quiet my mind and listen intently.

"The Inokine will use their mouths in the beginning. With several sets of sharp, hollow teeth, they latch on and use the sensory glands behind their tongues to taste emotion, in particular, fear. The more you give off, the more irresistible you become. It stimulates their arousal and sends them into a frenzy..." My throat goes dry and my tongue sticks to the roof of my mouth. I know what comes next. The proof was all over Xandria's legs when she first arrived. "They will not touch you while I am alive, Ajayla, I swear it. But if I should fall, get whatever you can and fight them off until Ren can retrieve you. You cannot allow yourself to be taken. Some things are worse than death..."

I shudder at the screams above us. It's horrific. My friends are *dying*. The heavy thud of feet and other large objects vibrate the walls around us. I breathe deeply, praying that Ren and the rest of the Illusians can defeat them quickly. Hearing the light patter of footsteps coming down the stairs to our right, I brace myself for the worst. Shock steals my words at the sight of Rett's familiar face peeking around the corner. He holds a single finger to his mouth, gesturing for me to be quiet, and turns the corner, disappearing again. Hope blooms in my chest. If anyone can find the keys to this shit hole and help us get out of here alive, it's him.

CHAPTER TWENTY-SEVEN

Ren

THEY ARE POURING in like vermin, infecting every surface with their filth, even crawling up the walls into the ventilation system to breach our perimeter. After intercepting a signal no less than five minutes before they arrived, Sol notified me, and I set everyone but Rivan, Orion, Nexx and Tao on defense. Those four remain hidden near the females. Our most vulnerable have yet to be found, and I want no more attention drawn to their location.

Initially entering the ship via the sanitation ducts, the lucky few who passed through the main hatch were swiftly dispatched by Ragar. Replaying his battle as I fight my own, I see the human mechanic has been injured, but she took down two of them herself. It seems my mate has chosen her allies well. Positioning myself in front of the ducts, Tor and I force the invaders to the far-left side of the compound, keeping them away from Naya and Jayla. I relax slightly being closer to her. They are untouched, and as far as I have seen, Naya remains strong and fully capable of defending them until the Inokine are under control.

All of my warriors are accounted for, but I cannot say the same for the other non-Illusians occupying the base. The Inokine are not interested in male prisoners. The heavy stench of human blood hangs in the air. They have already begun the systematic slaughter of all those who are dispensable. For my mate's sake, I hope the humans she warned have prepared themselves. Every life lost will affect her, and all those with blood on their hands will pay the price of her tears. A thousand-fold.

Feigning to my right, I grunt as I shove my blade in deep, twisting the edge so it sticks. Using the weight of the Inokine's body like a battering ram, I lift his rapidly dying form and slam it into the three headed for Tor's back. Smiling at me, he nods, the thick black blood coating his face and teeth making him look maniacal. Seeing the spoils of war dripping off his face inspires a new wave of energy thrumming through me. My enjoyment of battle is not what it once was. Not even the sweet taste of reckoning I feel with each abomination I cut down can compete with thoughts of my mate. I increase my fervor, dispatching them with greater speed, anxious to get to her.

Charging toward the two crawling out of the round shoots in front of me, I rip them from the orifice, sending them into the wall at my right. The scent of excrement permeates the air and masks the spicy tang of blood. How dare they sully it, I fucking love that smell.

Palming their faces, I relish the satisfying pop as my barbs burst through their soft palates, the panic swimming in their eyes for a brief second before the orbs cloud over in death. The Inokine trash squirm, clicking their tongues, begging for mercy, until they have no breath left to scream. I have none of what they seek.

Turning to face Tor, I count seven on him. He continues battling the six at his front as one hangs off his back, gnawing at his neck and shoulder. My lip curls in disgust at the way it mouths at him. Fucking savages. They never fight with honor, always biting at our ankles like quadruped animals.

Repulsed, I crush its skull with my bare hand. The release of his shoulder allows Tor to reach down and retrieve the blade at his hip. He slits their throats in one swipe and advances on the next group.

"They just keep coming, *Acia*. Shit, how many more can there be?" Tor yells over the fray. The floor is lined with bodies two deep, and they are still actively trickling in.

Bending down to impale the Inokine to my right, I twist toward him to avoid the blade of another.

"I do not know. Ragar has dispatched the twenty that tried to gain access from the front of the ship, and Fen and Nico have taken out at least three times that between the first and second floors. Ari and the others are freely roaming, maiming as they please. I checked in with Nexx, the females remain untouched." I grit my teeth and cut down another Inokine, annoyed by their numbers.

"And what of Naya and the *Aciana*?" he asks, throwing his blade behind him. It plunges into two Inokine and pins them to the ground. He leans over, braces with his foot and rips it from their chests.

"They remain unscathed, but we need to herd these pricks farther away. The last thing we need is for them to discover Naya's scent and seek her out. Let us move to the outer edge of the room and drive them upward. I will make Nico aware of the plan."

Tor uses the bodies as a wall, piling them on top of each other until they reach the ceiling in the middle of the room. Covering him from the front, I continue cutting down every third or fourth abomination as the rest continue up the stairs to where Nico and Fen are waiting to intercept them. Taking a second to survey the damage on the floors above, I access Fen's mind just as another wave of Inokine drop out of the refuse shoots.

I sense pain. Sharp and intense pressure all at once. An electrical impulse so strong, it causes the Inokine Fen is fighting to explode as it passes through him and into Fen's chest. That piece of shit saved his life. Nearly doubling over from the force, Fen remains on his feet and scans the room for the source of the hit. His gaze stalls on a large robed figure huddled over a human male, lapping at his thigh. The human wriggles underneath it, gurgling through the blood filling his mouth, sobbing in terror. The human's foot jerks, snagging on the corner of the creature's robe, pulling it partially off its shoulder.

What the fuck?

They brought the Haug? Recognizing it for what it is, Fen grabs his weapon then slides it through the base of the Haug's skull. The massive beast convulses, clamping down on the human's leg, and his scream intensifies. After watching the Haug fall to the ground, Fen withdraws the blade and wipes it on the leg of his pants. The human on the floor is seizing, gasping for breath. Fen turns away, then stops before ending the human's suffering by snapping his neck. It is a quick, kind death. Far less violent than the withdrawn suffocation he would have felt.

If one Haug is here, its siblings are not far. They may be basic creatures, but they hit hard as hell, and once controlled, can be utilized to manipulate the memories of whomever they latch on to. Their presence is unexpected, and my inability to calculate the extent of their involvement angers me. The Inokine only use those bottom feeders to guard their royalty. They have never been enlisted to assist with slave retrieval before. Haug are a rare mixed breed, only spawned when an Inokine is strong enough to survive a successful mating with a Quattra female. They produce their offspring in a set of four and are one of the few other races compatible with the filthy Inokine DNA. Quattra females often overpower and kill the males during intercourse, ending the act before the offspring can be conceived.

Hiding a Haug beneath an Inokine robe to disguise it as a simple foot soldier requires reasoning skills that far exceed

Inokine capabilities. Someone or something else is conspiring against us.

"*Acia*!" Tor yells across the room, pulling me from my thoughts. My body on autopilot, I jerk to the right, narrowly avoiding the jaws of an Inokine lunging at me. "*Acia*!" Tor calls out again. "Look out!"

CHAPTER TWENTY-EIGHT

Jayla

RETT STILL HASN'T COME BACK. Where the hell is he? Pacing the cage, I'm minutes from losing my shit. It's been over an hour since the Inokine arrived, and the screaming *still* hasn't stopped. It's only a matter of time before they find us, and I'm second guessing my decision to keep Ren away.

An audible gasp pulls me from my thoughts, and I turn to Naya just in time to catch her as she doubles over in pain, squeezing her skull between her hands as she convulses on the floor. The light bronze of her skin reddens, and her veins swell. She gasps again, and a long string of saliva dribbles from her mouth. I press my fingers to her neck to check her pulse. Her heart must be beating two hundred times a minute. Coming to with a tear in her eye, she sits up, wavering slightly, then climbs to her feet. Adrenaline pulses through me and I stare at her, unsure of what to do. I'm terrified.

What the hell just happened?

I've never seen her show an ounce of weakness, and watching

her writhe on the floor, completely vulnerable has me choking back tears.

"We need to leave. Now," she says, panting as she wipes away the spittle on her chin. Only seconds ago she was calm, and now the haze of aggression surrounding her makes my hair stand on end. The cold chill of dread covers me. Not Ren. It can't be Ren. No.

"What is it? What's wrong?"

"The bond has been severed, Ajayla." Her irises are blood red. Deeper and darker than before. For the briefest of seconds, her gaze churns with an emotion I never thought I'd see. Pity.

"What does that mean? I don't understand..."

Naya doesn't speak for several long moments, and tears gather in my eyes. There's no way Ren's hurt. There has to be another explanation.

"He's fine right? Ren is fine? I mean, of course he is. He's Ren." No matter how many times I try to speak the words into reality, nothing soothes the gnawing ache inside my chest.

"He would not have severed the bond by choice, Ajayla. Not unless his situation was dire. It is only you now. We must get you out and find Ragar."

My world goes silent. Naya grabs my face, trying to command my focus. I can tell she's speaking, but her words fall on deaf ears. Ren is gone. Pain radiates through me. My heart, my dreams, my future, shattering over and over. Unable to accept it, I withdraw into myself.

Everything hinged on Ren. I never once doubted he would keep me safe because in my mind, nothing could touch him. He's stronger, faster, and more intelligent than any being I've ever met. This entire time I was so focused on how *I* could help, knowing he would ultimately save us all, it never occurred to me his life was actually in danger. And now he's gone?

Abandoning me to test the bars for weak spots, Naya doesn't see Rett descending the stairs. He closes the distance between us quickly. I can barely hold back my tears but I have to keep it together. With Ren gone, the Illusians need all the help they can get. These are his people, his life's purpose, and I'll be damned if I let those pieces of shit take them from me too. Gathering myself up off the floor, I practically run at Rett, thankful he survived. Fighting back the frenzied panic rising in my throat and the deep overwhelming chasm of devastation threatening to swallow me whole, I force myself to ignore the pain.

"Hey, asshole, took you long enough," I snap. They may have taken Ren, but at least Rett is still alive. "Did you find a way to get us out of here?" I reach toward him to grasp his hand, but Naya wrenches my arm away with a hiss.

"Ow. What the hell, Naya!" I yell, rubbing my hand. "Rett's here trying to help us. Back off!"

Rett retreats a few feet as she places her body in front of mine.

"No, Ajayla. He is not." Naya spits on the ground at his feet, letting out a deep growl. I look between them, confused. What in the actual hell is going on?

I turn toward her. "What do you mean?" Looking to Rett, I cock my head. "What's she talking about? Seriously, can someone fill me the hell in? Because I'm two seconds away from ending both of you."

"Oh, girl. Don't be so dramatic. It isn't personal," he says through pursed lips, shrugging his shoulders.

"What isn't? I don't understand. You mean you aren't here to help us?" I scoot closer to get a better look at him, but Naya refuses to budge.

"Oh, honey. You just don't get it, do you?" Rett shakes his head and sighs, placing his hands on his hips. As the sound of multiple footsteps echo through the room, I look past Rett to see General Sterling and two hooded figures in black robes approaching. Naya stiffens and pushes me deeper into the cage.

"Rett, get out of—" I say but stop, as he turns toward the three of them and smiles.

What the actual fuck?

"See, they're all here and in one piece, babe. Just as I promised." Rett smiles at Sterling, then rolls his eyes at my shock.

"Fix your face, bitch, it isn't that complicated. Sterling and me, well... we're a thing. Turns out his goals are sort of my goals. We pooled our resources together, and boom. We made a shit ton of cash. I won't ever have to work again, and all I had to do was spy on you." I stare at the blue of Rett's eyes, trying to comprehend how he can be so nonchalant about betraying me. It's so far from the way a reasonable person would act it's almost comical. He really sees nothing wrong with what he did.

"You set me up?" I ask, still unable to wrap my mind around it. He's supposed to be my best friend. How was I so wrong about him?

He shrugs and looks over his shoulder at General Sterling.

"Hello again, Medic Shirley. I see you've stayed alive. Good for you." His lips spread into a wide grin as he claps his hands. "Okay, now. Play nice. When I open this cage, you'll be going with my friends here."

The taller of the two mystery beings starts to speak to the general. Their faces are hidden under the shadows of their hoods, and I can't understand their language. Sterling however, knows exactly how to communicate with them and nods his head.

"He asked if you are the one who mated Aren," Naya whispers as the general makes a clicking noise as he talks to the beings. The taller one holds out his gloved hand, and General Sterling hands him the key to our cage. The unknown *thing* inserts it in the lock but doesn't turn it before tapping the shorter one on the back.

"What did he say, Naya?"

Naya growls. "The general asked when the child would be delivered to him. The Inokine reassured him he is young, under ten, and will be available shortly. He is talking about Liral."

The general wants to *steal* a *child*? *That's* the package he was talking about? I know he's depraved, but a *child?* I don't even want to think what the general could to with a fully grown Illusian warrior under his control. And what a life with him would mean for Liral? No. Absolutely not. There's no way in hell I'm letting him get his hands on one of them. I don't care if I have to chew my way through these bars that asshole won't have him.

"Now ladies, if you will ex—"

With an outstretched hand, hood number two touches Sterling. There's a brief flash of blue, so bright it makes my eyes water, then the top half of Sterling explodes. The rest of him slides to the ground with a sick flopping noise.

Oh, shit, that's some refund policy.

Rett wipes the gore from his eyes. For several seconds he doesn't move, but then his brain seems to kick into gear, and he turns and tries to run. But only two steps later, the taller figure catches him, drops its hood, and latches onto Rett's face, knocking him down. Its wide jowls detach and swallow the entirety of Rett's mouth and nose. Now partially visible, the thing's hideous. Slimy gray, hairless skin. A spine that curves in on itself, forcing the thing's shoulders to draw in and hunch down over Rett's body.

I hide my face behind Naya's back. I can't make myself watch. Judging by Rett's frantic, muffled screams, whatever it's doing causes unimaginable pain. Despite knowing he lied and sacrificed the lives of our friends for money, the feelings I have for him linger. Watching him die in such a horrible way only makes the Ren-sized hole in my chest grow larger. After losing my mate and my best friend in the same day, I don't know how much more I can take.

"He will only feed for a few moments longer, Ajayla. You need to be ready to run," Naya whispers. The thing slurping on Rett's face pauses its assault, almost like it was so engaged in its meal it forgot we were there. Retracting its jaw, it releases Rett and flicks out its long, snake-like tongue to lick the remainder of blood off what used to be Rett's face. As it turns and refocuses on Naya and me, I get my first full view of the horrible being. No visible eyes, a round, sunken face, inverted nose, and rows and rows of razor-sharp teeth. It reminds me of the sharks living in the oceans back on Earth.

My heart is beating so fast, it burns inside my chest. My skin itches like hell. Even the sweat dotting my forehead itches something awful. Holy shit, I'm about to die.

"Listen carefully. We have little time." Naya speaks quietly in my ear as the robed figures approach the door. "Do not let them pin you down, Ajayla. Remain on your feet and fight. The Inokine cannot control themselves once they have tasted your emotion, and they will try to steal what is most precious from you. We are lucky the shorter of the two is a Haug. They are not concerned with mating needs, only consuming flesh, and this one appears to be well fed."

She points to the untouched remains of Rett's body. I guess the fact this thing isn't hungry enough to finish what the Inokine started is a good thing.

"Now remember, the glands at the base of their tongue are most important. If you can damage them, it might save your life." She spits her words out quickly as the hinges of the door squeak to life.

Kicking the door open with a loud thud, the shorter one blasts several bright blue impulses of energy from his hands rapid fire at Naya. She swirls and dances around the cage to avoid them. Too slow to catch her, the bright blue slowly dims as whatever energy reserves the Haug has begins to burn out. Trying to get out of the way, I dive to my left and push as far into the corner of the cell as possible. Naya has drifted far right to draw the Haug away from me.

Two wet, sticky hands reach through the bars and fist my hair so forcibly it nearly rips it from the roots and I realize my mistake. Backed against the opening of the bars, I'm too vulnerable. With a grip tight enough to pull my brows back and make my eyes water, the Inokine jumps up, forcing my chin down. Its feet land on my shoulders and it pulls at me like I'm an animal on a leash. As I turn my head, its tongue slithers toward me. Seconds before it connects, Naya abandons her grappling match with the Haug to extend her blade and sheer off the Inokine's right hand. Gnashing its teeth loudly at the pain, it releases its grip on my hair. Naya wrenches me toward her and out of the way, flinging my body into the middle of the cell as she turns to engage the Haug behind her.

As I right myself, Naya stills, her back toward me. *Why isn't she moving?* I force myself up, and pivot in front of her. My eyes widen as I see the outstretched hand pressed firmly against her chest. As if frozen in time, the bright blue glow emitting from the Haug's palm illuminates her body, like a flashlight under human skin. Her gaze connects with mine.

"Run," she mouths, before shriveling into herself, leaving nothing but a dry, desiccated corpse.

CHAPTER TWENTY-NINE

Jayla

THEY'RE ALL DEAD. Ren, Naya, Rett, and the countless others upstairs. They're all gone, and it's my fault.

If I hadn't opened the door...

If I hadn't fallen for Ren...

If I hadn't insisted on going back to the comm room...

They'd all still be alive. My breath rattles in my chest as Naya's withered form blurs in my watery vision. If I hadn't been an idiot and put myself in harm's way, Naya would have overpowered the Haug and we'd be with the others right now. She was a fierce warrior, massacring hundreds—if not thousands—of her enemies to protect her people, and a single second of my incompetence took her down. I was the distraction the Inokine needed to get her out of the way, and I'll spend the rest of my life, however short that may be, hating myself for my stupidity.

I hardly feel the Inokine pull at my body. Barely register the sticky heat of its tongue as it slithers up my cheek. Heavy breaths turn to grunts as it laps at my face, then climbs on top of me. I know what's about to happen, what it's about to do, yet my mind is so far gone, I can't muster the will to react.

As if it knows I won't fight back, the Inokine takes its time removing the gloves it wears to protect against the Illusian's venom. Its tongue roves all over my arms and hands as I lie there unmoving. The Haug quickly loses interest and returns to Rett's corpse, but the Inokine tugs at my waistband. Then at the shirt over my breast. Closing my eyes, I retreat deep within myself, trying to distance myself from what's coming. I let my thoughts drift to Rhia and her babe. Imagining how she and the surrounding females are coping with the loss of Ren. I thrust myself into the image. Swim deep into the realistic scene until I can see Rhia on a soft mat. Her beautiful face is pulled into a tight grimace. Her hands clutch the blankets at her side. The others are cooing and singing, doing their best to calm her. I imagine my hands smoothing her hair, pressing a cold compress to her glistening forehead.

I feel a distant tug at the leg of my pants. I need to be farther away, down deeper. I push my mind until I can feel the pain of Rhia's contractions. Hear the thrum of her heart in my ears. I hum to her, the opening bars of my grandfather's nursery rhyme. The wet sting of teeth on my fingers sucks me back toward reality. No. I can't.

Don't make me feel it.

I strain and fight against my mind to get back to the image of Rhia. Cementing myself there, I again begin to hum, louder now, praying the distraction of my voice will keep reality at bay. Rhia's eyes open wide and she looks around, searching the room, face to face. First Amina, then Dreya, Iana, Illaria, Xandria, Uni, and Vora, confusion twisting her features.

Vora. That's the unmated who refuses to speak to me. Uni must be Tao's mate.

"Ajayla?" she whispers. "Is that you?"

After hearing Rhia, Amina leans over her with a smile. "Do

not fear, Rhia. I felt her too. It seems the *Aciana* is more than we all expected."

What? They can hear me? Did I just access the bond?

Spiraling back into reality, my survival instinct rears up, stronger than ever. The fucking space rapist sucking on my fingers bites down hard, warning me not to move. My lungs seize, and a scream builds in my throat as I flail my arms and legs. Naya's words cycle over and over.

"Do not let them pin you down, Ajayla."

Sweat stings my eyes, blurring my vision, and making it almost impossible to see. The sudden influx of fear only excites the Inokine more. Every burst of energy, every small act of defiance, makes the creature lick and lap harder. Clicking its tongue to the gore-covered Haug, the Inokine yanks at my clothing in a frenzy. Frustrated with its inability to undo my scrubs one handed, it calls out what I assume is an order, and the Haug grabs both of my wrists to hold me down.

This isn't happening. This can't happen.

They pin both my arms and legs. I can't move. I scream, and with no other option, lift my head to bite at its face. The Inokine *laughs* at me while licking up and down my cheek. But that only makes me sweat more. Lifting its tongue, the Inokine tenses then jumps off of me, falling through the open cell door. Wiping furiously at its tongue, it screams as smoke begins to rise off its skin. Blisters bubble then burst as his entire body ignites in bright green flames.

Did I do that?

Looking up at the Haug, I gasp as its hands begin to sizzle. Stumbling backward, it brings them up to its face, confused. Not the brightest, it looks at me with anger and hurt brimming in its big black eyes. No matter how dumb it is, the fact that it just ate my ex-best friend and tried to help its Inokine buddy violate me really puts it low on my "give a shit" list. Succumbing to the burn just like the Inokine at my feet, the

Haug flails around on the floor until it's little more than a gelatinous blob.

Not willing to risk a second coming of these things, I grab the key out of the smoking remains and carefully lift Naya's corpse, carrying her out of the cage before I lock the door behind me. It's ridiculous, but everything inside me screams, "*Hide her!*"

I don't know if it's because I've grown attached to her or because she deserves to be honored for her sacrifice, but I carry her to the storage closet near the stairwell and gently lay her inside.

CHAPTER THIRTY

Jayla

STUMBLING UP THE STAIRS, I pause two steps from the top, and roll the gel-like sweat coating my palms between my fingers. *So weird. What the hell is this stuff? Poison?* I wipe the residue on my pants, then peek around the corner before jerking back and pressing myself against the wall. There are bodies *everywhere.* I take a deep breath and, this time, fully turn the corner. They're mostly dead Inokine, a clear sign that the Illusian warriors have been here. Relief floods through me until I recognize the still form slumped over in the corner. I can't remember his name, only that he worked with Rett in the kitchens. I consider climbing over the dead bodies and closing his cloudy eyes but can't gather the courage to do it.

I step carefully, afraid the Inokine underneath my feet might still be alive. Most of them are in pieces, and the walls and ceiling are so saturated with their black, oily blood, I worry it'll drip down as I pass. Fear marks every step.

The Illusians could leave me. I know Ren's gone, but my life here was over the minute I let their ship in. After spending so much time with Amina and the others, I've grown to love them as my own. My heart shudders at the thought of losing the small piece of Ren I have left.

Trying to remain unseen, I take the long way around to the females. This odd, gelatinous sweat, or whatever it is, continues to ooze down my face, and I shove a hand under my rib to ease the stitch in my side. Running through the hallway, I skid to a stop when I see a lone Inokine rounding up a group of three human females near a set of open storage lockers. Probably where they were hiding.

I turn to charge toward them but stop. *I don't have any weapons.* A terrified scream pierces the stillness of the hall, followed by the sounds of a scuffle, and an idea takes hold. I slide my hand across my brow to collect the sweat on my forehead. Unsure if it's enough, I reach into my sweaty cleavage.

Jackpot. I've never been so thankful for tit sweat in all my life.

Cupping my hand, I tiptoe toward the Inokine. For a second, I worry it'll notice me, but it's completely focused on the blond in its grip. She's screaming and squirming, trying to get away. The other two women are pulling at her but can't break her free. Undeterred, the Inokine latches onto the blonde's shoulder and bucks its hips in excitement. A chill skitters down my spine. *That was me.*

Enraged, I lunge, slapping the entirety of what's in my hand onto the side of its face. The reaction is instantaneous. The gray bastard releases the woman and jumps back, running around in a circle before bursting into flames. So, it isn't a coincidence. Is this the neurotoxin Naya warned me about? What was it she said? Something about only Keepers and alpha females able to inherit mating gifts? So, I got this from my bond with Ren?

"Are you guys okay?" I ask in a low whisper. All three of them look haggard, with tangled hair and pale skin. The blond is trembling, and the smell of urine wafts toward me as she tries to wrap her arms around me.

"Oh, no. Don't. I have no idea how I did that but I'm pretty sure I shouldn't touch you." I point toward the heap of flesh still burning on the floor.

"Thank you so much for getting that thing off of me." The other two women reach out and embrace her.

"Look, I don't know where the rest of them are, so you guys need to get out of sight. Go back to your pods." I motion to the large bite on her shoulder. "And make sure you put pressure on that thing." With a tight smile, I rush past them.

"Wait, no! Don't go that way." The blond points to the girl closest to me. "Remy just came from there, says there are tons of them through that door and some big ass scary dude fighting them."

Big ass scary dude? Outside of Ren, there's only one other Illusian who fits that description, Ragar. Ren usually allowed him to remain separate from the group, so I've only met him once, but even with Ren at my side, I couldn't stop inching away from him. After thanking them, I forge ahead anyway. I may not be strong like Ren or quick like Naya but there's one thing I have that makes me capable of great destruction.

Nothing to lose.

AFTER TAKING the stairs two at a time, my thighs burn and cramp from exhaustion. I take a moment to catch my breath, and shuffle towards my pod with my back to the wall. I look both directions, double checking it's clear, then scurry across the hall to enter the code for my door.

A loud beep rips through the air as the lock rejects my code. *Shit*! I must have hit a wrong key.

Calm down, Jayla.

My forehead feels cool against the door as I steady myself.

Just a few more steps and I'll be on my way to them. I start to re-enter my code but stop when I hear a loud thud behind me.

What. Was. That?

I stiffen, and my gut clenches painfully. Turning around, I recoil. Teeth. All I can see are rows and rows of sharp, gore-covered teeth and a tongue bathed in slimy, thick saliva. The Inokine looks up, sniffing the air. I have nowhere to go. My back's against the door and there's no way for me to escape. If I could just move my arm, reach out and touch its cold, gray skin, I might be able to kill it, but my body's refusing to move. It's *so* close.

The thick paste of slime coating its tongue stretches, then drips down onto my chest as the creature takes one long lick of my face. Chirping in excitement, it opens its mouth and lunges at me. I close my eyes and flinch, jerking my head to the side, when a loud blast of plasma singes my eyebrows. The Inokine explodes, splattering its inky blood all over my clothes and the walls around me. I fight to see through the cloud of smoke pouring off the charred bits of Inokine flesh strewn about, and as it clears, Serena comes into view, smoking plasma gun in hand.

"Where the fuck did you come from?" I ask, annoyed that even during an invasion she doesn't have a single red hair out of place.

"I think you mean '*thank you for saving my life, Serena.*'" She smirks as the mess all over the floors and walls comes into view. "That makes twenty-two," she says, raising her chin.

"Normally, I'd find something really sarcastic to say, but you did kind of just save my life. So, thank you, Serena." I pause for a moment, uncomfortable with how gross it feels to thank her. "But you're still a bitch."

A genuine smile crosses her lips. "Glad you're still in there, Jay. Try not to get yourself killed, all right?" She pauses, glancing over her shoulder. "I listened to you, you know. When you told me to prepare, I reinforced the armory, and over half the crew has barricaded themselves inside. You saved a lot of lives, Jayla. No matter what happens, I won't let them forget." Not waiting for a reply, Serena continues down the hall in the direction I came.

Re-entering my code, I burst into my room and grab as many supplies as I can find. If Rhia hasn't had her baby yet, she'll need everything I have and more. Not to mention any potentially wounded males. I pray I'm not too late as I race for the room at the end of the hall, skidding to a stop as Nexx suddenly appears in front of the door.

CHAPTER THIRTY-ONE

Jayla

WITH ALL THE exhilaration my tired body can muster, I race over to Nexx, nearly crashing into him. "You live, *Aciana*." Nexx presses his closed fist to his heart and drops to one knee. The sentiment in his voice nearly brings tears to my eyes. He's *happy* I'm here. I can't see Rivan and the other males, but I know they're close. I remember Ren mentioning they would stay hidden as long as they could. My heart shudders. *Ren.*

I stumble through the door, fatigue weighing me down. Amina is the first to touch me as I enter. I stiffen before remembering they're all immune to whatever's on my skin. Grabbing my hand and pressing it to her chest, she leans down and sniffs it. Her eyes widen, and a small smile tugs at the left side of her mouth.

"We felt you, Ajayla. We know you accessed the bond." The excitement in her voice is short lived as she watches Rhia pale mid-push. With no time to explain the situation, I drop to my hands and knees.

"How is she?" I ask, concerned by the amount of sweat on Rhia's brow.

"She cannot get him out. She has been pushing for hours, and he will not come, Ajayla. Normally Naya would turn the baby. None of us know how." Amina looks around the room at the rest of the worried females.

"Rhia, have you tried another position?" I ask, curious if maybe the baby is facing the wrong direction.

"Another position? I do not understand, Ajayla," Rhia pants, weak with exhaustion. I run my hand along the trembling muscles of her thigh. She won't tolerate being moved, and judging by her short, irregular breaths, holding herself up on all fours isn't an option either. She's growing paler by the second, and her lips are chapped from dehydration. She can't keep this up much longer.

"Okay, Rhia. I'm not sure how Naya does it, but I can try to move the baby myself if that's all right."

Rhia tenses as I lower myself between her legs and tries to pull her knees together. "I know this is uncomfortable for you, but we have to get that baby out. If you've been pushing for as long as Amina says, there's a chance the baby's in distress. Let me help you."

Nodding her head, she lets her legs fall open. The top of the baby's head is partially out and he's face down. I watch as Rhia pushes once more. The baby doesn't respond to her efforts to push.

I need to get this kid out now.

Donning the gloves I grabbed from my pod, I slide my fingers inside her to check his position. Rhia moans through gritted teeth as I push deeper, but her heart rate remains unchanged. Amina, who's monitoring the pulse at her wrist, confirms it. I marvel at Rhia's ability to control her body's response to pain. She's incredible.

Using my other hand to palpate Rhia's belly, I realize the

baby's shoulder is stuck on her pelvic bone, and if he's going to come out, he needs to go back in first.

"Rhia, hold still. The baby's stuck on your pelvis. I'm going to maneuver him out but it's going to hurt like hell." Rhia sucks in a deep breath and nods.

The pressure of knowing any additional pain could kill her wars with the knowledge that if I don't do something, the baby could die. Just as I'm about to begin, the sounds of muffled fighting ricochet into the room from underneath the door. Shit, the Inokine have found us. With panic spreading through the room, Rhia struggles further.

"This has to happen now. Push!" I press down on her belly and turn her baby with the hand inside her in one fluid motion. Grabbing the shoulders as they pass through the bounds of her opening, I use my body weight to pull him out and gather his bruised, blood-covered body into my arms. He isn't moving. Grabbing the towels I brought, I wrap him up and begin to rub him vigorously.

"He is not crying, Ajayla. Why does he not cry?" Rhia whimpers as Amina and Dreya try to soothe her. I can't control the tears pouring down my face. I've lost too many people I love today and I won't survive losing this baby.

I leave him connected to the cord while I try to stimulate his breathing. *It's not working.* Frantic, I press on his little chest and breathe into his mouth. His skin grows duskier.

No, this can't happen.

There's a loud thud on the door, and the fighting outside intensifies. Panicking at the thought of the Inokine breaching the door before I can save this little life in my hands, I try again to help him breathe and suction his little nose.

"Please... Come on little one... *Please,*" I beg under my breath. Suddenly, what I can only describe as a miniature battle cry erupts from his lips, and pink infuses his pale cheeks. I wrap him up and place him on Rhia's chest while we cut the cord and finish taking care of her needs.

With no time to celebrate, Amina, Dreya and I carry Rhia and the baby into the bathroom at the back of the pod. It isn't much safer, but it's the farthest point from the hall and will at least keep them out of sight. Grabbing anything we can find, the females and I barricade the door. I lean back against the counter, taking a second to process everything that just happened. The baby and Rhia are both alive. Now, I just need to keep everyone else safe.

I press my ear to the door, trying to gauge the fight outside. Something hard smacks into the metal and startles me, and I bump into Iana behind me. Spinning around, I reach out to catch her but find her utterly still, staring at the ceiling. I try to follow her gaze until the ceiling groans loudly. There's no way they can tunnel their way down from the floor above unless...

"Um, what is that?" Illaria asks, pointing to an eerie blue glow where a moment ago, the tiles were gray.

"Get out of the way! Move now!" I yell as the ceiling in the left corner of the room gives way and showers us with debris.

"Rivan, help!" I scream, hoping he can hear as the bodies of several Inokine drop in from the hole above. In full protection mode, Dreya and the other mated females engage them, grabbing whatever they can find to throw and swing at them. There are six, maybe seven, but I can still hear scratching and skittering above us. My heart jumps.

Oh, no you don't, you sneaky prick.

I sprint toward Xandria. She's huddled in the back of the room, near Illaria, and there's an Inokine headed straight for her. Her panicked gaze locks on mine, begging for help. She's been through this before and almost didn't survive. I'm not letting that shit happen again.

Rivan and Nexx drop down from the ceiling behind us. I lunge for the Inokine. Underestimating the distance, I shove my hands into its open mouth instead of slapping its cheeks. Pain radiates up my arms as its razor-sharp teeth flay the tender skin of my fingers and palms. I dig my heels into its sides, trying to right myself, but am lifted off my feet as it stands to full height. Out of options, I extend my fingers, squeezing the Inokine's slimy tongue, hoping I can find its glands. The bones of my wrist make an audible crunch as it closes its jaws in one final act of defiance. I scream, trying to wrench my hands away, but only manage to further impale them on its sharp teeth.

I can't breathe. The agony is overwhelming, mind altering. Tears stream down my face. My hands are shredded, as well as several very important veins in my wrists. I hold onto the Inokine's tongue until it crumples to the ground and then collapse beside it.

Unable to even blink, I stare at the blood pouring from the thing's mouth. Red blood. My blood. I'm floating. Separating from my body. Going somewhere far away. Somewhere I'm safe. A sudden pain drills into my head. Ripping me apart from the inside, only to knit me back together and rip me apart again. It's all consuming, taking and giving at the same time. Fighting against it, I do my best to guard my mind, terrified if I give in, I'll lose all memories of Ren along with my sanity.

As the Inokine's jaw releases and starts to burn, the pressure on my wrist lets up. I could probably pull my hands out. But I'm tired. So, fucking tired. If I can just lie here a moment longer, maybe I can get up and rejoin the fight.

I've never felt this much pain. I didn't know anything could hurt this much. My heart, my body, even my soul longs for rest as I continue to mourn the loss of Ren and our future. It hurts to breathe without him, like my lungs can't fully expand knowing he's gone. I tried to be strong for him, for Naya, knowing that even during moments of desperation they would have wanted me to stand tall. Lifting my gaze, I see the Illusians fighting over me, protecting me. Nexx, Orion, Tao and Rivan are battling vigilantly to keep the Inokine away from me. Even the unmated females have started to drive them back but more of them continue to pour in. The barricade is still in place, forcing them to drop through the ceiling one or two at a time.

Letting my eyes close, I stop fighting the pain and pressure banding around my head. I don't care anymore. It can have whatever it wants as long as it leaves me the hell alone and lets me sleep in peace. The pain subsides as soon as I stop resisting, and I gasp.

Ren.

The door bends and whines before exploding off its hinges, blowing back the barricade and knocking down the Inokine in its path. Like something out of a nightmare, Ren storms in, carrying the severed heads of two Haugs. He looks like a beast possessed as he finds me lying in a pool of blood on the floor. The room seems to swell with rage, and the power radiating off him as he barrels through Inokine to get to me is palpable. Without even bothering to look at them, Ren clenches his jaw and sends the remaining forty or so Inokine to the floor, all squirming in pain. A thin stream of blood trails from his nose.

He's... pushing himself... too hard.

Leaning over me, he snaps the Inokine jaws wrapped around my wrists. A deep sense of gratitude and relief overwhelm me, and I throw myself into the bond, digging in and opening the channel wide. I need him to know how much I love him. I need him to know how much I want and appreciate him, and despite wanting to murder him for his "roll over and play dead" act, I also want him to know how much I need him. He's mine, and he better not ever fucking leave me again.

The entire group of Illusians sways off balance, nearly knocked back by the sheer potency of my love and lust and the connection between us.

Oops.

I sent my feelings to everyone, not just Ren. The influx of forbidden emotions is too much for the unmated females.

Sampling something out of their reach sends them into a violent frenzy. They take their rage out on the Inokine still flopping around on the floor until there's nothing left but oily piles of skin and bone.

It's about time someone allowed them to blow off a little steam.

CHAPTER THIRTY-TWO

Ren

MINE. She is mine, and they have fucking broken her. How could I have let this happen?

"Where have you been?" Jayla asks, as I pull her into my arms. Her voice is weak, and there is no warmth in her skin. Clammy and stained with blood, her hands are torn apart, chunks of missing flesh exposing the white of the bone beneath it. The bleeding has slowed in my presence, but the wounds continue to seep. With my remaining energy directed toward controlling her pain, I scan the room once more to ensure there are no Inokine living. The unmated dispatched those I left to suffer.

Placing my mate on the counter gently, I assess every inch of her, categorizing her wounds and etching them into my subconscious. My hands tremble with fury. Brushing them against every wound, every marred piece of flesh, my rage flares, begging to be released. Someone will pay for each bruise on her skin. Each cut. Each slice. For every scar she carries, I will make them suffer a thousand-fold. I will find everyone involved, and when I am finished with them, they will pray for death.

Looking up at me with eyelids so heavy I cannot see the color underneath, my wounded Queen's lips move.

"I thought you were dead. We all did." Her voice is rough and weak, bearing the weight of her emotional turmoil. My absence has hurt her deeply. I should not have stayed away so long.

I check the pulse in her neck. It is faint, far quieter than I like. Knowing there is only one way to accelerate the healing process, I grab her still bleeding wrists and bring them to my mouth. The bitter taste of Lumin coating her skin surprises me. It seems my little *Skara* really does carry a bite.

"What the hell are you doing?" she croaks, eyes wide with disgust and confusion. She tries to pull her wrists away, but I hold firm and continue to lick the wounds.

"Oh, gross, Ren. Don't you know how dirty your mouth is? I get you're into kink, but this is where I draw the line." Her voice is louder now, stronger. It's working. Moving her torn wrists closer to her eyes, I watch for the moment understanding dawns.

"Of course your spit can heal me." She laughs hysterically. "Why the hell wouldn't it?" I don't miss the twinge of annoyance lacing her tone. I should have mentioned it earlier, but outside of our first mating, she has required no help to heal. I must be better at telling her things.

"Look around, *Skara*. All mated pairs can heal each other this way. Those who have yet to pair are far easier to kill. It is one reason so much emphasis is put on selecting a mate."

Fully numbed from the pain of her injuries, she pushes up on her elbows and watches Dreya and Nexx do the same. I follow her gaze as she observes every single mated pair behaving in a similar way.

"Well, I'll be damned. That must be why a bunch of them healed so quickly after you arrived." I nod my head, then continue cleaning her wrists. "That's weird as hell. I'm not opposed to licking you, Ren, but you're taking a shower first. You smell like complete ass." Her lips curve into a thin smile as she lies back and lets me finish.

I grunt at the thought of her tongue on my skin.

Ari bursts into the room as I bandage her wrists, and I turn to him for a report. "*Acia* Ren, it is good to see you." He presses his fist to his chest. It's swollen, misshapen appearance will need to be addressed. There will be time for that later. Not interested in pleasantries, I nod for him to continue.

"The Inokine are mostly controlled. Fen is scouting as we speak. I have not seen Ragar, but last I overheard from the humans running by, the female mechanic helped him disable the Inokine ship, preventing them from evacuating those already chained within its hull."

His eyes stray from mine to Jayla and then to the floor. Good. He remembers what I will do to him if he touches what is mine.

"Tor has already scanned them, *Acia*. Your Life Giver is not among them but…" he pauses as if to brace himself from my rage, "Injari and Urina are."

"And the dead?" I ask.

"The non-Illusian casualties are extensive. As for our numbers, we had only one fall…" I recognize her absence as soon as Ari says the words.

Naya.

Guilt and pain explode across the bond and my mate's face twists in agony. My protective instincts flare. Naya remained true to her promise, and my mate no doubt believes the loss is her fault. If she knew the depths of what I have uncovered, she would feel even worse.

"I watched her die, Ren. She was trying to save me, and that thing pressed its hand against her chest." Jayla sucks in a ragged breath. "She died protecting me." She sags into my arms, then jerks up. "Her body! You have to go get her body. I don't know what you guys normally do but…"

"The husk remains intact?" I interrupt, surprised. If the damage is not too extensive...

"Yes, I hid her out of sight." She buries her face in my shoulder, and her eyes begin to leak. I should not have kept Naya's true nature from her. Lifting her in my arms, I look to Nexx first, then Dreya.

"Bring Liral, we must go to her immediately." Needing to do something, anything to ease the devastation overwhelming my mate, I lift her in my arms. "Take us to her, *Skara*." With a strained voice and tear-soaked eyes, she leads us to Naya's husk as she recounts the events leading to Naya's fall. I do not mention that I have already seen it in her mind. She feels compelled to pay tribute to Naya's honor. The genuine display of respect only makes me want her more.

Despite my strongly voiced opposition, I lower Jayla to her feet so she can show us where she hid the body.

"I don't know why I did it. Why I felt the need to hide her there. It didn't seem right leaving her. I wanted her to be somewhere safe. Oh, Ren, I'm so sorry. She's dead, and it's all my fault..." She collapses against me and her knees give out from the weight of her grief. Easing her to the floor, I kneel beside her as she wails. Tipping up her chin, I pull her gaze level with mine.

"Do you know why I have chosen to call you *Skara*?" She shakes her head silently.

"*Skara* is the name of one of the most vibrant flowers in all of Illusia. It is resilient, surviving no matter the climate." She sniffles, running a hand across her wet eyes. "What makes this flower so unusual is that it is not only the most attractive of all the growing things but also the deadliest. Capable of killing a fully grown male with a single prick of its barb, it requires the utmost care if it is to be acquired safely. Many warriors have died foolishly because they chose to underestimate its strength. That is what I see in you, my *Aciana*, a beauty and ferocity that knows no bounds. Do not discount your instincts, my *Skara*. Your choice in hiding Naya's body will give us the ability to restore her life."

"What? What do you mean 'restore her life'? I saw her die, Ren. She's gone. See for yourself."

Leaning in to press my lips to her cheek, I stand up and pull her with me, guiding her to where Nexx hovers over Naya's husk. I once again help my mate lower herself into the seated position. Nexx and Dreya look at me cautiously. This ritual has never been witnessed by non-Illusian eyes and is the last of our gifts still unknown outside of our ranks. If knowledge of what our young can do is revealed, there will be no stopping our enemies in their thirst for us. Trusting in the sanctity and strength of our bond, I do not hesitate. She is my queen and will lead all of Illusia beside me.

"You can begin," I instruct them. Liral, eager to help, removes the knife from the sheath his father presents to him and slices the blade across his palm.

"No, don't!" Jayla reaches for him.

"It is okay, Ajayla," Dreya assures her. "This is a great honor." Liral does not flinch, does not shed a single tear. The look of intense pride passing between Dreya and Nexx is not unfounded.

Kneeling next to Naya's withered body, Liral presses his hand to her chest letting his blood saturate her pores. Moving his palm to her mouth, he squeezes his fist, grimacing slightly at the pain, but remaining focused on his task. Finishing the ceremony by pressing his much smaller hands to each of hers, Liral initiates the rejuvenation and Naya's heart begins to beat.

Jayla stares at Naya as her body begins to utilize Liral's blood to heal, allowing her own organs to replenish and return to their original state.

"How... how is this possible, Ren? I don't understand... I saw her die. You're telling me all you need to do to save her is get one of the children to bleed on her?"

Nexx's jaw clenches at such a simple characterization of the sacrifice Liral has made. He lowers his eyes, and his jaw loosens after I growl in warning. I will not tolerate any resentment directed toward my mate. She is still learning our ways and will not be held to a higher standard than that to which we hold our own. Screw that. She is not held to any standard. There was no female for me before her and there will be none to follow her. She can make her own standards. She can make her own fucking rules.

Cupping her chin, I draw her against my chest, wrapping an arm around her. "Mated pairs are designed to sustain each other, and it is our bond that allows us to do so. Naya will never mate. Her kind are born without the desire or ability to complete a pair. Their sole purpose in life is to serve and protect. Just as we are connected, Keepers possess a bond of their own with the young and aged they guard. The only true way to end them is to destroy their bodies. Keepers sacrifice their lives for those they protect and in return when needed, the protected sacrifice a small amount of their blood, their life, as a gift of restoration.

"So, Liral just shortened his life?" Her rigid posture relaxes and her gaze floats between mine and Liral's.

"Yes, by a fraction, approximately one of your Earth weeks. But it is shortened just the same."

She stills for a moment, and I watch as her mind tries to process the complexities of my race—of *our* race. Even I do not understand how our mixed mating will continue to affect her. It is clear she carries some sort of alpha trait within her lineage, or she would not have been able to produce Lumin. Not only that, but after witnessing the events leading up to her injuries through Amina's mind, I see how she accessed the bond. She should not have been able to do so. No female ever has.

CHAPTER THIRTY-THREE

Jayla

IF REN LOOKS at me like that one more time, I swear I'm going to reach up and poke him in the eye. Normally him staring at me like he wants to eat me alive would have me ready to crawl all over him, but after that bullshit death scare from earlier, I can't decide whether I want to punch him in the throat or jump on top of him and rip his clothes off.

Who knows, maybe I'll do both.

Unhappy about the constant stream of anxiety thrumming through our bond, Ren slips into Ragar's mind to give me an update on Leandra. She and Sol went to the armory to check on the humans who had barricaded themselves inside. Ragar refused to leave his post and ordered her to stay, but she told him to screw off and went anyway. He reluctantly followed. Apparently after witnessing Leandra put down two Inokine with nothing but a wrench and a blowtorch, he won't leave her side.

Ragar and Leandra? This should be interesting...

With those two now clearing the area of remaining Inokine so the crew are safe to come out, Sol ventured off to gain access to the Comm Room to restart the system. He intends to sift through the correspondence saved in the queue to look for evidence of anyone else's involvement in the attack.

The few remaining Inokine that cross our path on our way to the ship die quickly. Ren is in full-on butcher mode. He's furious about whatever kept him away, and finding me in a pool of my own blood left him one broody, ultra-aggressive grouch ass. His lust for violence has everyone on edge. He's practically itching for a fight, and even Ari is smart enough to keep his eyes directed anywhere but at me. To make matters worse, the not-so-little lust bomb I accidentally sent through the bond has made the unmated, even Amina, barely tolerable to be around. After Naya went all sea monkey, the task of controlling the pissy, sexually frustrated females fell to Dreya and those with mates. They don't appreciate it.

The landing bay is eerily quiet. Ren sniffs the air and cocks his head. Several of the males fan out between the entrance and the main control hub in the center of the floor. It appears empty, but since Ren refuses to put me down and let me walk, I can only see so far. The wide hatch of their ship remains closed, and the bodies of the Inokine Ragar ripped apart are piled on one another like a makeshift funeral pyre. Everything else is just as it was before we left. Yet, something in the air unsettles me. My instincts are screaming that the danger isn't quite over yet.

After convincing him to put me down, I hobble over to the controls with Ren at my side, only to find the wiring I ripped out earlier has been repaired. Sol must have grown bored waiting. That should save Zone a few hours of work. Well, if he's still alive. Tapping on the main screen to pull up the radar, I make a note of the two ships attached to our exterior walls. *Wait, what?* I turn to Ren as my eyes narrow in confusion.

"I thought the Inokine only brought one ship?" I ask, pulling at his hand to get him to pay attention. He's on high alert, consumed with scanning the room. Something isn't sitting right with him.

"Yes, one ship," he mutters as he continues to try to pinpoint what's out of place. Noting their leader's discomfort, several of the other warriors have already begun to search for threats. All the females are huddled together with Rhia and her baby in the middle. Orion has been assigned the task of caring for Naya while she continues to reanimate. He holds her close to the other females. Nexx and Rivan stand on either side, shielding them from harm.

"There are two, Ren. Something or someone else is here." Pure dread gathers in the pit of my stomach. It could be a UCom ship. Ren and the other alphas that led before him devoted their lives to keeping their people hidden, and if UCom has discovered that they're alive, none of them are safe. Ren may be strong enough to slaughter an army single-handedly but there's no way we can outrun UCom's never-ending reach.

Finally focused on the screen, Ren clenches his fists. "Do not move, *Skara*," he whispers to my mind as he silently takes off.

After several long minutes waiting for Ren and the others to scour the room for something to kill, I make the impromptu decision to run into my office. Rhia's baby still hasn't been checked out properly, and Ren doesn't need me for whatever's going down. Running the fifty feet from the control panel to my office door, I yank on the handle, tripping over something hard on the floor. I twist, trying to right myself, but end up slamming face first into the desk. Grabbing my forehead, I lean against the cold metal with my eyes closed.

"I'm fine! I'm fine... keep doing what you're doing," I yell, knowing Ren is probably two seconds away from plowing into the room and creating a scene. Trying to keep the dizziness at bay, I breathe deeply until I catch a familiar scent. *You've got to be kidding me.*

I open my eyes slowly, hoping the smell is just wafting off the dead bodies outside but stiffen as I see the Inokine inches away from my face. It's wounded, a large pulsating stream of black goo pouring out of a gash on its neck, dripping all over my thighs. I spread my legs to avoid the splatter then jam them closed. *Not such a good idea, Jayla.* How lucky for the Inokine. It escaped Ragar's death pile by crawling in here, only to be hand delivered a human snack right before it dies. I close my eyes, sending Ren a silent SOS, and throw myself to the side as its head explodes all over me. *Seriously? Again?*

Disgusted by the amount of Inokine blood in my mouth, I wipe the errant chunks of flesh away and get to my feet. Ren stands in the doorway, chest heaving. "Damn it, Ren. Couldn't you have done your mind thing a little less violently? I practically ingested his face. And did you have to be so damn loud? My ears are ringing." Don't get me wrong, I'm grateful he kept me alive for the thousandth time, but seriously, that was gross as hell. Irritated by his silence, I continue to stare at him until I realize he isn't looking at me but rather, behind me.

"Seriously, what is so important..." My whiney tirade fades away as I come face to face with the barrel of a smoking gun. Not just any gun, but one of the archaic metal types they used to sell on Earth long before the ban. No one in their right mind would risk shooting an actual bullet inside a space station. Modern weapons are designed not to penetrate walls, and while I can appreciate that this knock-off cowboy saved my life, he also could have killed us all in the process.

Idiot.

I start to yell at them both, but then realize Ren's holding him there, controlling his mind and preventing him from moving an inch.

"Ren, let him go." The man's face continues to turn red as the veins bulge beneath his pale skin. The white of his bushy eyebrows and handlebar mustache stand out against his now ruddy, aged complexion. It takes me a second to realize Ren isn't just controlling his arms and legs, he's stolen the man's ability to breathe. What a terrible way to die.

"Ren!" I yank on his arm again. "Let him go, he can't breathe..." Still no response. Ren's eyes are wide and as black as the void outside. Part of me worries my almost dying again has pushed him over the edge into a rage he can't control. Taking a second to clear my thoughts, I force my way into his mind like I did before. If this guy dies before we can figure out why he's here, he takes what he knows along with him.

"Let him go, Ren! We need to question him!" I yell, letting my words bounce around his skull as loudly as I can.

Wavering slightly at the volume of my voice, Ren releases the man and lets him fall to his knees, choking and gagging. Appearing out of nowhere, Ragar hauls the stranger up by the lapels of his jacket and drags him out of the room. Shit, I hope the guy keeps his mouth shut. Ren kills things because he's angry. Ragar just does it for fun.

Ren's gaze flicks from the now-empty space to me and the giant red welt now throbbing in the middle of my forehead. The look on his face is primal and so raw, my body quivers with the urge to flee. His shoulders tense, and the sharp angle of his eyes softens, rounding out to form the catlike orbs I've grown to love. He reaches for me, placing his hands on my lower back and pulls me against his chest. Using his touch to dull my pain, he rubs the tip of his nose along my jaw and lightly scrapes his teeth over my collarbone.

"You should never fear me. You are my life, my *Aciana*." He licks along the long edge of the bone and bites down hard on my tender skin. Redirecting his gift from pain manipulation to torture, he sends a wave of pure sexual pleasure through me that floods my panties and makes my body arch toward him in anticipation.

Since when can he do that?

It's been a while since I've had him all to myself, I couldn't care less about how filthy I am. I need him. *Now.* I tip my head up to find his lips, seeking their punishing heat, only for him to stand still, keeping his lips on my shoulder where he bit me. *What the hell?*

"I told you not to move," he taunts as he laps at the tiny rivulet of blood he drew, closing the skin. A small gasp escapes my lips as the warmth of his breath on my neck makes my nipples hard with excitement. *Wait, wait... Wasn't I pissed at him?* Letting his hands circle around my butt, he squeezes tightly. Continuing to torment me, he applies the faintest pressure to the back of my sex, then curls his fingers, separating me through my clothes. *Oh, I am down for this. So, so very down.* Just as I'm about to rip off his clothes, he removes his hands and holds them up in surrender. *Wait, what? Oh, screw this. I'm about to beg for that dick.*

Backing away from me, he grabs my hand, pulling me along with him toward the door. "Maybe next time, you will listen when I ask you to wait."

My jaw nearly hits the floor. Seriously, I almost die, and he's punishing me by restricting my dick privileges? Who does that?

"That was so wrong. So, so wrong."

He slaps my ass as we cross the threshold.

A few feet away, Leandra smacks Ragar on the shoulder and points to the bloody man on the floor. Aww, hell. He wasn't bloody five minutes ago.

"Can't you just let the man speak! How are we supposed to get anything out of him if you shatter his jaw!" she exclaims, leaning over to help the man up. The females huddled together by the ship stare openly at the exchange. No one talks to Ragar like that. In fact, most are afraid to speak to him at all. Growling at her closeness to him, Ragar nudges her out of the way and offers his own meaty hand instead. The man stares at it for several seconds before accepting it. Well, he has balls, I'll say that much, I would have just stayed on the floor.

With Orion, Nexx and Sol crowding around him and Ren closing in, the man looks like a spooked animal about to run.

"Thank you for saving me..." I blurt out, trying to find something to diffuse the tension in the room.

"Just in the right place at the right time, ma'am." He smiles through his blood-stained teeth. His eyes are kind, the type of blue that reminds me of the bluebonnets back on Earth, but the worry lines around his face hint at his demons. He's older, probably mid-sixties, and dressed like something out of one of the Westerns my grandfather used to watch. The guy has a major cowboy fetish, and he looks the part right down to the starched blue jeans and hideous pearl snap shirt. Cotton crops haven't been utilized for almost a century. Where in the hell did he even find it?

"You will not speak to her again." Ren's voice is low and laced with malice. One wrong move and he's going to snap.

"Why are you here?" he asks.

The man looks to me for help, like he knows no matter what he says, Ren won't like the answer.

"Stop it. Whatever you're doing. Give me back my sight." The man panics and blinks his eyes furiously.

"Look at her again and it will be permanent. *Why are you here*?" Ren stresses the question as the last remaining shred of his control threatens to snap. The man's shoulders visibly relax, and he focuses on Ren once more.

"I heard your call for help. Well, I read it actually. Not often I see a text alert, especially as far out as the Landu Pass, so I thought I'd better check it out."

Ren remains silent but continues to stare him down. The longer Ren eyes him, the more the man fidgets until, eventually, the dam breaks. "Look, I followed Sterling here. I've been looking for someone, and last I heard, he knows where she is. I promise you'll never see me again. Just let me go find the general and then I'll be out of your way."

My eyebrows nearly jump off my face when he says the word "she."

"I tracked him from his last post. He dropped off UCom radar after taking a small group of their men. My guess is the ones he took were already involved in all the terrible shit he's into, but somewhere along the way, I lost him. I turned back around to retrace my flight path and saw your transmission. I hacked into the UCom logs, and your station was listed as down for repair, which didn't make any sense. By the time I got here, those things were everywhere. I took cover and waited."

"What do you know of Sterling and his motives?"

"I know that UCom has failed to draft charges despite more than fifteen different reports of sexual misconduct and aiding slavers. I know he has clearance way above what a normal general should have and he's somehow involved in the disappearance of hundreds—if not—thousands of females. My granddaughter has been missing for six months, and he knows where she is. I have to find her. She's only seventeen."

"He's dead," Ren says callously. My heart drops at the shock, disappointment, and defeat blanketing the man's face. Sometimes I forget Ren doesn't know how to *human*.

"You killed him?" the man asks, anger bleeding through the tears in his eyes as he stares at Ren.

"No, human. The space trash he colluded with took his life," Ren replies, spitting on the floor.

"How unfortunate for both of us." The words sound innocent, but the implication is enough to make Ren and the other males narrow their eyes in irritation.

"Why is that unfortunate for me?" Ren asks, raising a brow. At least he has the decency not to be condescending.

"Because my granddaughter was supposed to be handed off to the same people who purchased your stolen females."

Oh, shit.

Snarling, Ren rips the man off his feet and shoves him into a nearby wall. "Choose your words wisely, human. What do you know of my kind?"

"Not much. My sources didn't tell me who or what they were. Just that they had purple eyes like the ones over there." He nods his head in the females' direction but doesn't dare take his eyes off Ren. "When I saw them, I put two and two together."

"Who is your source? How does he know this?"

"He's a smuggler, just small stuff though, none of the heavy shit. He isn't into that. He got wind of someone needing a reinforced freighter. Apparently, the people they needed to transport were more violent than they were expecting. Sterling was supposed to be the one to set it up. He was the middle man with all the connections. I swear that's all I know!"

Dropping the man, Ren turns around to face us.

"Ragar, collect him." He nods toward the man now slumped on the floor. "He is coming with us." The man doesn't even fight as Ragar grabs his ankle and drags him toward the hatch of the ship. "We are leaving immediately. There are many things I need to tell you about what I have uncovered today, and this place is not secure."

Ren strides toward me and lifts me into his arms. "We must go retrieve your things, *Skara*." With only a brief glance at the others, Ren carries me back toward my pod. Choosing to show, rather than tell me, Ren opens his mind and allows me to see where he's been. He told me when I first discovered the bond, that I might see things I didn't want to, but I didn't believe him. Despite all the violent things I've seen him do in the past twenty-four hours, I never imagined anything would shock me now.

I was so wrong. So terribly wrong.

He collected the rest of the general's men. Held them together and used the two Haug he captured to aid him in ripping them apart from the inside out. That's why he disconnected from us. He used whatever ability the Haug have against them after he split their skulls and removed the parts of their brains that gave them the ability to resist. One by one, he invaded them, pulling apart everything that made them who they were, piece by piece, until he had consumed every memory their fragile minds possessed. It isn't their pain that devastates me. Their wails of misery don't come close to what Ren found hidden deep within their minds. As he laces together the fragments for me, confusion and betrayal shred my illusion of reality and rip a gaping hole in my chest.

Looking up at Ren as he wipes the tears from my eyes, I make him one promise. No matter how bloody our combined hands have to get, I will follow him into the darkest places and fight alongside him until the monsters responsible for all the suffering and torture our people have faced are brought to justice.

Dead or alive, we'll find them. No matter how long or how hard they pray for mercy, they'll suffer for what they've done.

To be continued in Unwelcome: Her Illusian Warrior #2.

THANK you so much for taking the time to read Unexpected. The characters in this book demanded to be written, and I am head over heels for Ren and Jayla. I hope you love them as much as I do.

The second book in their story, ***Unwelcome***, is available now, and you can one-click it here. There's also a very special excerpt from Unwelcome on the next page. So stick around.

Oh, and don't worry about cliffhangers. The entire series is available now!

For all the latest news on the Illusians and all the other races of beings I write about, join my Facebook group, Annalise's Word Fiends. Also, don't forget to sign up for my newsletter. You'll get early access to sneak peeks and cover reveals, and there just might be a contest or two as well.

Have a question? Just message me! I'm always excited to hear from you. Don't be shy! You can find me on Facebook, Instagram, or at my personal website www.annalisealexis.com

I look forward to hearing from you.

XOXO — Annalise

P.S. Turn the page for a special excerpt of Unwelcome: Her Illusian Warrior #2.

ONE-CLICK TODAY!

UNWELCOME - SNEAK PEEK

Chapter 1 — Jayla

Time seems to slow as I sit in the shower waiting for Ren to finish collecting my things. I think on some level, he knows I need time to work through the tangled mess of emotions swirling around in my head. The sound of the water splashing off the floor and the warmth of the steam help to ease my overwhelming anxiety but do very little to blunt the sharp stab of anger pulsing through me. So many people are dead.

General Sterling and his men?

Dead.

The hundreds of Inokine slavers he snuck on board?

Dead.

My former best friend who colluded with Sterling?

Yeah, he's dead too.

More than a dozen people I spent the last year of my life with are sprawled lifeless on the floor, and for what? Some extra meal rations? Money and sex?

Nausea rises in my throat, and my heart aches for their suffering. I want to scream. Beat my fists against the wall and demand a higher power explain how something like this could happen. But I cry instead, letting the water wash away the evidence of my tears. It's all so senseless.

I loved Rett like a brother, and he betrayed me. He betrayed all of us. His eyes held no remorse as he stared at me through the bars of the cage holding me prisoner. He even had the audacity to act like it wasn't a big deal. "It was just business," he'd said. "*Nothing personal.*"

Getting sold out by your best friend to a group of sadistic sex traders feels pretty fucking personal.

My skin crawls as I teeter back and forth between anger and sadness. Empathy and outrage. Rett was such a piece of shit, but I loved him, and the misery I feel over his violent death pisses me off even more.

It would be so much easier if I could just hate him.

My life has gone from systematic boredom to uncontrolled chaos in less than two weeks, and I'm freaking out. The Illusians are alive. Not only that, but I'm mated to their alpha. I'm their *queen,* for crying out loud. The answers my family spent their entire lives obsessing over just fell into my lap, and all I want to do is pick up my comm and call my father but I can't. Because like many of my friends, he's dead. Gone. And I'm still here, guilt ridden and confused.

What the hell happens now?

The Illusians are leaving, returning to their nomadic lifestyle to hunt down those who betrayed them. Leandra and I are fleeing with them. Any second now, we'll be excommunicated and labeled as Unwelcomes. Me, because I let the Illusians board and broke UCom rules, and Leandra... she'll be charged with aiding and abetting no matter why she agreed to help. Neither of us are safe. It won't matter what Sterling did or how many lives we tried to save. We're both guilty in the eyes of UCom law, and we're as good as dead if they ever get their hands on us. We have to leave.

Even if I had the choice to stay, I still wouldn't. I knew the moment I laid eyes on Ren my life would never be the same, that I could never be without him. The depth of despair I felt when I thought he was dead affirmed that feeling by showing me the difference between living and being alive. I can breathe without him, I just don't want to.

I sag against the shower wall, held captive by a combination of exhaustion and dread. The skin of my fingers is pruning, and the water's gone cold, but I can't summon the energy to get up. The shower door creaks and steam billows out as Ren reaches in and pulls me to my feet.

"Sol has returned with news." His words are softer than normal. I guess my ugly shower cry was louder than I thought.

"What did he have to say?" I step into the towel and his outstretched arms. The raging storm of misery clawing at my chest ebbs, and the tighter his hold, the safer I feel. Ren's my home. Everyone and everything else can just go to hell.

"He scanned the communications from the past six months, and none mention our presence. The general's preference for making under the table deals will work in our favor. We still officially do not exist."

My eyes mist as the heat of his breath tickles my neck. Hours ago, I mourned him. Suffocated under the weight of his death, believing I'd never feel this again. But here he is. Alive. Holding me. I nuzzle against him, beyond thankful to have him in my life. "Everyone here knows you guys showed up. Sterling made sure the entire crew hated us. How long do you think that's going to last?"

"Sol took care of it. He met the human you call Serena on his way back to us. Apparently, she was more than happy to convince the remaining survivors to leave our involvement out when filing their official reports."

I take a deep breath and hold it in. There's only one way she'd agree to do it. "She's taking all the credit, isn't she?" I snort in annoyance. Only Serena.

He chuckles. "Yes, that was part of the deal. Sol took all security footage of us and left only the parts featuring her involvement. He also left her the currency stick I found hidden when I interrogated Sterling's men and instructed her to divide it amongst those still living as payment for their silence."

I shudder, knowing what Ren considers interrogation. "You really think no one will tell?" I'm genuinely curious. There's no way in hell this stays quiet.

Ren sighs, kissing my forehead. "No *Skara,* I am not so naive. Word will spread of what happened here, and it is only a matter of time before our existence becomes public knowledge. My goal is to successfully retrieve our missing and find somewhere safe for you to rest without worry before the Inokine and the Universal Community seek us out."

Ren leans into my hand and closes his eyes. The wiry stubble on his face feels rough against my fingers as I trace his jaw. "Let's go find our people then." I smile, holding his gaze a moment before pulling away to head back into my room.

Ren catches my hand and yanks me back into his arms. "We need to disclose what I found. I have yet to allow the others to interact with the two rescued females from Xen's group, but they will be reintroduced to our population once they have settled. Both of them will be able to speak about those involved once they awaken. It is important the circumstances surrounding their abduction come from us." His tone is firm but kind. The worry lines around his eyes grow deeper as he waits for my answer. I know we have to tell them. They deserve to know. I'm just not ready for them to hate me yet.

Injari and Urina, the two Illusian females discovered in the Inokine ship, were rabid and uncontrollable when Ragar freed them from their chains. Bruised, bloodied, and naked, both females scratched and tore at his flesh, even biting him, until Ren forced them to sleep. They were so far gone, they didn't even recognize him. With Naya out of commission, the only way he could safely get them back to the ship was to keep them sedated with his gifts. He assured me after searching their minds for pain, there were no external wounds that required immediate attention. The internal...well, nothing within my power can fix those.

"Can we just wait a little longer? Maybe until tonight?"

Ren tilts my chin upward to meet his gaze. His calm eyes, the palest of blues at their center, help soothe the ache in my soul. "As you wish, my *Aciana*. As you wish."

ACKNOWLEDGMENTS

First of all, as always, thank you so much for picking up this book and taking a chance on me. Your support means everything, and I appreciate each and every one of you. To my main bitches, Ashley and Sara, thank you for your continuous support and uplifting advice. To Mandy, Lesley, Hailey, and my team of alpha and beta readers, you guys rock. A huge thank you to my editor and friend Patricia @ The Novel Fixer, you really are one in a million. Lastly, to my husband Chris. I love you, now go make me a sandwich.

ABOUT THE AUTHOR

Annalise Alexis is a free-spirited mother of three who lives with her husband and kids in the heart of Texas. A huge fan of Firefly, Gilmore Girls, and anything with Jason Momoa, Annalise combines her love of all things sexy and strange by writing in several genres including: science fiction romance and paranormal romance.

Don't forget to join her newsletter for snippets, sneak peeks, and all the things. You can also find Annalise's Word Fiend reader group on Facebook.

You can find Annalise on the web at http://annalisealexis.com

ALSO BY ANNALISE ALEXIS

Her Illusian Warrior

Unexpected (Her Illusian Warrior #1)

Unwelcome (Her Illusian Warrior #2)

Unmatched (Her Illusian Warrior #3)

Shared Survival

Saxon

Made in the USA
Monee, IL
29 December 2023

50598580R00154